Rashi's Daughter,
Secret Scholar

This volume is dedicated to our wonderful children,
Miryl and Ari.

*"Great is the Torah, for it confers life upon its practitioners,
in this world and in the World to Come."*
—Pirkei Avot

Gittel and Alan Hilibrand

Rashi's Daughter,
Secret Scholar

MAGGIE ANTON

2008 • 5768
Philadelphia

JPS is a nonprofit educational association and the oldest and foremost publisher of Judaica in English in North America. The mission of JPS is to enhance Jewish culture by promoting the dissemination of religious and secular works, in the United States and abroad, to all individuals and institutions interested in past and contemporary Jewish life.

The Jewish Publication Society
2100 Arch Street, 2ⁿᵈ floor
Philadelphia, PA 19103
www.jewishpub.org

Design and Composition by Claudia Cappelli
Manufactured in the United States of America

09 10   10 9 8 7 6 5 4 3 2

Library of Congress Cataloging-in-Publication Data

Anton, Maggie.
  Rashi's daughter : secret scholar / Maggie Anton. – 1st ed.
      p. cm.
  Adapted from the author's adult novel, Rashi's Daughters, Book I: Joheved.
  Summary: In eleventh-century Troyes, France, Joheved, the eldest daughter of a respected teacher and Bible commentator, studies Talmud after her days of helping run a household and the family winemaking business, but worries that her future husband will agree with those who believe women should not be scholars.
  ISBN 978-0-8276-0869-6 (alk. paper)

  1. Jews–France–History–11th century–Juvenile fiction. [1. Jews–France–History–11th century–Fiction. 2. Judaism–Customs and practices–Fiction. 3. Rashi, 1040-1105–Fiction. 4. Family life–France–Fiction. 5. Education–Fiction. 6. Sex role–Fiction. 7. Troyes (France)–History–11th century–Fiction. 8. France–History–Medieval period, 987-1515–Fiction.] I. Title.
  PZ7.A62945Ras 2008
  [Fic]–dc22
                                              2008008769

JPS books are available at discounts for bulk purchases for reading groups, special sales, and fund-raising purchases. Custom editions, including personalized covers, can be created in larger quantities for special needs. For more information, please contact us at marketing@jewishpub.org or at this address: 2100 Arch Street, Philadelphia, PA 19103.

ھ

In loving memory of my mother

Anne S. Anton Einstein

Like Rashi,

a teacher of teachers

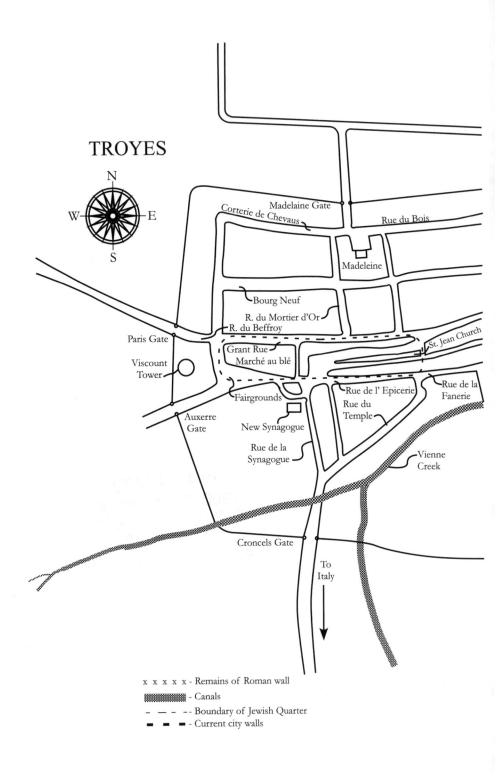

TROYES

N
W E
S

Madelaine Gate
Corterie de Chevaus
Rue du Bois

Madeleine

Bourg Neuf
R. du Mortier d'Or
R. du Beffroy

Paris Gate
St. Jean Church

Viscount
Tower

Grant Rue
Marché au blé

Fairgrounds
Rue de l' Epicerie
Rue de la
Fanerie
Rue du
Temple

Auxerre
Gate

New Synagogue

Rue de la
Synagogue

Vienne
Creek

Croncels Gate

To
Italy

x x x x x - Remains of Roman wall
- Canals
- — - -- Boundary of Jewish Quarter
- Current city walls

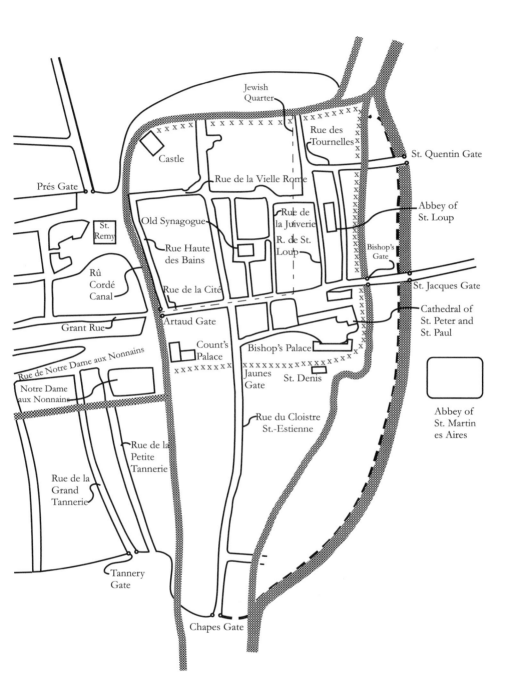

Jewish Quarter

Rue des Tournelles

St. Quentin Gate

Castle

Prés Gate

Rue de la Vielle Rome

Abbey of St. Loup

Old Synagogue

Rue de la Juiverie

St. Remy

R. de St. Loup

Bishop's Gate

Rue Haute des Bains

St. Jacques Gate

Rû Cordé Canal

Rue de la Cité

Cathedral of St. Peter and St. Paul

Grant Rue

Artaud Gate

Count's Palace

Bishop's Palace

Rue de Notre Dame aux Nonnains

Jaunes Gate

St. Denis

Notre Dame aux Nonnains

Rue du Cloistre St.-Estienne

Abbey of St. Martin es Aires

Rue de la Petite Tannerie

Rue de la Grand Tannerie

Tannery Gate

Chapes Gate

Acknowledgments

I offer my thanks and love to my husband, David, who listened patiently to countless stories about Rashi and his daughters, who read and critiqued countless drafts, always giving me excellent advice, and to my children, Emily and Ari, who for the most part cheerfully tolerated their mother's obsession. Last, but certainly not least, I want to thank my niece, Mallory Russell, for all her excellent help and suggestions.

One

"Come here, kitten." Joheved wiggled a piece of string in front of the synagogue woodpile. "Come out and play."

Her younger sister, Miriam, tossed a few small pieces of cheese near the string and the two girls waited. Soon a small gray tabby crept out toward the cheese, followed by its gray and white sibling. Next an orange striped kitten stuck its head out, and finally another gray tabby.

"Don't throw them any more cheese," Joheved whispered. "Make them come to us."

Miriam held out her hand, and soon two of the kittens were licking the cheese off it. Joheved's mouth watered, but there wasn't enough cheese for both her and the kittens.

"Now," Joheved hissed.

She dived for the gray and white kitten as Miriam grabbed the other. But it was too fast for her.

"Ow," Miriam yelled as the gray tabby scratched her hand to free itself.

A moment later the four kittens were hiding under the woodpile and Miriam was crying. "Now what are we going to do?" she wailed. "It will take weeks for them to trust us again and we have to catch them before Papa comes home at Shavuot."

Joheved sat down on the ground and blinked back tears. It was Mama's idea for them to catch a pair of kittens. The whole thing started a month ago, during Passover, when Papa stayed up so late studying that he was too tired to put his books away when he went to bed. Either that or he fell asleep while he was studying; Joheved never found out which. In any case, he left his manuscripts out all night, and when he woke up the next morning, it was clear that mice had eaten some of them.

1

Joheved winced as she remembered how he'd cursed and thrown a dish at the mouse hole. And that was just the beginning of that terrible morning. Grandmama Leah heard the crash, came downstairs, and started yelling at him. She scolded her son Salomon that it was his fault for not putting his things away and for having a tantrum when he should have known that mice would eat any parchment he left lying around.

Grandmama Leah continued to berate her son. "Do you realize how much new dishes cost? Do you think they grew on trees?" She carried on about how little money they had, and now she had to buy new parchment as well as new crockery. "Have you no consideration for all the sacrifices I made so you could study at the Talmud academy in Mayence?"

Poor Papa. He just stood there in silence; he couldn't talk back to his mother. When Grandmama Leah finally had her say, or at least ran out of breath, he was so upset that he bashed his fist against the wall. Joheved could still hear the sound of wood splintering.

He hit the wood so hard that he broke his hand. Grandmama Leah could see at once that he was in terrible pain and sent Joheved to fetch the doctor. In the end, Papa's hand swelled up terribly, and it hurt him the whole time he was home.

He had no sooner left for Mayence than Mama took Miriam and Joheved aside after services and asked them to follow a certain calico cat that lived at the synagogue.

"That cat used to be pregnant, but now she's thin again," Mama told them. "If you can find where she's hidden her kittens, maybe you can catch one or two for our house. Then Papa won't have to worry about mice anymore."

They followed the cat for days until they finally found her hiding place under the woodpile. Then Mama gave them some small pieces of cheese to feed the kittens to start taming them. At first all Joheved and Miriam could do was put the cheese down and stand back while the mother cat hissed at them. But eventually the kittens got used to the girls' presence and began playing with their strings.

Miriam's continued sobs interrupted her sister's reverie. "Joheved, we need to go home. My arm is bleeding."

"Just wrap it with the bottom of your chemise for now," Joheved said. "There's a well on Rue de la Cité. We can wash there."

2

"But my chemise will get all stained."

"Then use mine." Joheved held up the corner of her underskirt as they headed toward the street.

Miriam pressed her other hand against the wound. "That's no use. I'll still end up wearing it when you've outgrown it."

"We can't give up on the kittens," Joheved said. "Not after they've gotten used to us feeding them."

"Maybe we can ask for some meat scraps at the butcher's again. The kittens really liked that."

Joheved sighed. It was true that butchers sometimes had scraps left over in the afternoon; most women bought their meat in the morning. "I hate begging there. The butchers must think we want the meat for ourselves."

"Then stay outside and I'll go in by myself."

None of the butchers the Jews usually shopped at had any scraps that afternoon, but two days later they were in luck. As soon as Jacques saw the girls, he called out, "If you can wait, I'll have something for you." He stepped out into the street and looked around. "I have to catch a suckling pig first . . . for a christening."

Pigs roamed most streets in the Jewish Quarter of Troyes. Their owners, who weren't Jewish of course, knew those pigs were perfectly safe, that none of them would "accidentally" disappear into a resident's stewing pot. As long as the pigs stayed out of their courtyards, the Jews tolerated them in their neighborhood. It kept the roads cleaner.

Down the street, a sow and five piglets were busily rooting around where someone had just emptied a pail of garbage. Jacques grabbed a feedbag and advanced on the pigs. Before Joheved could count to ten, he threw the bag over the piglets and snatched up one of them. He carried the squealing creature back to his shop, where Joheved and Miriam waited outside until the piglet's squeals abruptly ceased.

"Here you go." He handed them a small package and smiled. "Good luck catching a kitten."

"That's how we can do it," Joheved said, her eyes shining with excitement. "We'll find an old blanket or sheet and throw it over them while they're eating."

Miriam clapped her hands with glee. "Then they won't be able to scratch us either."

"We'll wait until tomorrow. Then they'll be really hungry."

Sure enough, they arrived home after services the next day with a kitten apiece, one orange striped and one gray and white, rolled up in an old sheet. Their hands were scratched, but they didn't care. Now Papa wouldn't have to worry about mice.

Yet when Rabbi Salomon ben Isaac came home for Shavuot, the festival in late spring that commemorates the Israelites receiving the Torah at Mount Sinai, he scarcely noticed the kittens. The grapevines were about to flower, as they did every year at the end of May, and by this time the springtime work in the vineyard should have been complete. But not all the ground between the vines had been hoed free of weeds, and worse yet, leaves still remained on last year's sterile wood—leaves that would only consume the plant's needed sap.

After the festival, instead of leaving immediately for Mayence, Salomon continued to labor in the vineyard with his family. Once the vines flowered, more leaves would need to be removed, this time from the new fruiting wood so that each bunch of baby grapes was exposed to sunlight. And no sooner would the final piece of land be hoed than they would need to start again at the other side.

Summer was Joheved's favorite time to work in the vineyard. The earth between rows was soft and warm, squishing pleasantly between her bare toes as she and Miriam attached the grape-laden stems to their trellis. The leafy vines were only slightly taller than the girls were, offering excellent conditions for hide-and-seek games. It was also fun to look for caterpillars and snails hiding among the leaves. But they couldn't bring themselves to squash them with bare feet, so they took the bugs to Grandmama Leah, who saw the small foragers as thieves and furiously dispatched each one with a stamp of her booted heel.

Joheved disliked hoeing; her back and arms always hurt after a day of it. Papa apparently didn't like hoeing either, because she often saw him hacking angrily at the weedy ground. Once she heard him curse when he accidentally dug too deep and dislodged a grapevine's roots.

"When is Papa going back to Germany?" Joheved asked her grandmother one afternoon. He had never stayed into the summer before.

"He'll be leaving any day now," Leah replied as she tied a new shoot to the trellis with a piece of straw.

But two weeks later, when the Hot Fair opened, Papa was still in

Troyes. When Grandmama Leah again told her that he would be leaving sometime soon, Joheved decided to ask him herself. Instinct told her to ask him privately, but it was difficult to find the right time. He remained after services with the Jewish merchants who attended the fair, and he stayed out late at night with them as well, so she was asleep when he came home.

She knew better than to disturb him when he was studying, but it seemed that his head was always bent over some manuscript. Joheved had peeked inside one of them when he was outside using the privy in the courtyard, and while she could recognize the Hebrew letters immediately, it took a while to realize that the words weren't Hebrew, but Aramaic, the same as in Grandmama Leah's *Targum* translation of the Torah.

But unlike reading the Torah, which Joheved did easily now, she couldn't understand what this manuscript said. She knew most of the words, but the text didn't make any sense. As she read further, she could see that many words seemed to be missing, but before she could figure anything out, she heard Papa at the door. She quickly returned the manuscript to where he'd left it and bolted for the kitchen.

In the vineyard it was difficult to see him among all the vines, but her opportunity to confront him came in midsummer when she was thinning the leaves surrounding each cluster of grapes not far from where he was hoeing weeds. She only knew he was there because she could hear him.

It sounded like he was crying.

Joheved crept around the end of the row and there was her father, leaning on his hoe, his shoulders shaking as he wept. She immediately stepped back, hiding herself behind the vines, and waited for him to quiet. Then she poked her head out.

He was hoeing again so she gathered her courage and approached him. "Papa?"

He sniffed a couple of times before responding. "What's the matter?"

"Nothing's the matter. I was wondering if you're going back to Germany after the fall holidays?"

"No." He sighed and it looked like he might start crying again. But then his voice hardened with anger. "I have to stay here at least through the winter, to make sure the vineyard gets pruned properly for a change."

Joheved ran back to where she'd been trimming leaves. She didn't know what she'd done to annoy him, but she was sure Papa wouldn't want to talk about it.

Joheved thought that Papa might return to Mayence when the pruning was done, but by then Mama was pregnant, which meant even fewer people to work the vineyard. He didn't leave after Passover either; the baby was close to being born by then. Huddled in their mantles, Joheved and Miriam helped in the frigid vineyard as much as possible. The calendar might say it was springtime, but it never seemed to get warm, not even at noon.

One night the cold forced Joheved awake. Sure that Miriam was comfortably wrapped in more than her share of bedding, Joheved reached out for the covers, only to find them still in their proper place, topped by the rough blanket that Mama had woven from their first clumsy attempts to spin thread from raw wool. There wasn't a hint of morning light, so Joheved snuggled under the covers, determined to ignore her discomfort and find sleep again. Her feet were freezing, but getting up to find her hose would just make them colder. If only she and Miriam could have a charcoal brazier in their room at night.

She sighed.

Why did Mama and Papa have to be so secretive about being poor? Did they think they could protect her from poverty by never mentioning it, by telling her that only babies and old people needed their rooms heated once Passover was finished? A girl in her twelfth year was old enough to be told the truth. Joheved rubbed her feet against each other to warm them and bumped into something small lying at the edge of the bed. The room's silence was broken by purring.

Joheved nudged the cat and moved her feet onto the warm spot the creature had occupied. Pleased at this solution, she listened to the small noises outside as she waited for sleep to overtake her. Every so often, the clip-clop of horses' hooves or crunch of cartwheels echoed on a nearby road. What errands kept someone away from home at this hour, when the demon Agrat bat Machlat and her eighteen myriads stalked the night outside?

Joheved shivered and pulled the blankets tighter around her. She had just about drifted off when a low-pitched moan, like someone in pain, jerked her back to consciousness. But this noise wasn't from outside; it was coming from just beyond the bedroom door. Terrified of what had to be an approaching demon, Joheved dived under the covers and grabbed for Miriam.

And felt no one.

A frantic search proved that Joheved was alone in their bed. Convinced that the demon who had somehow taken Miriam was coming for her, she recited the words she'd been taught to say if evil spirits ever threatened her.

"Be split, be accursed, broken, and banned, you son of mud, son of clay, like Shamgaz, Merigaz, and Istemaah," Joheved whispered through chattering teeth, and then, because incantations said three times were the most powerful, she repeated it twice more. Heart pounding, she waited.

And waited. The cat, still purring, nosed its head under her hand, eager to be scratched. Her fear slowly dissipating, Joheved began to feel both relieved and foolish. How often had she watched the cats chase their invisible prey? Surely no cat would lie so contentedly in her bed if demons lurked nearby.

The world was plagued with evil spirits: from Ashmedai, King of Demons, and Shibeta, who strangles children with croup or whooping cough, to the *cauchmares* who bring on bad dreams and little Feltrech, responsible for tangling a sleeper's long hair at night. There were more demons than there were people. Most feared of all was Lillit, whose prey was women in childbirth and their newborn babies. And Mama was due to give birth any day now.

Mon Dieu, what if Mama was having the baby right now?

Two

Was that where Miriam had gone? It would be just like her little sister, too, leaving her to miss out on all the excitement. The cold forgotten, Joheved jumped out of bed. She groped her way along the wall to the pole holding their clothes where, in fact, only her own were hanging. She hurriedly slipped her long linen chemise over her head, making for the doorway at the same time.

Across the landing from where she stood, the door to her parents' room was ajar, and sure enough, a lamp was lit within. Light came from downstairs as well. Joheved tiptoed toward the brightness before her. She had almost reached her parents' doorway when she heard the moaning again, this time followed by a familiar voice, low and melodic, a voice identical to Mama's, except for a slight German accent.

"Miriam, it would be a great help to me if you could keep counting between your mama's pains." The voice belonged to Aunt Sarah, Mama's widowed older sister. "We can tell how soon the baby will come as the number you count gets smaller."

Mama was having the baby! And Miriam was in there as well. Joheved was filled with a whirl of feelings—happiness and excitement, anxiety and fear, plus some righteous indignation that everyone had been quite ready to let her sleep through it.

She stepped boldly into the room and then stopped short. "Oh, what's that smell?" The air was pungent with a strange odor, not unpleasant, but sweet and spicy. It made Joheved's nose want to sneeze.

Mama lay in bed, her eyes closed and her right hand clutching the protective amulet she always wore around her neck. Her long dark hair was disheveled, spread loosely on the pillow. She appeared to be sleeping, except that she opened her eyes after hearing Joheved's voice and gave her older daughter a wan smile.

Joheved stared at her mother. "Why is Mama's hair is spread out like that?" Mama was fastidious about her appearance, her hair always kept out of sight under her veil.

"Aunt Sarah says that it's important to have nothing tight or constricted near the childbed, especially not the mother's hair," Miriam said, proud of her newly acquired knowledge. "It makes it easier for the baby to come out."

Sarah turned around and said firmly, "Hush. Your mama needs to rest between pains, and I don't want you disturbing her. Joheved, you can sit next to Miriam and keep count with her." Her voice softened to the gentle tone Joheved was accustomed to. "What you smell is the fennel I've scattered around the floor. It sweetens the air and wards off evil spirits."

A chastened Joheved edged toward the chest where Miriam was sitting. When her sister slid only a handbreadth to the side, Joheved shoved Miriam over, forcing Aunt Sarah to give her nieces a quick frown of reproach. They had barely settled down when Rivka began to breathe faster and clutch at the bedclothes. A groan escaped her lips. Then, as suddenly as it began, whatever had disturbed her was gone. Her grimace faded and she reached for the amulet at her throat.

Aunt Sarah looked at Miriam questioningly, and Miriam replied, "Five hundred. I counted to five hundred that time."

The dread that gripped Joheved was fading now that Mama seemed calm again, but her heart was racing and her stomach felt funny. She had completely forgotten about the counting.

"Don't worry, Joheved, Mama always does that when the pains come, but then they stop right away." Miriam gave her older sister a reassuring hug. "What's the matter? You look like you're going to be sick."

Joheved did feel ill. Was having a baby always like this, one agonizing pain after another? And when the time came, would it be like that for her, too? "Miriam, is it . . . ?"

"You two go outside and chat," Aunt Sarah interrupted, motioning them toward the door. "We don't need a count between every contraction." Sympathetic gray eyes focused on Joheved's pale face. "Don't worry. Your mama is doing fine. By the time the sun is up, you'll have a new brother, may the Holy One bless us, or sister."

They went out into the hall, their bare feet moving quietly over the rushes on the floor, and Miriam leaned casually against the wall. "How long have you been in there?" Joheved asked her little sister, whose confident posture and calm demeanor made her seem quite grown up.

"Not long. I only did a few counts, all over five hundred, and Aunt Sarah wasn't interested if I counted more than that. She says that things won't begin to happen until I get below two hundred, that Mama's birth pangs will get stronger and last longer, until finally she's in pain most of the time." Miriam straightened up and gestured with her hands. "Then we get her out of bed, onto the birthing stool, and she pushes the baby out. Isn't it exciting? I can't wait for the baby to come!"

Joheved's nose wrinkled in distaste. "How can you stand it?"

"You mean how can I stand Mama having a baby?" Miriam recalled how her sister preferred to pluck a chicken rather than gut one, although it took a lot more time. "Probably because I'm not squeamish like you."

"I mean, doesn't it bother you to see Mama in pain?" Joheved said. "Besides, you're not doing much except counting."

"I think it's wonderful, and Aunt Sarah let me make up Mama's special drink. It's got the most amazing ingredients in it: myrrh, cinnamon, and savin, all mixed together in wine with honey." This was a rare opportunity for Miriam to outshine her sister.

"When the baby's about to come, I'll be able to do more. Aunt Sarah says I can be her assistant. A laboring woman shouldn't be left alone, on account of demons, so I can run downstairs to fetch things, or I can tend to Mama if Aunt Sarah has to go do something. I might even be a midwife like Aunt Sarah when I grow up." Thank goodness she wasn't such a coward like Joheved.

Joheved didn't need to be reminded that Mama was in danger. She wanted to ask if Aunt Sarah had said anything else about demons, particularly about Lillit, but she didn't like her little sister thinking she was ignorant or scared. Besides, it was best to speak of demons as little as possible.

"If you're a midwife, you won't have to worry about money. It's not like making wine, where you never know if you're going to have a good harvest or not. Women are always having babies."

"Aunt Sarah probably does all right." Miriam lowered her voice, loath to provoke the Evil Eye. "She's the only Jewish midwife in Troyes and only has herself to support."

Joheved matched her sister's furtive tone and whispered, "I hope

Mama has another girl, not a boy baby."

Miriam had also been hoping for a baby sister, but all the same, it was shocking to hear the words from Joheved's mouth. She peered down the hall, not wanting to be overheard. "I've been praying: please don't let Mama die in childbirth and please, make the baby a girl."

There, it was out in the open. Miriam felt guilty about praying that second part; she was pretty sure that Papa, and Mama too, was praying for a boy. "I don't think Papa would pay us any attention if he had a son."

"Not that he pays that much attention to us now." Joheved agreed with her sister, but she didn't want to tempt any evil spirits to harm the baby, no matter what its gender. "Let's go see how Mama is doing," she said. She didn't really want to watch her mother's painful progress, but her parents' room was warm.

They returned to find Aunt Sarah wiping Mama's face with a small cloth. "Rivka, your daughters are here." She motioned for them to stand on either side of the large bed.

Mama took hold of their hands and gave each a gentle squeeze. "Now I have my guardian angels watching over me." She smiled up at them. "This is a woman's greatest blessing, when she can bring forth new life. This is what the Holy One created us to do. I pray that I may live to see you two give me grandchildren."

Perhaps she wanted to say more, but she stopped and gripped their hands tighter. Right then Joheved wanted nothing more than to get away from the bedside, but Mama held her fast. Joheved shut her eyes rather than watch up close as Mama went through another contraction, clenching her hand tighter and tighter until it was all Joheved could do not to cry out herself. Yet Mama just moaned softly, and suddenly the pressure on Joheved's hand relaxed.

Joheved opened her eyes to see the room starting to spin around her. She felt Aunt Sarah's strong arms supporting her just as her legs began to fail, then helping her over to the storage chest. She could hear Miriam counting, "Five, six, seven, eight," and she felt awful, not only because of her head, which was starting to feel less dizzy, but because she realized that she was more of a hindrance than a help.

"Joheved, we don't really need two people up here to count," Aunt Sarah said gently. "Why don't you go downstairs and keep your papa company. He must be lonely and worried down there by himself. We'll call you when the baby's been born."

Feeling rejected and useless, Joheved slowly made her way down the circular staircase. Only a faint light came from below, and she took each step carefully. Papa was seated at the dining table facing the hearth, staring into the fire. In the dimness, his brown hair looked black and his gray eyes were hooded under dark brows. He was stroking his beard like he always did when he wanted to think, and it seemed as if he was looking at something far away.

Uncertainty stopped Joheved's descent. She didn't dare interrupt him, but she couldn't return to Mama's room; she'd just been expelled. Maybe she should go back to bed?

The room's walls and furnishings had disappeared into the night. Illuminated solely by the flickering flames and an oil lamp on the table, Salomon sat alone in a vast darkness, manuscripts spread before him. In isolated monasteries across the continent, a few monks laboriously copied ancient texts, but Europe had lost the knowledge of Greek philosophy and science. Yet the Jews, despite the bleak intellectual atmosphere of the time, kept the light of their forbearers' wisdom burning bright. Salomon himself had spent the last fifteen years studying at the elite Talmud academies in Germany.

As his sister-in-law had intuited, at this moment Salomon was feeling both lonely and worried. It was the first time he'd been present when Rivka was giving birth, and it was a terrible, solitary vigil. In Mayence when a *chacham*'s wife was in labor, his students gathered at the scholar's house. To protect her from demons, they brought a Torah scroll with them and chanted Psalms until the baby arrived, all night if need be. But Salomon had been back in Troyes less than a year, and when Rivka went into labor, he felt reluctant to ask any local men to keep him company.

So he sat at the table, trying to keep his attention focused on the Torah commentary he was writing. Several times he had fought the urge to stand up and pace the room. It was so quiet upstairs. Hearing Rivka's cries earlier had been bad, but this silence was worse. He tried to calm himself and get back to his studies. His sister-in-law was an excellent and experienced midwife; she'd warn him if things were going badly.

If only he were still in Mayence, surrounded by students. But no, he was trapped in Troyes, his mother no longer competent to manage the family's vineyard. He returned to his manuscripts with a sigh. He would have to be satisfied teaching invisible students, the ones he imagined might someday read his *kuntres*—commentaries—and learn from them.

Salomon heard someone coming down the stairs and jumped up to receive the news she brought him, sending the cat that had been asleep at his feet scurrying off in a huff. But rather than the midwife, it was his elder daughter, Joheved, standing timidly at the bottom of the stairs. Her two long braids were coming undone and she was barefoot. Dressed in a rather threadbare chemise that barely covered her knees, her arms hugging herself, she seemed a forlorn figure. He recalled that a girl's chemise ought to be ankle length and felt a pang of remorse. His daughter had probably been wearing this one for years.

Three times a day, as part of the prescribed liturgy, Salomon prayed for the year's produce to be blessed with abundance. If the Holy One blessed him with a decent wine harvest this fall, he might finally be able to afford new clothes for his family at Rosh Hashanah, the Jewish New Year. Especially for his older daughter, who appeared to be growing out of her old ones before his eyes. She was already taller than Rivka, on the threshold of womanhood. Sadness came over him again. How was he ever going to afford a dowry for her and her sister, when he scarcely had the money for food and parchment? And now another mouth to feed.

His immediate worries suppressed his future ones. "So, *ma fille*, what news do you have for me?"

"Everything is fine, Papa. Aunt Sarah says the baby should come before dawn." Joheved shivered in her thin chemise. It was much colder downstairs than in Mama's cozy bedroom.

"Come closer to the hearth," Salomon beckoned to her. "We don't want you to catch cold."

Joheved approached the fireplace, but feeling shy, she stopped at the far side of the table. She could feel, rather than see, his deep-set eyes scrutinizing her. What was he thinking, this stranger who was her father? She was still getting used to his being home. Except for Passover, Shavuot, and Rosh Hashanah, when Papa had returned for a few weeks at a time, their household had been completely female.

Even now, except for meals, they hardly saw each other. Papa went to synagogue in the morning, labored all day in the vineyard, and worked on his manuscripts after *souper*. Maybe she could ask him about demons. He was a scholar.

"Papa, why does Lillit hate newborn babies so much?"

Surprised by her question, yet hungry to be teaching again, Salomon chose to answer his daughter exactly as he would have for one of the young students at the yeshivah. She has a right to know about Lillit, he told himself. She'd be a mother herself one day, Le Bon Dieu willing.

"Lillit was Adam's first wife. Because she too was created from the dust of the ground, Lillit insisted on equality with her husband. They quarreled, and she left him." Joheved's rapt expression encouraged Salomon to continue. "Three angels were sent to capture her, but when they did, she refused to return. They threatened her, yet Lillit preferred being punished to living with Adam. Now she takes her revenge by harming new mothers and their babies, boys before their circumcision and girls until they're twenty days old."

Joheved was appalled. She had vague memories of Mama having other babies who died, and she recalled a neighbor woman who had died in childbirth last year. She grabbed her father's arm. "What can we do to protect Mama and the baby, to keep Lillit away?"

Tears were forming in his daughter's blue eyes and Salomon felt ashamed for frightening her. He should know better; a good teacher gives lessons appropriate for his student's level.

"The Almighty has given us powerful tools of protection, *ma fille*. Your mama is wearing the amulet her mother gave her, my tefillin are wrapped around the top of our bed, and as soon as the baby is born, he will be given an amulet with those three angels' names on it. In addition, I am here praying and studying Torah. Don't worry—the Merciful One will guard our pious household."

Papa's calm words reassured her. He was home now and that would make the difference. Joheved didn't want to jeopardize the closeness that had suddenly developed between them, but she had to ask another question. "Papa, you called the baby 'he.' Are you praying for a son?"

Salomon hesitated as he considered how best to answer. He did not see how he could give an honest explanation, one that did not compromise his integrity as a teacher, without using the Talmud as its source. But teaching Talmud to a girl?

He began to argue with himself: I can't teach Joheved from the Talmud, women aren't allowed to study Talmud. *Yes, you can. You know it isn't actually forbidden. And didn't you yourself take notes at the yeshivah although all study is supposed to be oral?* Women certainly don't study at the yeshivah. *Yet the Talmud itself mentions learned women, often the daughters of scholars.* She won't understand Talmud; women are light-headed. *Joheved might understand; she knows the Bible, both in Hebrew and Aramaic. Your mother saw to that.* If only I had a son to teach. *Well, you don't have one, and if you want to teach your children, you'll have to make do with her.* But a father's obligated to teach Torah to his sons, not to his daughters. *It doesn't matter that you're not obligated to teach her. You want to teach her. Don't deny it.*

Watching his daughter's chin begin to quiver with rejection, Salomon realized that he wouldn't disappoint Joheved or himself. He could no more refuse to teach an eager student than he could stop breathing, and if it was sinful to teach his daughter Talmud, then let the sin be on his head.

He smiled down at Joheved and said, "Just when I was sighing over not having any students, the Merciful One has provided me with one. Tell me, do you know what Talmud is?"

Her father's long silence had worried Joheved. But he didn't look angry. She had no idea why he was asking her about Talmud, but she answered, "*Oui*, Papa, it's the Oral Law."

Salomon nodded his head. "That's right. When Moses, our teacher, received the Torah on Mount Sinai, it was in two forms, the Written Law, which we read in the synagogue, and the Oral Law, which was taught in person from teacher to student. Moses taught it to Joshua, and so on down to the earliest rabbis. After the Holy Temple in Jerusalem was destroyed, Rabbi Judah the Prince worried that too many scholars who knew the Oral Law had been killed, that it might be forgotten. So he ordered the Oral Law, called the Talmud, to be recorded. Do you understand?"

"*Oui*, Papa. Grandmama taught me and Miriam all about it."

"That's right, she wrote me about what good students you were." He paused and stroked his beard before continuing. "Talmud has two parts, Mishnah and Gemara. Suppose you wanted to find all the laws in the Torah concerning a certain subject, let's say the Sabbath. Judah the Prince knew that was difficult, so he wrote the Mishnah, which takes the laws from all over the Torah and arranges them by topic."

Joheved nodded as he spoke, so he continued. "But Mishnah is only a small part of the Talmud. Most of Talmud is Gemara, which records the sages' discussions about the meaning of the Mishnah. Don't worry. You'll understand better when you see it."

When you see it! Joheved couldn't believe her ears. Papa was going to teach her, a girl, Talmud! Terrified, yet fascinated, she didn't dare do anything to interrupt him, to give him a chance to reconsider what he was doing.

She nodded her head and squeaked out, "*Oui*, Papa."

Salomon got up from the chest he was sitting on and rummaged around inside it. He pulled out a large volume, bound in leather, which had seen much wear, and he thumbed through it until he reached nearly the end. Joheved could see that the pages were covered with Hebrew script. She leaned forward to get a better look.

Chuckling at her eagerness, he said, "This book, the Talmud's first tractate, is called *Berachot*, 'Blessings.' It concerns, as you might surmise, the laws of prayer. Here in the ninth chapter, we have a Mishnah that answers your question. See if you can read it to me. It shouldn't be much different from reading Scripture."

He pointed to where the characters were written slightly larger than the rest of the text. Joheved was afraid that, like before, she wouldn't be able to understand it, and that Papa would realize it was a mistake to try to teach a girl Talmud. Yet she was excited and curious, too. She sighed in relief when she saw that the text was in Hebrew, not Aramaic.

Three

Heart racing, Joheved began reading the Mishnah aloud.

If a man cries out (to God) over what is past, his prayer is in vain. If his wife is with child and he says, "May it be Your will that my wife bear a male," this prayer is in vain.

Salomon gave an inward sigh of relief; Joheved had read the text without difficulty. "And you understand why these prayers are in vain, for no purpose?"

Joheved gulped. Had she and Miriam sinned when they prayed for a sister? "If the wife is with child, then it is already either a boy or a girl, and no prayer can change that," she said slowly.

"*Oui, ma fille.*" Salomon replied. "But while it is true that these prayers are empty or useless, they are not forbidden, because it is man's nature to pray these things."

Joheved sighed with relief and continued reading the Gemara, her father helping her with the missing words.

From the third to 40th day, he should pray that it will be a male. From the 40th day to three months, he should pray that it not be deformed. From three months to six months, he should pray that it not be a stillborn. From six months to nine months, he should pray for a safe delivery.

Salomon was more pleased with his daughter. "According to this view, the baby's gender is not determined until forty days, so one may pray for a boy until then. Of course," he quickly added, "if the parents desire a daughter instead of a son, they may also ask during this time. And praying for a safe delivery at nine months is what we should both be doing right now."

Joheved closed her eyes and tried to concentrate on Mama in the room upstairs. But she couldn't stop thinking about what had just happened. Papa had taught her Talmud and she had understood it! And there were so many tractates of Talmud. Who knew what amazing things were written in them? As fervently as Joheved prayed for her mother's safety, she also prayed that today would be the first of many such study sessions with her father.

Salomon decided that this would not be the only time they studied together. He would teach Joheved any Mishnah and Gemara she wanted to learn. And not just Joheved; he would teach Miriam too! Then his two daughters could learn the texts with each other.

Salomon knew he had made the right decision when Joheved turned to him with anxious eyes and asked, "When will you teach me more Talmud, Papa? I want to learn what the Rabbis say about everything, not just about prayers."

"*Ma fille*, we can study together every night. We'll start with blessings and see how things go after that."

It would have been difficult at that moment to say which of them felt happier. Their joy was shattered by Rivka's scream, followed by the thin wail of a newborn baby. Father and daughter stared at each other for a moment. Then Joheved raced for the stairs and almost collided with Miriam coming out of the bedroom.

"A girl, the baby is a big, healthy, girl!" Miriam was so excited, she was almost dancing. "Mama is fine, too," she added before disappearing back into the bedroom.

When Salomon and Joheved were finally allowed to enter, Rivka, her hair neatly tucked under her veil, was soothing the baby with a mother's own best remedy. The room smelled different now; something sweet was smoking in the charcoal brazier.

"A pleasant smell encourages the baby to come out quickly, so Aunt Sarah burned some rosemary," Miriam explained before Joheved could ask.

Obviously all was well, and Salomon recited the traditional *Shehecheyanu* prayer of thanksgiving, said on those happy occasions when something is done for the first time. "*Baruch ata Adonai* (Blessed are You, Lord our God), King of the World, Who has kept us alive, sustained us, and brought us to this season."

Aunt Sarah's dawn estimate for the baby's arrival had been accurate, for no sooner had Salomon finished the blessing for seeing his youngest daughter for the first time than Troyes's many church bells began their daily cacophony. When all was silent, Rivka gave her daughters the necessary instructions to keep her household running smoothly.

"Go downstairs and tell Marie that the baby has come. She'll know what to do. While she's helping Grandmama Leah get dressed, you two stoke the fire and get breakfast ready." Rivka paused and shifted the baby to her other breast. "There should be some oatmeal stirabout that just needs to be heated, as well as some stewed fruit. And for Heaven's sake, put some clothes on."

"Don't you worry about breakfast," Aunt Sarah told her nieces once they were out in the hall. "I'll prepare it myself." Anticipating the early morning birth, she had bought some special foods for what she hoped would be a celebration. And celebrate they would, even if the baby was another girl. After all, Rivka had come through the birth safely. Not only that, which, the Merciful One be blessed, was plenty to be happy about, but Miriam had shown unexpected promise as an apprentice midwife.

Sarah was more pleased when she reached the kitchen and found that Marie, the young maidservant, already had a fire burning in the fireplace. Two kettles hung on the hearth from a toothed iron rack, the large copper one full of water. There were some smaller pots standing on tripods above the flames, their warm contents giving off enticing smells.

"When I heard the babe crying, I knew I'd better get things ready down here right away," Marie said, her high voice happy and excited. "I've heated up a kettle of ale for the mistress, the best thing for getting her milk flowing. Is it all right for me to bring her some on my way up to dress Mistress Leah?"

Sarah smiled at the servant's eagerness to see the new baby. "You're a great help to this family, Marie. Warm ale is just what my sister needs. Take your time with Mistress Leah. The girls and I will see to breakfast."

Once their hair was braided, Joheved and Miriam accompanied their aunt to her house on the other side of their shared courtyard. There Sarah filled their arms with fern fronds. "Ferns have a certain force such that evil spirits avoid it. So when a woman gives birth, we place its fronds around her bed and the infant's cradle."

When they returned to the kitchen, they heard Grandmama Leah's voice screeching upstairs. "You robber, you stole my favorite brooch. You should be ashamed of yourself, stealing from the hand that feeds you. You ungrateful wretch, you thief."

"You're mistaken, Mistress. I never took your brooch, I've never taken anything of yours."

In a few moments everyone except Rivka had assembled in Leah's room. The gray-haired matriarch surveyed her audience with satisfaction. "Salomon, I insist that you fire this thieving girl at once." Leah pointed at Marie. "She's stolen my brooch and probably more besides that." Leah addressed her son with the authority of one who brooks no arguments.

Without waiting for his assent, she gave her orders to the sobbing maid. "Pack your things and leave my house this instant. I won't share my roof with somebody who steals. For all we know, you're in league with a band of rogues just waiting to cut our throats in the night and take away everything."

Marie broke into tears and tried to run from the room, but Salomon caught hold of her arm and led her into the hall.

"Don't worry, Marie, we know you didn't steal anything." He then addressed the distraught girl in a softer voice. "My wife and child must not be left alone. Please keep them company while I sort this out."

But it was too late. Rivka was limping down the hall toward him, the baby in her arms, her eyebrows knit with trepidation. Before she could speak, Leah began a new tirade, this time directed at Sarah.

"What are you doing here? How dare you enter my bedroom?" Grandmama Leah pointed her bony finger at the midwife. "Don't think for a moment that I don't know what you're up to. You've been putting a curse on Rivka for years to keep her from having any more children, so she'll be barren like you."

This was so patently absurd that the family stood paralyzed, uncertain how to respond to Leah's indictment. Arguments were futile, but Miriam realized that her grandmother's latest grievance might be the key to distracting her.

"Grandmama, Aunt Sarah's here because Mama had the new baby last night." Miriam made her voice sound as cheerful as possible. "She had a baby girl. Don't you want to see her?"

"What baby?" Grandmama Leah looked warily around the room, suspecting a conspiracy to keep this important information from her. "Nobody told me anything about a baby."

Miriam took Leah by the hand. "Aren't you lucky, Grandmama? Now you have three granddaughters instead of two. After all, odd numbers are good luck and even numbers are bad luck."

"A boy would have been luckier," Leah muttered, but she took the baby in her arms and allowed herself to be led from the room.

"I guess I'll be leaving too," Aunt Sarah said, giving her sister a quick hug. "I'll check on you after breakfast, when everyone's gone to synagogue."

His mother and sister-in-law gone, Salomon sighed and surveyed the scene. Near the door, his diminutive wife was patting the distraught maidservant who towered over her. Rivka looked close to tears herself.

He'd deal with Marie first. Then they could look for the brooch. "Marie, please calm yourself. You mustn't even think of leaving us, not now when we need you so much. Not with both the new baby and my mother to take care of." He tried to keep the anxiety out of his voice. "How long will it be until your fiancé finishes his cobbler's apprenticeship?"

"Just a few more years, Master Salomon, not more than three."

"Surely, you can remain with us for that small amount of time. It would hardly be worth it for you to start again somewhere else when you'd be leaving in a couple of years anyway."

Marie nodded and headed for the stairs. Salomon turned to Rivka. "Now where do you think my mother put that brooch? I suppose we'll have to search her usual hiding places."

He had hoped that such clear confidence in Marie's innocence would cheer those left in the room, but the mood only became more somber. Rivka and Joheved looked at each other apprehensively, as if each expected the other to save her. Salomon waited for a response, but the nervous silence continued and neither one would meet his gaze. His wife and daughter were hiding something.

He fought to control his temper; if he frightened them he'd never discover their guilty secret. He held out his hands and appealed to Joheved. "*Ma fille*, please tell me what's the matter. It can't be that bad." At least, he hoped it wouldn't be.

Joheved couldn't refuse her father's direct request. "Papa, Grandmama's brooch isn't lost." She took a deep breath and spoke quickly, her eyes fixed on the floor. "Grandmama took it to Avram the goldsmith last spring, before you came home. He loaned us enough money to make a nice Passover."

Salomon stepped backward as if he'd been punched in the stomach. "I see," he said slowly. "Is Avram the only one in Troyes we owe money to, or are there more?"

Rivka shook her head, too mortified to speak. Tears filled her eyes and slid down her cheeks.

"Now, now. Let's not be so glum. What's done is done." Salomon gave his wife an encouraging smile. At least they weren't too badly in debt. "We should be celebrating the birth of our new daughter."

When they got downstairs, Miriam and Grandmama Leah were waiting for them at the breakfast table. Contentedly cooing at the sleeping baby in her lap, the old woman showed no signs of ill will toward Marie, who was ladling out the stirabout. Leah turned and admonished the latecomers. "You'd better come and eat, or we'll be late for services this morning."

The sun was clearing the city walls as Grandmama Leah and Salomon set off for weekday services, Miriam and Joheved following behind them. Rivka and the new baby wouldn't leave home for at least two weeks, not until the child had been safely named in the synagogue. From her kitchen window Sarah watched her nieces close the courtyard gate behind them, and then she slipped back to her sister's house.

"Oh Sarah, what am I going to do about Leah?" Rivka put her head down on the table and wept. "After what she said here about you and Marie, I can't bear to think of the things she might tell others about us."

"Don't worry, Mistress," Marie said. "Mistress Leah would never air her dirty laundry in public."

"And I'm sure I would have heard if people were gossiping about your family." Sarah gave her sister a reassuring hug.

Rivka allowed the two women to lead her upstairs. "But what about the shopping?" She let Marie take the baby while Sarah helped her use the chamber pot. "The grocers will cheat Leah if she can't remember any prices."

"They will not," Marie said proudly. "Mistress Leah may be forgetful, but she can tell right away if somebody is trying to cheat her. Besides, Joheved remembers all the prices for her . . . she's a clever one, your Joheved is."

"Rivka, let your husband worry about Leah." Sarah tucked her sister in bed and adjusted the fern fronds. "You need to relax. Get some sleep now."

But Rivka wasn't tired. She looked down at the sleeping baby and then up at her sister. "Who do you think she looks like?"

Sarah couldn't help but smile. "With that curly hair and her cute little nose, I think she'll grow up to be pretty like you."

"Joheved and Miriam may be plain, but they're good girls, pious and hardworking, may the Holy One protect them." Rivka's voice was filled with pride. Then she lowered her voice so Marie couldn't hear. "I am glad that they take after Salomon rather than me."

Both girls clearly had their father's high forehead, strong jaw, and thick brown hair. They also had his deep-set, intelligent eyes, but Joheved's were blue like Rivka's while Miriam's were more hazel.

Sarah looked at her in surprise and Rivka said, "That way no one will ever doubt that he's their father, no matter how much time he spent away from home."

"How can you possibly worry about such a thing?" Sarah shook her head in disbelief. "You're one of the most virtuous women in Troyes."

"It doesn't matter how chaste a woman is, people will still gossip about her," Rivka said, covering a yawn with her hand.

Sarah yawned herself, then strode over to the shutters and closed them tight. "That's enough talk. You should be sleeping while the baby is asleep, and I want to catch up on my rest, too."

Salomon's family didn't have to walk far to reach the Old Synagogue, as opposed to the New Synagogue in the market district that had been built during Grandmama Leah's lifetime. Located on Rue de Giourie in the oldest part of Troyes, the Old Synagogue was constructed of stone, like the count's castle, the cathedral, and the Abbey of Saint Loup, all built before Charlemagne.

As they hurried past the abbey, Miriam babbled excitedly about the birth she'd just witnessed, but her sister scarcely heard her. Grandmama Leah's missing brooch was forgotten as Joheved remembered herself in front of the hearth, studying Talmud with Papa. She basked in her new knowledge, like a miser admiring a chest of gold.

"Joheved, what's the matter with you? Haven't you heard a single word I've said?" Miriam was seething with indignation. Here she was, trying to tell her older sister all the amazing things that happened when a woman gave birth, and Joheved wasn't paying the slightest attention. "You just don't want to admit that there's something I know that you don't."

In fact, the few words Joheved did hear had convinced her that the less she knew about childbirth the better. Let Miriam prattle on about how babies were born, she knew something better. "You're not the only one exciting things happened to last night."

"What are you talking about?" Miriam grew suspicious of her sister's self-satisfied smirk.

"Miriam, you'll never guess. While you were helping Aunt Sarah deliver Mama's baby, Papa was teaching me Talmud!" Joheved took a deep breath and waited for Miriam's response.

"What? Papa wouldn't teach you Talmud, nobody teaches Talmud to girls. Girls aren't supposed to learn Talmud!"

Joheved reveled in her sister's agitation. "He did too teach me Talmud. We studied the ninth chapter of Tractate *Berachot*, about prayers you say when a woman is pregnant. I read it myself and didn't have any trouble at all. And Papa said he would teach us, both of us, more of *Berachot*, a little each night. So there!"

Miriam was torn between admiration for her sister and shock at how their father had broken tradition. But no matter how scandalized she might feel, if Joheved was going to study Talmud, then she would, too. Before she could say anything else, they reached the synagogue doorway. Under their grandmother's watchful eye, Joheved and Miriam tried to adopt the proper attitude of reverence and thankfulness. And that meant no more talking.

They entered into a small anteroom, which offered a view of the sanctuary a few steps below. The focal point of the room was the *bimah*, a raised area along the eastern wall. Here stood the ornate carved wooden cabinet that held the Torah scrolls, as well as a table on which the scroll was opened to read that week's portion of Scripture. A row of tall windows facing the central courtyard provided illumination.

Stairs from the entry, their banister worn smooth by the hands of women climbing them for generations, led to the women's gallery, a deep balcony along the width of the sanctuary opposite the *bimah*. As usual, the other girls had spread themselves over the back benches so that Joheved and Miriam would have to sit by themselves in the front row.

"Just ignore them," Grandmama Leah advised her granddaughters when the other girls snubbed them. "You don't want to associate with such ignorant people anyway. They'll just distract you from important matters like learning to make wine and manage a scholar's household."

That was easy for Grandmama Leah to say. Leah was learned enough to lead the women in prayer, she ran her own vineyard, and her son was a *chacham*. Let the silly girls gossip and giggle in the back. Joheved liked sitting in the first row, right at the balcony's edge; then she could watch the services below.

Word of Salomon's newborn daughter swept through the congregation. Never acknowledged aloud, giving birth was a risky undertaking. Of the roughly one hundred Jewish families in Troyes, nearly every one had lost a baby, and many had a mother or sister who'd succumbed in childbirth.

After services Salomon found himself surrounded by men he barely knew inquiring about Rivka and the baby's health, while upstairs the women listened eagerly as Miriam related her experience at the birth. Eventually the crowd thinned as people returned home for *disner*, the midday meal.

Grandmama Leah kept tapping her foot and saying, "We really need to get going," or "It's time to leave." But she refused to leave without Salomon, who was deep in conversation with Isaac ha-Parnas and his son, Joseph.

The *parnas*, leader of the Jewish community, was probably the most important Jew in Troyes, and definitely one of the richest. He was responsible for paying the communal taxes to Count Thibault and for making sure that every Jewish family contributed their fair share. He also headed the committee that administered the community charity fund.

Watching the three men in earnest conversation, Joheved didn't dare interrupt them. Perhaps her family's financial circumstances were so dire that Papa had been forced to apply to the *parnas* for assistance. Yet Grandmama Leah was growing increasingly agitated.

It seemed like ages before Salomon finally noticed his daughter's desperate glances and excused himself for a moment. "You can leave now and tell Rivka that I'll be along shortly."

With this dismissal, Leah allowed Joheved and Miriam to walk her home. Along with other Jews in Troyes, their family lived in the Broce-aux-Juifs district, located at the center of a triangle formed by the Abbey of Saint Loup to the east, the count's palace to the south, and his castle to the north. The Jews' houses, like others in town, were timber post-and-beam structures surrounding a central courtyard. Each story jutted out above the other, and because they had a tendency to lean as they aged, it was sometimes possible for a woman on the third floor of one house to hand an item to her neighbor in the house across the street.

The narrow alleyways below were graded like a **V** with the highest level immediately next to the houses and the lowest point in the center. Garbage of all sorts was thrown into the middle of the road, with the hope that a rainstorm would soon wash it into the nearest waterway. Pedestrians tried to walk as close to the buildings as possible, leaving the vile median to those on carts or horseback. Shopkeepers found this arrangement convenient since it forced passersby close to their open windows, from which they called to the potential customers to advertise their wares. Joheved and Miriam were used to ignoring the clamor.

"Do you really think it will be all right for Papa to teach us Talmud?" Miriam was trying to recall exactly why girls weren't taught such things, but she couldn't think of anything except that it just wasn't done. "What if somebody finds out?"

"Who could possibly find out? I doubt Papa will tell anyone, and if we don't say anything either . . ."

Miriam was not reassured. "Grandmama?" She pulled on Leah's sleeve. "What happens to women who study Talmud?"

Even knowing this conversation would be forgotten before they got home, Joheved was flooded with trepidation. But Grandmama Leah didn't ask Miriam why she wanted to know. She merely wrinkled her nose and replied, "Any such masculine activity will certainly cause a woman's womb to wander, probably so much so that she develops hysteria. Not that anyone teaches Talmud to girls."

Joheved had no idea what hysteria or a wandering womb was, but she was willing to risk them both. Once home she helped Marie prepare some baked fish and vegetable stew for *souper* that evening, to be eaten with the cheese pies and fruit pastries that a couple of women had dropped off earlier. The family was surely planning to retire early, but if she and Miriam tidied the kitchen quickly, Papa might still have time to teach them Talmud. Joheved steeled herself not to feel too disappointed if he was tired and wanted to put off more study until tomorrow.

But Salomon was not about to skip what he anticipated would be a most gratifying experience. After *souper*, he surprised Rivka with his offer to put the girls to bed so she could rest, and as soon as she was upstairs, he got out Tractate *Berachot*. First they reviewed what Salomon and Joheved had done earlier. Then he instructed the two girls to help each other learn the text by heart, just as study partners in the yeshivah did.

"Copies of Talmud are rare," he said. "And no yeshivah student is considered proficient in a chapter unless he can recite it by memory."

From that night on, each evening after Rivka and the baby went to sleep, learning Talmud became Joheved and Miriam's secret bedtime ritual. The door to higher Jewish education had been opened for them, and they were eager to enter. That this knowledge was traditionally reserved for males only made it more enticing.

Four

For the next two weeks Joheved and Miriam had unprecedented freedom to explore outside the Jewish Quarter. Troyes, with over ten thousand inhabitants, was one of the largest cities in France and there were lots of interesting avenues to investigate. The girls spent most mornings on the bustling Rue de l'Epicerie, home to the various food vendors.

They hurried past the butchers and poulterers, lingered at the pastry shops and bakeries, and elbowed their way through the peddlers touting everything from fish and cheese to milk and honey. But they didn't need to buy anything except staples. Thanks to the congregation's generosity, an array of savory dishes awaited them each day when they returned from synagogue.

One day Papa was waiting for them when they got home. "Isaac ha-Parnas has offered me a business partnership, and he wants to discuss the details over *disner*. If your mother feels well enough, we'll go a week from Thursday."

Isaac ha-Parnas was a widower who lived with his son's family on Rue de Vielle-Rome. An invitation to dine with him was an honor; the prospect of a business partnership was incredible.

Before the girls could say anything, Grandmama Leah declared, "I'm too tired, you go without me."

Salomon rolled his eyes in frustration. There was no point in telling his mother that the meal wasn't today; she was stubborn as a mule when it came to doing anything beyond her usual routine. He sighed in resignation; it was probably best for her to stay home anyway.

Joheved and Miriam wished they were going immediately. But Monday and Wednesday were unlucky for new undertakings, and Tuesday, under the influence of Mars, was associated with enmity and destruction.

Finally the day arrived. Rivka had changed clothes three times before finally settling on wearing her newest weekday *bliaut*, or tunic, over her embroidered *Shabbat* chemise. Miriam and Joheved, dressed in their best, were nervous too.

"Mama, are you sure it's all right for you and the baby to go out?" Miriam asked as they passed the old synagogue. "It's barely been two weeks since she was born."

"I'm sure your new sister, Rachel, will be fine." Rivka looked down at the sleeping baby and fingered the amulet around her neck. "I fed her before we left, and I'm perfectly capable of sitting and eating at somebody else's house instead of my own."

As they walked along Rue de Vielle-Rome, the breeze brought an occasional whiff of some mouthwatering odor. Joheved's stomach growled, and she hugged her belly in embarrassment. She'd eaten a good breakfast, but now she was starving.

"I see that we are just in time." Salomon gave her a wink. "Here is the house with the blue door, just as Isaac ha-Parnas directed me."

"Remember your manners, girls." Rivka straightened their clothes and tidied their braids. "Don't speak until you're spoken to and don't talk with your mouths full."

The door was opened by a hulking manservant, as much a guard as a butler. Joheved scarcely noticed the man as she surveyed her surroundings. The linen wall hangings in the main room, or *salle*, were dyed a sunny golden yellow, unlike those at home, which were left in their natural undyed state. Everyone except peasants used wall hangings to shut out drafts, but how extravagant to expend costly dyes on them.

Several people at once could have walked through the massive fireplace at the far end of the *salle*. A large trestle table was set up on a raised floor in front of the hearth, all the better to show off the intricate carvings on its legs. Their hosts sat in matching high-back chairs. Joheved could not have described any of this elegance; she was overwhelmed by the delicious smells coming from the kitchen. Her stomach growled again, and she pressed her arms into her belly harder to silence it.

Isaac ha-Parnas and his son rose to greet them. Despite her limited knowledge of clothes, Joheved could tell that they were as well dressed as they were well fed. Isaac's *bliaut* fell nearly to the floor in luxurious blue velvet folds, while Joseph's, made of similar material, was knee length. Despite the rich fabric and jeweled belts they wore, both men were so plump that Joheved was reminded of two bulging sacks of flour, each tied loosely in the middle. Both men had neatly trimmed beards and bushy eyebrows, so bushy that they appeared to be two fat caterpillars above their eyes. Each man had a large emerald ring on his left hand—the green stone of Zebulun was reputed to increase goodwill and bring success in trade to those merchants who wore it.

"Length of days and years of life and well-being shall they bestow on you." Salomon addressed his hosts with the traditional visitor's greeting from Proverbs.

"Rav Salomon, I greatly enjoyed this morning's Talmud lesson." Isaac took Salomon's arm and led his guests toward the table. "Your explanations brought out several points I hadn't considered before." He inclined his head to Rivka. "I'm particularly honored that you, Mistress, would rise from your childbed to dine with us. My daughter-in-law will be delighted to have feminine companions at the table for a change."

At that moment, a stouter woman entered from the kitchen, followed by two young boys giggling and jostling each other. Joheved recognized Joseph's wife, Johanna. If her husband's torso resembled a sack of flour, Johanna's ample hips and bosom made her look more like a sack of pumpkins tied in the middle. Her round face broke into a grin when she saw them and she hurried forward, her bulky frame moving with surprising grace.

"I'm so glad you could come. I apologize for not visiting yet, but I hope your family enjoyed the fish pies I sent over." She embraced Rivka and cooed at the infant in her arms. "Your baby is adorable, may the Holy One protect her. I can't wait to hear all about her."

"These are my twin grandsons, Menachem and Ephraim, boys who never slow down, except when they're asleep." Isaac patted each of their heads affectionately. "I'm sure you're all hungry. Come, let's eat."

He led them to a stand containing several wooden and metal basins, where they were to wash their hands. Joheved and Miriam hung back; they disliked the gooey soft soap made of mutton fat. Youngsters were always the last to wash, and at home the towel was inevitably clammy and slimy with leftover soap by the time the final girl used it. Joheved and Miriam constantly bickered over who got to go first.

Today, under their father's stern gaze, they reluctantly made their way to the washbasin. But there was no greasy soap container in sight. Instead there was a small cream-colored ball, sitting on a wooden tray. They watched, fascinated, as Mama turned the ball this way and that in her wetted hands, then rinsed them off and dried them on one of two large towels.

"It's made in Italy, from olive oil," Isaac ha-Parnas explained proudly. "It's called Jew's soap."

"Why do they call it that?" Salomon asked. "Do the Italian Jews make it?"

"I don't know who makes it," Isaac said. "But Jews in the south won't use other soaps because they're made from pork."

"There's perfume in it, too," Johanna added, bringing her hand to her nose. "So your hands smell nice when they're clean."

Joheved followed their mother's lead, using a separate towel from Miriam, and sniffed her hands appreciatively when she was done. This fancy Jew's soap had to be expensive.

The men and women sat down at opposite ends of the table. Joheved's mouth watered with anticipation to see each place set with a trencher, a thick slice of day-old bread; this meant sliced meats were sure to be served upon it. Once everyone was seated, Isaac led the blessings, which the servants recognized as their signal to begin serving the meal.

First came a poultry and vegetable stew, served in small two-handled bowls. Joheved knew her mother was watching, so, despite her hunger, she broke off some bread, then slowly and deliberately mopped up her stew from the bowl she shared with Miriam. The twins were fidgeting, tearing up their bread into small pieces, but not eating much of the stew.

As Johanna admonished them to stop playing with their food, Miriam whispered to her sister, "They can't be full already. Maybe they're waiting for something better. . . ."

Her voice trailed off in awe as a servant brought a roasted leg of lamb, still on the spit, before their host, who began slicing pieces onto the trencher in front of Salomon. Another servant laid a tray of roasted onions and turnips on the table, while a third refilled the adults' wine goblets from a large jug.

All except Rivka's, who indicated that she preferred the well-watered wine that the children were drinking. At the women's end of the table, Johanna was eager to hear Rivka's description of her recent confinement, and retell, in turn, the difficulties she had experienced with the birth of her twin sons. Miriam plied Johanna with questions, while Joheved, who had begun salivating the moment she smelled the roast lamb, was losing her appetite.

Not babies again. Since Rachel's birth, they'd been inundated with female visitors who brought gifts of food and a great desire to share their own childbirth experiences. All she'd ever hear about was babies if it weren't for Papa teaching her Talmud. Maybe that's what the men were discussing now. Without taking here eyes off her mother, Joheved turned her attention to the head of the table, but the men were talking politics.

After what seemed like hours of talk about babies and politics the meal was nearly over, but no one appeared in any hurry to get up. Johanna smiled proudly as two servants entered, one with a tray piled high with small pies and the other with bowls of raspberry preserves. Joheved watched as Papa and Mama each dipped a pie in the preserves, and then eagerly followed suit. The flaky pastry was filled with a mixture of spiced meat and raisins in a sweet wine sauce. It was even more delicious than the lamb.

All were wiping their hands on the tablecloth when Isaac got down to business. "Tell me, Salomon the winemaker, what did you think of the wine we had today? Don't worry about hurting my feelings."

Salomon picked up his wine goblet, as if examining its workmanship. "Frankly, the wine was adequate, but by no means up to the high quality of your food. The first wine was inferior to the wine served later, probably made with grapes that had not completely ripened before harvest. The second wine may have been excellent a few seasons ago, but it has aged poorly."

"You know wines as well as you know Talmud," Isaac said, slapping his hand down on the table. "The first wine was from Rheims, the best I could find from last year's harvest. The second was from your own vineyard, a few years back."

Isaac leaned forward and fixed his gaze on Salomon. "A week ago, I asked you how much good wine you could make if you had unlimited resources. It was not an idle question."

The whole table waited in expectant silence, and Joheved

suddenly realized that she needed to use the privy. But she couldn't leave the table now and miss Papa's answer.

Salomon didn't need time to consider his reply. "I have often asked myself this question," he said. "Much of a successful harvest is in the hands of the Almighty. The weather, after all, is not in my control. But to increase the yield of my vineyard, I need people to help me. My family and I were not able to prune the entire property last winter, yet only those vines that were well pruned will produce useful grapes this summer." He shook his head sadly.

"These pruning helpers needn't be Jewish." Salomon spoke louder and faster. "Anyone can work in the vineyard and the grapes still be made into kosher wine. But once the grapes are harvested, the wine production itself must be done by Jews."

"What about this year?" Isaac raised his voice as well, and he pointed his finger at Salomon. "If you are telling me that you can do nothing to boost your current harvest, then how about getting grapes from another vineyard, perhaps an Edomite's?"

Edom was the name used in Genesis to describe descendants of Esau, and the Talmudic rabbis adopted that name for the Roman rulers of Israel. It was one of the more benign names that Jews called the Christians they lived among.

Joheved squirmed in her seat. She desperately wanted to excuse herself from the table, but she had to see if Papa and Isaac could reach an agreement.

"I could doubtless make more wine this fall if I had more grapes and more Jewish workers. But not just anybody's grapes will do!" Salomon shook his finger back at Isaac. "I must first inspect the vineyard. And I will not accept any grapes I haven't tasted." He finished the wine in his cup and set it down firmly on the table.

"Naturally, nobody would expect you to make good wine from bad grapes," Isaac said soothingly. "Now here's my offer." He paused, the eyes of the room upon him. "I'll find a suitable source of grapes and provide all the Jewish workers you need. For my effort I get half the wine made from those grapes. You can keep the other half, as well as any wine coming from your own vineyard."

Salomon's eyes widened and his jaw dropped. "You will assume the entire monetary risk for half the profits?" When Isaac nodded his confirmation, Salomon grinned at the others and joked, "If I had known he was so desperate for good wine, I would have bargained harder."

Joheved couldn't ignore her full bladder any longer. A flustered whisper to Mama and then Johanna was motioning for a maidservant, who quickly led Joheved through the kitchen and past the garden. And not a moment too soon, Joheved thought with relief, as she closed the door and sank onto privy's seat.

As she looked around she let out an impressed "Oh." On the seat next to her sat a basket of the softest moss she had ever felt. Johanna must send servants a good distance out along the river to find it so fresh and velvety. At home, Marie didn't have much time to search out moss for the privy, and sometimes the riverbank was picked over already when she arrived. It was worse in the winter, when all they had was straw. Joheved was sure the parnas's family never used straw.

She went back into the kitchen to wash her hands. Dark and disgusting places usually harbored evil spirits, and one demon in particular, the Shaydshel Betkisay, was known to inhabit privies. People who neglected to wash after doing their business might inadvertently allow the demon into one of their body's openings. Heaven forbid she should touch her eye and induce blindness or wipe her mouth and bring on the flux.

When Joheved returned the table Joseph was speaking, and she helped herself to another pie. "Our entire Jewish community is desperate for good kosher wine and probably most of northern France as well. If Troyes had such wine for sale, we could entice more merchants to our Champagne fairs."

Johanna was frowning at her husband, who swallowed a few times before taking a last look at his wife's stern visage. "Rav Salomon, I have an offer for you as well," he said. "I'd like you to tutor Menachem and Ephraim. I would pay you ten livres a year."

The twins froze as Salomon stared at them. Joheved shot her mother a worried glance. What was wrong with these boys that Joseph would offer ten times the going rate to teach them?

"My sons are smart, perhaps a little too smart for their own good." Joseph was almost pleading. "They question and question and question. Their teacher complains that they do not respect him, so he beats them." He turned and frowned at the boys. "Things have gotten so bad lately that they refuse to go to school at all, and their teacher merely responds, 'Good riddance!'"

Salomon smiled to himself as he listened to Joseph's appeal. They didn't need to bribe him. He would have jumped at an opportunity to have students again, even such young, and possibly rebellious, ones. "I accept your offer, Joseph. I'm sure I can turn these two into scholars." He grinned at the twins. "Anyone who asks so many questions is already on the proper path."

When Salomon announced his acceptance, Rivka nearly wept with relief. Ten livres would lift them out of poverty, and if the wine business went well, they could hire another servant to help care for Leah. At the least there would be linen for new chemises and wool to knit new stockings.

Suddenly the baby started to fuss. Rivka tried to rock her youngest daughter to sleep, but this only succeeded in agitating her further. As the baby's cries grew louder, Rivka looked around helplessly, her gaze shifting from Rachel to Salomon and then back to the baby again. At this juncture Johanna earned her distraught guest's eternal gratitude by announcing that she'd like to accompany Rivka home and help her carry back a few gifts of food.

Joheved hoped she and Miriam wouldn't be forced to leave with the women, and when nobody made that suggestion, she remained seated at the table. Miriam was torn; she had enjoyed the women's conversation, and Johanna had answered her questions about the twins' birth without condescension. But if she left now, only Joheved would get to hear whatever the men talked about when the women were absent. Miriam decided to stay as well.

Suddenly Joheved felt Isaac ha-Parnas's gaze upon her. Her blue eyes met his and he asked her gently, "Joheved, you are Salomon's oldest child, *oui*?"

Joheved was so surprised to be addressed by her host that all she could do was nod. "I believe you to be a clever girl," he continued. "So I'd like to tell you a little story, more like a parable, and you can tell me what you think when I'm done."

Joheved swallowed hard and nodded. What did the *parnas* want from her?

Five

"Joheved," Isaac began, speaking with the same tone of voice parents use when they tell bedtime stories. Mama told her and Miriam tales of Reynard the Fox and his animal associates, while Grandmama told them stories about the people in the Bible, but they both used the same kind of voice.

"Let's say you were a merchant and you came to a new town just before the Sabbath. The inhabitants welcomed you and gave you hospitality. You saw that they were well dressed and had fine homes. What would you think about doing business with them?"

An easy question, thank goodness. "I'd think the town might be a good place to do business. Since the people looked prosperous, they could probably afford to buy things from me."

Isaac beamed his approval and motioned for a servant to refill the wine cups. "The next morning, you went with them to synagogue. But when they removed the Torah scroll from the ark, you saw that the Torah's mantle was not made of fine material with beautiful embroidery, but was torn and shabby." Isaac shook his head disapprovingly. "And there were no silver ornaments to decorate it, no adornment of any kind. Now what would you think about doing business there?"

Joheved smiled. "I'd think that since these people didn't honor the Torah scroll, they might not honor what was in the Torah. They might cheat or steal. I probably wouldn't be so eager to trade with them after all."

Again, the *parnas* questioned her. "Let's say you go to a town with a great Torah scholar. You want to study with him, and you also think that you might do some business there. The residents are well dressed, except for the scholar, whose clothes are old and worn." The gray caterpillars that were his eyebrows rose and he nodded slightly at her, urging her to speak quickly.

Joheved knew she'd better answer before her father objected. "I'd think that the townspeople didn't respect Torah scholarship. Otherwise they'd see to it that their scholar had enough business to support himself." Of course, that was why the *parnas* had offered Papa a business partnership. She took a gulp of wine and, feeling a little tipsy, grinned boldly at Isaac. "I would especially think this if his wife and children weren't well dressed, because a true scholar might be too absorbed in Torah study to care about his own clothes."

Isaac may have been pleased with her reply, but Salomon was livid. "Now listen, you two. First of all, I am not the great Talmud scholar you believe me to be, and it is an insult to my *maîtres* in Mayence to suggest that I am remotely their equal. Second, I have every intention of buying my family new clothes in time for Rosh Hashanah. I am not too absorbed in study to care about their looks."

As Joheved shrank back in her seat, Isaac frowned and Salomon apparently realized that he had protested too strongly. He gave a small bow in Isaac's direction and added, "I know your intentions are good, but I am not worthy of such honor."

Isaac saw no point telling Salomon about the many merchants who had attended last year's fairs, stayed after services to study Talmud, and asked him again and again if this new *chacham* would be there again this year. These merchants, the ones he hoped would form the core of a yeshivah in Troyes, would soon be here for the Hot Fair. New clothes at the New Year would be too late.

Despite her father's anger, Joheved thought about how wonderful it was to study Talmud with him. What if some of the Jewish merchants felt the same way? Like her, they couldn't go to a yeshivah. Maybe studying during the fairs was their only chance. She knew what she needed to say, what might make her father see how important he was.

Isaac saw the sudden eagerness in Joheved's eyes, and he hoped that she might safely say to her father what he could not. "What is it, Joheved?"

"Papa, surely there are Jewish merchants who love Talmud, but can't go to Mayence to study with your *maîtres* there. At least when they come to our fairs, they can study with you. And wouldn't all that trade be good for Troyes?"

Hearing the passion in her voice reminded Salomon of their study sessions. Joheved was right. Even great scholars left the yeshivah eventually to earn a living. Perhaps he could attract a few intelligent minds to his city, then they would attract more, and soon there might be a center of learning here, at least during the Hot Fair months of July and August and again for the Cold Fair in November and December.

"Very well, Isaac, I will accept that you and my daughter think I'm a *talmid chacham* because you don't know any better. And I'll grant that perhaps some merchants who come to the fairs to study Talmud will be disappointed if my family and I are not dressed in the latest fashion."

"Salomon, every Jew in Troyes will thank you." Isaac slapped him on the back. "You see, Thibault forbids any foreign merchant from selling directly to another at his fairs. All transactions must be handled by a local middleman."

"With a portion of the sale going into the count's coffers, as well," Joseph added, winking at Salomon as he drained his cup. Still, if all these learned foreign merchants came to Troyes, there would be plenty of profit to go around.

Isaac lifted his cup in Joheved's direction. "Salomon, your daughter has a mind like a jewel," he said. "What a wife she will make for some lucky man."

Isaac was about to suggest that he would be happy to help Salomon find a bridegroom for Joheved among the merchants and their sons at the upcoming Hot Fair, when the air was split by the first note in the clangorous dialogue of bells that kept time in Troyes. The Cathedral of St. Pierre, the bishop's church, had the right to ring first, then the count's chapel, followed by the Abbey of Saint Loup. Only after these three finished could the bells at the numerous other churches and abbeys chime in. No one could speak over the din.

When the echoes of bells ringing in their heads had finally quieted, Salomon stood up. "Where has the time gone? Here it is midday already and I have work to do in the vineyard."

Isaac took Salomon's arm and walked them to the door. "I'll let you know when I find a source of grapes for your inspection."

Joseph added, "I will bring the boys to you after services on Sunday, while the moon is still waxing." Everyone knew that the waxing moon advanced growth and development, just as the waning moon promoted decay. It went without saying that no student began lessons with a new teacher on a Monday, Tuesday, or Wednesday.

All that week Joheved savored her lessons with Papa. At *Shabbat* services, she felt a special pride when the Torah was read and she remembered what she had learned from him. But pride in her knowledge was mingled with shame about her appearance. Until Isaac ha-Parnas had encouraged, almost ordered, Papa to buy the family new clothes, Joheved hadn't thought much about how hers compared with other girls'. And on the Sabbath, Jewish women wore their finest clothing.

Joheved tried to concentrate on her prayers, but found herself surreptitiously surveying the occupants of the women's gallery. The other girls had colored *bliaut*s, and like usual, they were chattering together in the back. One of them glanced up, noticed Joheved staring, and glared back. Then she whispered something behind her hand and several of the girls giggled.

Joheved knew what the girls said about her and Miriam, that the two of them dirtied their hands working outdoors among the vines, that they were no better than peasants. And they dressed like them too. She and Miriam, with their brown *bliaut*s and unadorned chemises, looked like common sparrows in a room full of peacocks. It didn't help to remind herself that she studied Talmud, while the other girls didn't know Hebrew. Especially since the rest of her family didn't dress well either.

Grandmama Leah wore a violet silk *bliaut*, but it had seen better days. Mama had been wearing her dark red wool one for as long as Joheved could remember, yet at least it had elaborate trimmings. But even Mama's best embroidery could not prevent Papa's clothes from looking old and faded. Every year Mama carefully took them apart, cleaned them, and sewed them back together with the inside out to make them last longer.

Thus he managed to make do with the same weekday outfits he had worn as a student, while his Shabbat *bliaut* was the one he had been married in. Faced with a choice between new clothes and more parchment, Papa bought the parchment. Thanks Heaven he'd accepted Isaac ha-Parnas's belief that foreign merchants might judge Troyes's Jewish community based on how their family dressed, no matter how unfair that judgment might be. Now Joheved and Miriam would get to accompany Johanna to the Hot Fair when the cloth market opened.

The Champagne region's six fairs were the most important trading centers in France, some said in Europe, with the Hot Fair of Troyes the most celebrated of all. Throughout the province brush was cleared back from the roads, which were then patrolled by the count's men. Troyes's streets were clean, or at least cleaner, tavern and hostel keepers lay in supplies for a flood of guests, and an army of officials made sure that all went smoothly.

Mama never liked the fair; it was crowded and noisy and attracted all sorts of unsavory people. She wouldn't hear of Joheved and Miriam going there alone, saying, "Seeing all those fancy goods will make you greedy and covetous, and knowing that we can't afford to buy them will only make you unhappy."

But now, finally, the opening day of the cloth market, they were not only permitted to attend the fair, but would be escorted there by no less a personage than the *parnas* of Troyes and his daughter-in-law. And not just to look, but to buy! Joheved woke up early, and at breakfast Rivka had to remind Miriam and her several times not to bolt down their food. After synagogue, they forced themselves to be patient as Johanna discussed the arrangements with Salomon and Isaac.

Joheved and Miriam tried not to rush their patroness, but she seemed to sense their eagerness and hurried along, chattering to them about the different kinds of fabrics they would find. When they entered the cloth hall, which was actually a large tent, the girls stopped, overwhelmed by the visual feast. The tables were covered with a kaleidoscope of colored bolts, ranging from uncolored and little finished, through green and brown, to the brightest shades of yellow and scarlet. All around was the pleasant hubbub of buying and selling. Mama had been right about the noise level, but her daughters found it exciting, not annoying.

Johanna smiled at their appreciation. "Isn't it beautiful?"

Joheved found her voice first. "I never imagined there could be so many different colors."

Miriam was quiet a bit longer, and then realized that Johanna was waiting for her reply. "It's like an indoor rainbow. I could just stand here looking and be happy."

Joheved's earlier impatience was replaced with hesitation. "There are so many tables. How do we know where to start?"

Johanna smiled to herself. It would be fun to teach the girls how to tell the difference between grades of wool, to recognize fine fabric when they felt it. For the first time in her life, she regretted not having any daughters.

"We won't shop at every stall, my dear," she said. "There are certain merchants whom I trust, and we will deal with them. But you can stop and look whenever you like."

Though wool predominated, there were other materials for sale, and they stopped briefly at stalls selling cotton and linen. They lingered longer at the silk merchants, fingering the slippery smoothness and admiring the bright colors. Many of the silk dealers were Jewish, and most of them knew Johanna. Each insisted that he had the most beautiful silk cloth, exactly what she was looking for.

"Shouldn't we start looking at the woolens?" Miriam asked, turning back the way they'd come. "What if Papa gets here and we haven't found what we like yet?"

"Don't worry." Johanna spoke with an authority the girls had never heard their mother use. "If we haven't found just the right thing when your Papa arrives, we'll send him off to the vineyard and tell him to come back later."

They soon reached the wool dealers' area. There were tables for each of the different towns, and Johanna explained how an expert could recognize at a glance the cloths of Douai, Arras, Bruges, or Ypres. The Flemish towns carefully guarded their reputations, so only their finest cloth was exported to the Champagne Fairs.

As they wandered among the stalls, the girls stole glances at the exotic foreigners. Many spoke in unknown languages, but to Joheved's surprise, she recognized some Hebrew conversations. Several times, she or Miriam found what they thought was good cloth, but Johanna, while praising their discernment, insisted that they continue their search. It was just as well that something had delayed the men's arrival. Services had been over for some time.

They separated to cover more ground and Joheved was drawn to a vigorous bargaining session going on a few stalls away. The two men involved were a study in contrast. The seller, standing behind his table of merchandise, was freckled with auburn hair. He was fashionably dressed in a red *cote* with yellow hose. His outfit might be considered striking, except that the buyer's was outright flamboyant, a robe of brilliant green silk, tied with a blue sash. This man had swarthy skin and a short black beard that tapered to a point. His hair was almost completely hidden under a turban of the same material as his robe. Buyer and seller furiously gestured with their hands, heads nodding or shaking, oblivious to those around them. To Joheved, they looked like a sparrow and a raven, involved in some bizarre mating dance.

She stopped short when she realized that, despite the dark man's strange accent, they were speaking Hebrew. Their argument was fierce, but they weren't angry. It was not about the quality of the fabric, only about cost, and somehow both seemed to understand that an agreement would ultimately be reached. Most potential buyers eagerly found fault with the merchandise; the cloth had been stretched, material left out all night in the damp to increase its weight, the wool dyed by the piece rather than by its thread. But this fabric was acknowledged to be exceptionally fine; the dispute was over its price.

Joheved was intrigued—what was this wonderful stuff? She stood quietly nearby, her attention focused on the two men. Soon Miriam noticed her sister standing there transfixed and joined her. When the merchants saw that they had an audience, they increased their theatrics, unable to resist showing off to the little dears who apparently understood everything they said.

"You won't find anything finer at this entire fair, and you know it." Sparrow, the seller, shook his finger at Raven. "These sheep are rare, they give less wool per animal than most, but require just as much pasture. My supplier is entitled to a fair profit." Actually, Sparrow had already paid the supplier an excellent price. It was his own profit that mattered.

Raven knew this. He had come from the land of the Saracens, carrying rare spices and jewels, on a journey short of miraculous. Pirates had not attacked his ship, highwaymen had not assaulted him on land, and in Provence he had joined a caravan of Jews who seemed to know somebody in charge at each of the toll places on their route. If his return was anything like that, he stood to make a small fortune. Even if his return trip had the usual amount of expenses, he would still arrive home with a tidy sum.

"I have come a great distance, and I must return a great distance." Raven waved his arm expansively. "I cannot pay you so much that it was not worth my coming here. I have a large family who depend on my support." He thought fondly of his three wives and several daughters who would be thrilled with this beautiful cloth. He had already decided to keep some of it.

Sparrow understood that the strange merchant had a large amount invested in the trip. "All the more reason for you to buy my best woolens. The more expensive the goods you bring back, the more profit you can make."

Back and forth they went, Sparrow extolling his wool and Raven insisting that he could not afford it. The seller lowered his price, the buyer countered, and the debate continued. Joheved and Miriam watched from behind a nearby table until Joheved noticed a familiar *bliaut* and looked up to see Johanna standing next to them.

"Johanna, you came just in time. I think we've found the finest wool at the fair."

"If Nissim's sheep are as excellent as he says"—she looked the seller in the eye—"then you are probably right."

"Mistress Johanna, I am overjoyed to see you again." The Sparrow, whose name was now Nissim, bowed low. "And who are these charming young mademoiselles?" He knew she didn't have any daughters, and these girls were dressed too poorly to be members of her family anyway. But they obviously weren't servants.

"The older one is Joheved, and the younger is Miriam. They are daughters of Rav Salomon, the winemaker, Isaac's new business partner. In fact, I expect both men to join us any time now."

Both merchants made small bows in the girls' direction. Raven coughed delicately, and Nissim remembered his manners. "Pardon me, sir. Allow me to introduce Mistress Johanna, wife of Joseph ben Isaac ha-Parnas of Troyes."

"*Shalom aleikhem*—peace be to you—. I am Hiyya ibn Ezra of Cairo." The Egyptian Jew spoke in halting, heavily accented French. "I am honored to meet you."

"Peace be to you as well, Hiyya ibn Ezra. You are a long way from Egypt," she said, switching easily to Hebrew. "I hope our fair will be worth your lengthy journey." She turned to Nissim. "I myself happen to be in the market for some wool cloth, so I'd like to see what your fabulous sheep have produced."

Giving Hiyya a helpless look, Nissim retrieved a covered bolt from under the table and carefully unwrapped it. Miriam couldn't repress an awed exclamation, and the three females leaned forward for a closer examination. The wool was dyed a deep burgundy, yet the color was clear and not the least bit muddy. Johanna caressed the fine cloth and held up a length to the light. She put her face in the material and smelled it.

"This is fine fabric indeed. I'll take enough to make five *bliauts*, one man's, two women's, and two girls', and perhaps some extra for cloaks as well." She turned to the two merchants. "What was your last asking price and your last offer?"

When she heard their answers, she announced that she would pay him exactly halfway between the two amounts. She then turned to Hiyya, "I expect him to give you a better deal, since you're buying much more than I am. But I'll act as your middleman for only half the usual fee, which will make it less painful for him."

If Hiyya was surprised at her boldness, his expression didn't show it. He was a stranger here and this woman was obviously someone important. Hadn't Nissim introduced her as related to the *parnas*? And the girls as the rabbi's daughters?

As if to confirm this, Isaac and Salomon strode up and joined them.

Hiyya ibn Ezra greeted Isaac with the respectful politeness expected toward a community leader. Salomon, however, he met with joy. "Rav Salomon, I am so glad to meet you at last." Hiyya pumped his hand vigorously. "Three things induced me to make this journey. That in Troyes I would be able to buy excellent steel swords and fine wool, as well as study Talmud with their *talmid chacham*. I have not been disappointed in two of the three, and I expect to find the swords soon. Ever since my yeshivah days, I have never understood that difficult section in Tractate *Sanhedrin*. This week you explained it, and I am in your debt."

"You are too kind." Salomon colored brightly. "It is a complex passage, and I only explained it so well because you and that fellow from Provence questioned me so relentlessly."

Joheved had never seen her father look more pleased or more embarrassed. Isaac winked at her and whispered, "I told you so."

"Papa, Papa, we've found the most wonderful cloth. It's so soft and smooth, almost like silk." Miriam nearly knocked him over with her enthusiastic embrace. "And guess what color it is? The same color as wine!"

Salomon kept his arm around his daughter while Nissim proudly presented the material for inspection. Salomon groaned inwardly. The finest wool at the Hot Fair, and he was obligated to buy it, even if took him years to pay Isaac back. Nissim, expert trader that he was, read Salomon's emotions like an open book and tried to figure out how he could diplomatically undercharge the scholar while still maintaining his previous price for the Egyptian.

Isaac ha-Parnas bent over and addressed Joheved. "Speaking of wine, the reason we were delayed is that we were visiting the Abbey of Montier-la-Celle. They have an excellent vineyard. Even your father was impressed. The monk in charge has a green thumb when it comes to raising grapes, but admits he has no such talent for winemaking." Isaac paused dramatically. "Montier-la-Celle's abbot has agreed to trade us his grapes to make into kosher wine, in exchange for an equal amount of regular wine, which I can easily obtain for him."

Nissim saw his opportunity. "I will take payment for this wine-colored cloth with a cask of your kosher wine, payable at the Troyes Cold Fair." He would buy additional casks at that price as well, higher than anyone had paid for Leah's recent vintages.

Hiyya quickly offered to pay 5 percent more for Salomon's wine. To ensure that Jewish scholars had adequate time to study, the community was obligated to see that every avenue of profit was made available to them. This was definitely the time to buy, before the other merchants who studied with Salomon became aware of his profession.

"Gentlemen, please restrain yourselves." Salomon gulped in alarm. "The grapes are still on the vine. I cannot guarantee that I will be able to produce any wine at all this year, let alone wine of the quality your offer requires."

Hiyya ibn Ezra held up his hand to stop Salomon's objections. "I am a merchant who is used to taking risks. The ship carrying my spices may sink in a storm. My caravan may be robbed, my agents captured and held for ransom. If I am willing to expose myself to these dangers and many more, do you think I worry about the possibility that your vineyard will fail, with only a few short weeks left until harvest?"

Six

As much as Joheved and Miriam longed to visit the fairgrounds, the next day they had to go to the parchment maker's. Papa used a great deal of parchment to write his *kuntres*, his Talmud commentaries, but full pages were expensive. Most tanneries sold scraps at reduced prices, and one tanner in particular had a daughter, Catharina, who enjoyed the sisters' company and often set aside the best pieces for them. Catharina didn't have any visitors her own age. The tanneries gave off such a dreadful smell that most people chose to stay as far away from their streets as possible.

When the girls arrived at the shop, Catharina jumped up from her work to greet them. "I'm so glad to see you. Foxes attacked the sheepfold at a manor near Ervy. The lord wants to salvage what he can, which means we'll be getting a wagonload of sheepskins, and, wouldn't you know it, my brother won't be home for days."

"So here we are, with all these skins coming in together, and just me and my father to work them," Catharina said as they collected the scraps she had set aside for them. "If you help us, you can have some of the parchment when it's ready."

"I suppose so," Joheved said slowly. She had no idea what it took to make vellum, except that it was sure to be a smelly process. "Will it take long?"

"Only a few days. Especially if you both come."

"We'll have to ask Papa's permission, of course," Miriam added, a bit more enthusiastic than Joheved. "But I expect he'll be eager for more parchment."

"And you won't be getting odds and ends," Catharina called out as they began walking home. "You'll have lots of full pages."

"Think. We'll be able to bring home folios of parchment." Joheved walked faster. Papa would be so surprised with their good luck.

"But now that Papa has a teaching job and a wine partner, he'll probably be able to buy all the parchment he wants."

"I don't know. Did we actually promise to help or did we only say we'd ask Papa?"

"Ask Papa what?" Salomon said as he opend the courtyard gate for them. Embarrassed at being overheard, they had no choice but to explain their dilemma. He made his decision quickly. "You must certainly help make parchment if you said you would."

There was enough distrust between the Jews and Edomites as it was; he didn't want anyone saying that his daughters had made an agreement and then broke it. "I believe I will help as well. The parchment maker has been kind to us, and now I can return the favor. And I am curious to see how the stuff is made. After all, Torah scrolls are made of parchment."

That evening, Rivka was still wide-awake after feeding the baby, so she decided to kiss her daughters good night. Finding their bed empty, and annoyed at her husband for allowing them to stay up so late, she went downstairs to complain. It took only a few moments of listening to realize what Salomon was discussing with her daughters and she could not restrain her temper.

"Salomon, are you out of your mind? How can you consider teaching our daughters Talmud? What will everybody think?" Joheved and Miriam sat in stunned silence as she ranted on. "Once you get them studying Talmud, they won't have any time to learn how to run a household—they won't want to learn how to run a household." Her voice rose even higher. "Don't you realize that no man will want to marry a girl who is more learned than he. We'll never find them husbands!" Rivka put her hands on her hips and stared stonily at Salomon. "I won't tolerate it, I tell you, I won't."

At first Salomon was just as shocked as the girls. But whatever misgivings he had about this endeavor, he was not about to be cowed by his wife. "If I want to teach my daughters Talmud, I will teach them Talmud!" he thundered, banging his fist down on the table. "It doesn't matter what anybody else thinks."

Rivka cringed and slowly backed away. "It obviously doesn't matter what I think," she muttered as she stormed off to bed.

Too upset to study anymore, Joheved and Miriam quietly let

Salomon tuck them in. He admonished them to be sure that their chores were done before they studied, so their mother could find no fault with them. Miriam eventually drifted off to sleep, but Joheved lay awake.

It hurt when Papa and Mama argued. Would they get along better now if they hadn't lived apart all those years? She remembered how anxious Mama always became as the festivals approached, and how relieved Mama acted after Papa finally left. Probably she'd feel that way too if her husband spent most of his time at a yeshivah far away and only came home three times a year . . . except she didn't want a marriage like her parents'. But she had to marry somebody, and who else but a scholar would agree to marry a girl who studied Talmud?

CLANG! CRASH! Joheved had just finished braiding her hair the next morning when she heard the violent sounds coming from the kitchen below. Uh oh, Mama was banging the pots around something awful. She must be really angry.

The clanging sounded even louder as Joheved cautiously entered the kitchen. Miriam was already inside, trying to calm the fretful baby, while at the other end of the room, their mother brandished two copper skillets as if they were weapons. Just as Joheved reached her sister's side, Salomon burst in.

He still had on his tefillin, the small boxes containing words of Torah that pious Jewish men wear when they say their morning prayers, and his face was bright red against the black leather box tied to his forehead. Joheved and Miriam shrank from his furious presence.

"Would you mind keeping quiet? I'm trying to pray." He stood stiff as a statue, his fists tightly clenched.

Rivka's reply was defiant. "I'm trying to make breakfast."

Salomon took several steps in his wife's direction and raised his right hand. She in turn held the pans up between them. As his daughters watched in dread, he stopped and stared at the tefillin box tied on his bicep and its leather straps that wound down his arm. Then he lowered his hand and said in a voice as hard as steel, "Woman, you can bang your pots as much as you like, but I will not stop teaching my daughters Talmud!" He pounded his left hand on the table, sending the crockery skittering across it.

Rivka burst into tears. Joheved could barely keep from crying herself. Had her parents been possessed by demons? In desperation she gave the baby a pinch, and the room was immediately filled with the infant's howls.

Salomon could see that he would be surrounded by weeping females if he didn't soften his stance. He inwardly cursed his short temper and watched his wife fumbling at her chemise, trying to quiet little Rachel with her breast, and he felt ashamed. He knew she'd have to calm herself in order to nurse properly, so he waited until the baby was sucking before he spoke again. "Rivka, I cannot stop teaching our daughters now that I know how eager they are to learn."

Rivka sighed in resignation. "Very well then, teach them whatever you think is appropriate, but please try to be discreet." She emphasized the word *discreet*.

Did Salomon understand the importance of discretion? Everyone else knew how much the demons hated Torah scholars. Did he realize his selfish need to teach might make Joheved and Miriam their target? As if the world wasn't dangerous enough. Rivka reached up to stroke the amulet around her neck.

"Don't worry, Rivka, Torah study confers divine protection." Salomon leaned down and spoke softly to her. "And I promise to find great scholars to marry our daughters, so they will have husbands more learned than they are."

Rivka rearranged the dishes in their previous position and the family managed a calm breakfast. Salomon reminded her that, after services, they would be working at the tanner's.

Joheved was still thinking about her parents' fight when they turned onto Rue de la Petite Tannerie. Catharina was waiting for them at the door to her father's shop. "I was afraid you wouldn't come," she said, hugging Joheved, then Miriam. "Papa is already down by the canal, setting up the frames."

Catharina led them down a well-worn path through cattails and rushes toward the Rû Cordé canal. A few years ago, to improve sanitation, Count Thibault had ordered a canal dug off the Seine. Tanners relocated onto two streets near where the canal exited under the town walls, thus sparing Troyes's inhabitants from drinking their effluent. The canal was not without its undesirable effects; city authorities regularly fished out the bodies of careless drunkards.

As far back as she could remember, Joheved had been warned to stay well away from the river's edge. She worried that the ground near the canal might be slippery and muddy, but to her relief, much usage had tamped the trail solid. There were even clumps of fresh green moss growing nearby. Perhaps they could collect some later to take home for the privy.

They reached a clearing where the sheepskins lay in small piles, surrounded by swarms of flies. The stench of decomposing animal remains assaulted them, and Catharina quickly moved them upwind to where her father was fastening one of the raw skins into an open wooden frame. The stink was not so bad there, but Joheved had trouble breathing and began to cough.

"Here, take a deep breath of this." Catharina's father thrust a damp handkerchief at her. The pungent smell of vinegar replaced that of dead sheep and Joheved's head cleared.

"*Merci*, I feel better now."

"Let me explain what we'll be doing today." The parchment maker held up four fingers. "Parchment is made in four stages. The first one is getting the skins attached to these wooden frames and into the river. We also need to scrape the wool from the outsides and the flesh from the insides, but if we can't get it all off today, it can be done later."

"I'm fairly handy with knives," Salomon said. "I've been pruning grapevines for years."

"Excellent. The girls can pin the skins between the frames, then you and I will clean them up and get them into the water."

He was surprised that the Jewish scholar was also a winemaker; the cathedral and abbey scholars who frequented his shop seemed to do nothing except write their manuscripts and pray. And they looked like it, too, all pale and flabby. But Salomon was sinewy and tanned, apparently used to hard work outdoors.

They soon made an efficient team. Joheved and Miriam grabbed opposite ends of a sheepskin and pulled. When they stretched it as far as they could, Catharina slid a frame around the skin and closed it tight. Then the framed skin went to one of the men, who scraped it with his knives until the girls announced that the next frame was ready. At that time, no matter how much or little had been cleaned from the skin, he dropped the frame into a holding area that the parchment maker had prepared in the shallow water.

The day grew steadily warmer. Joheved pushed her vinegar-soaked handkerchief up on her forehead to catch the sweat forming there, and Miriam removed hers entirely. "I can't believe it, but your father was right," she said to Catharina. "I can barely smell the sheep skins anymore, although you'd think they'd really stink now that it's gotten so warm."

Joheved cautiously sniffed the air. "Maybe the vinegar in our noses has stopped us from smelling anything?"

Catharina laughed as they tried to figure out if their noses still worked. "I have an idea. I'll find some flowers and a dead fish, and you see if you can tell the difference between them."

The parchment maker laughed too. Not only was his daughter happy, but the piles of sheepskins were shrinking rapidly. "You probably don't smell the skins because there aren't so many of them. I believe we can get them all into the frames by tomorrow afternoon. And in this heat, that's not a moment too soon."

He added emphasis to his statement by splashing himself after he dropped his latest frame into the canal. Then he grinned at the sweating girls and sent a gentle stream of water in their direction. They rewarded him with squeals and giggles.

Salomon was trying to work efficiently, but he could only manage to scrape the skin three times on each side before a new frame was ready for him. A breeze coming off the river afforded some relief from the heat and stench, but his chemise was drenched with perspiration. He watched with amusement and envy as his daughters got wetter and wetter.

Joheved and Miriam heard a sudden splash as something heavy fell in the water. They anxiously scanned the work area for their father, and just when they were sure the river demons had seized him, he resurfaced and waved to them from the middle of the canal.

"Miriam, look." Joheved grabbed her sister and pointed toward the water. "Papa's all right. He's swimming!"

The parchment maker stared at Salomon in amazement. It never occurred to him to bathe in the river. He knew that Jews went to the public baths regularly, but most Christians avoided immersing themselves in water for fear of the demons lurking there.

Salomon swam gracefully toward the shallow water where his daughters stood waiting for him. "Papa, Papa, I didn't know you could swim." Miriam wanted to hug him, but he was so wet that she just clung to his hand instead.

"I didn't mean to startle you." He pushed his wet hair back off his face. "My father, Isaac, may his merit protect us, taught me how to swim in this same river when I was a boy. And on hot days in Mayence, the yeshivah students often go swimming together in the Rhine. You see, there is a Mishnah in Tractate *Kiddushin*, which says that a father is obligated to teach his son to swim."

"Oh Papa, can you teach us to swim?" Wouldn't it be wonderful, swimming around in the cool water on hot days?

"Non, Joheved. A father is only required to teach his sons to swim, not his daughters." Salomon spoke in a voice that brooked no discussion. Men and boys went swimming naked, which made it an inappropriate activity for girls.

When Joheved's face fell in disappointment, he added, "Considering how your mother feels about demons, I can only imagine the fuss she'd make if I took you into the water. She's already angry enough at me for teaching you Talmud."

The afternoon passed swiftly and the next day went just as smoothly. As the parchment maker predicted, they were able to finish well before sunset. When the girls set off to collect moss to take home, Salomon asked when they should return.

"I don't see any reason to burden you further," the parchment maker replied. "After these skins have sat in the Seine for several days, they'll be soft and fairly clean. I'm sure my son will be home in time for the second stage, when we move the frames into troughs of lime solution."

"But I'd like to see the complete procedure, even if I can't help much. What happens after the skins sit in the lime? Could you use help with the next part?"

The parchment maker stepped into the water to attach a net over the frames to keep hungry fish away. "After they've spent two weeks in the lime water, we scrape each skin clean of all remaining wool and fat. This is easier than what we did today, because the lime causes most of it to come off in the troughs. Then we rinse the skins in the river and put them back in lime for another two weeks."

"What happens when they're finished with the lime?" As much as Salomon wanted to participate in the entire process, he couldn't make a commitment for months of work. He had new students to instruct and the vineyard to tend.

The parchment maker understood the hesitancy in Salomon's voice. "Next comes the third stage. We let the skins dry, all the while cleaning them with pumice, chalk, and water. Then they're ready to be thinned, which is the final step. Sometimes it takes months before we're finished. We take our time and work carefully, until all that remains is to trim the parchment and fold it into sheaves."

Salomon felt around the frames to make sure that the netting covered his side completely. "So when should I come back for the third part?"

"Just wait for a rainy day when it's too wet to work in your vineyard. You'll be welcome to join my family in the workroom, thinning and scraping the skins into parchment."

The summer weather remained excellent, much to Salomon's consternation. The better the climate and the more luxuriant his plants' growth, the more the vintner fretted over possible disasters awaiting him. A late frost would cut down his tender buds before they flowered, and too much rain could hamper fertilization by washing away the pollen. Then, if midsummer was cool and humid, mildew would destroy the grapes before they'd begun to grow.

Salomon could only pray for the warm, calm weather that facilitated the critical flowering and fruit-set. Thus far this year the Creator obliged him; the young grapes hung heavy on the vines, slowly becoming translucent. But peril still threatened. A sudden hail shower could crash down with a summer storm, and the result would be destruction of leaves, shoots, and grapes.

This summer Salomon divided his time between tending his vineyard and tending his new young students. The first thing he had to do was teach Menachem and Ephraim to ask questions, to shower him with their most difficult queries. He did this by asking them questions in return, and not just academic ones.

Why didn't the lions on Noah's ark eat the other animals? What did Abraham say to the Holy One when he was told to sacrifice his son? How did Sarah die? How did Rachel help her older sister, Leah, marry Jacob first? If all the cattle in Egypt died in the fifth plague, where did the cattle come from that were smitten with boils in the sixth plague?

Why wasn't Joseph buried in Egypt? Why did Moses break the tablets containing the Ten Commandments?

Joheved and Miriam loved this part of studying Torah, when Salomon told them about the people in the Bible. Midrash, he called them, stories that explained so much more than the original text. Judging from Menachem and Ephraim's rapt expressions, Joheved could see that they loved it too. She and Miriam would sit near the kitchen, listening carefully as they silently spun thread, embroidered, or did mending. They knew their father expected them to question him at bedtime, more vigorously than the boys did. Still they were careful to give no indication of how closely they followed their father's lectures. Although Rivka no longer spoke of it, the girls were sure there'd be trouble if their studies became public knowledge.

No matter how much Rivka disapproved of her daughters studying, she had to admit that their spinning and needlework had improved greatly. Joheved in particular had become quite adept at spinning flax into thread for weaving linen. Mending and embroidery required frequent attention, but without looking, Joheved could draw out fibers from the mass of flax on her distaff, twist them together into a continuous strand, and wind it onto her spindle. The process was tedious, but her hands took on a life of their own as she listened to her father teach Torah.

In the morning Joheved and Miriam attended services, and after *disner* they accompanied their grandmother for the short walk beyond the city walls to the vineyard. From their vantage point atop a small rise, the vines' bright green foliage was easily identified among the golden fields of grain. The road was surrounded by tall stalks of wheat, soon to be cut, and the remains of oat fields already harvested. Here and there livestock grazed on fallow land, which would be enriched with their manure.

Despite Grandmama Leah's failing memory, she still knew exactly which leaves should remain and which ones pulled off to allow maximum sunlight to reach the grapes. She lectured them continuously on the importance of careful foliage control as if neglecting to trim leaves properly were a moral failing.

"You must have enough leaves to feed the growing grapes, but shaded branches produce thin, soapy wine." Leah tore off several offending leaves and let them flutter to the ground.

In another part of the vineyard, the men hired by Isaac ha-Parnas were working on the vines that Salomon's family had not been able to prune last winter. These plants were unlikely to produce grapes worth pressing this season, but their leaves still had to be trimmed. Joheved and Miriam, remembering how their grandmother had antagonized previous workers, tried to keep Grandmama Leah occupied far away from the *parnas's* employees.

One day Grandmama Leah suddenly started screeching, "Someone's stealing my grapes!" She picked up a discarded branch and, shaking it at the men in the distance, began running toward them. "Keep away from my grapes, you thieves! Get out of my vineyard!"

"Grandmama, stop! Wait for us!" Joheved and Miriam took off after her, but she was amazingly agile for her years and eluded them among the vines. "Nobody's stealing your grapes. Those men work for us."

Salomon managed to catch up with her before the workers could make out what she was shouting at them. "It's all right, Mama, it's all right," he repeatedly reassured her, using his most soothing voice. When she grew calmer, he tried to distract her. "Mama, look at those gray clouds. Do you think it will hail?"

Leah stared at the darkening sky and declared, "Don't worry. This storm will only rain gently for a few days, which is just what the vineyard needs."

"Perhaps we ought to be getting back home then." Salomon sighed, unable to hide the sadness he felt whenever he was forced to confront his mother's deterioration. Most of the time he tried not to dwell on her condition; it was too depressing and there didn't seem to be anything anyone could do to cure her.

Seven

When night fell Salomon was still thinking about his mother. The air was sultry and humid, leaving Troyes's inhabitants feeling damp and poorly rested when the church bells woke them at dawn the next morning. It was drizzling when Salomon's family left for services, and by *disner*, the rain was coming down so heavily that Salomon announced that they might as well help the parchment maker finish his skins. Joheved and Miriam drew their cloaks tightly around them and set out with their father down the muddy street toward the canal.

They walked carefully along the road, staying as close as possible to the buildings where the jutting second floors offered a narrow shelter for pedestrians below. The girls tried to keep well away from the center of the street, where the running water was moving faster and faster, taking with it all the garbage that had accumulated since the previous rainstorm. As they hurried along, they encountered servants emptying the fetid contents of their masters' waste pits into the small creek that had recently been the road. They grinned at each other to acknowledge that they had managed to avoid that odious chore.

The parchment maker was at home with his son and daughter, each working on sheepskins stretched out on frames. He greeted Salomon cheerfully and waved them over to dry out in front of the hearth. Then he showed Salomon how to scrape the skin clean with various small knives, to remove even the tiniest blemish on its surface. At the same time, Catharina taught the girls to rub the scraped skin with pumice to make it soft and smooth. Soon they were all busily occupied.

The parchment maker's son announced that he had recently done business with a Jew who raised sheep nearby. "His name is Samuel and he has a small estate near Ramerupt. He was glad to find a tanner who would deal with him regularly because his son's a student who needs a lot of parchment." The youth smiled at Salomon. "I happened to mention that we had a Jewish scholar in town who frequently bought from us, and the man nearly attacked me with questions about you."

Salomon's eyebrows raised slightly. "Really now. What interest could a man who raises sheep have in me?"

"First off, he was curious how long you've lived in Troyes because he couldn't remember any scholars here. I said you'd grown up here but only moved back again last year."

"I don't think I know him." Salomon stroked his beard. "I wonder if his family comes to Troyes for Rosh Hashanah."

"I doubt it. You see, he asked about your family and nearly jumped out of his chair when I mentioned your daughters." The son laid down his knife, grinning widely. "He wanted to know how many unmarried ones you had, how old they were, what they looked like. I told him about your girls and asked why he was so interested. Did he perhaps have an unmarried son himself?"

Joheved felt herself getting warm and moved her chair away from the fire. Catharina and Miriam were looking at her strangely and Salomon gave her a quick glance before encouraging the speaker to continue.

"So Samuel admits that he does have a son yet unmarried, his youngest boy, the same one who needs all the parchment, who is away studying in Mayence." The parchment maker's son leered at Joheved, apparently enjoying her discomfort with the subject. "But I must apologize. I neglected to ask for his son's name."

Joheved was greatly relieved when Salomon ended the conversation by announcing that he needed silence to concentrate on the skin he was scraping. As she smoothed the pumice along her nearly finished parchment, Joheved tried to sort out her disconcerting feelings.

Of course she'd be the first to marry; she was the eldest. And it was her father's job to find her a suitable husband. So why was the subject so embarrassing? Why did it bother her to hear people discussing a prospective match? Joheved had no answer for herself, only the knowledge that the more she considered the question, the more embarrassed she felt. She caught herself continuously polishing the same area of parchment far thinner than necessary, and in dread of tearing the precious material, she resolved to stop daydreaming and pay full attention to her work.

The rain continued in fits and starts, sometimes raining so hard that Salomon stopped his knife and listened long enough to ascertain that it was only rain he heard, not hail. Then, with a sigh of relief, he'd begin working the skin again. The end product was indeed parchment, and he was pleased that he could visualize the entire process.

A sudden increase in the room's illumination made the occupants realize that the rain had halted.

"Papa, I think it's stopped raining for a while," Catharina said, laying aside the skin she'd been working. "I need to do some shopping for *souper* and it was raining too hard to go out earlier. Maybe I should go now while it's let up some."

Before her father could say anything, her older brother rebuked her. "You should have gone in the morning, rain or no rain. Now the bread won't be fresh and the best meat will be gone. Papa spoils you too much, letting you put off your chores."

The parchment maker scowled at his son. "I don't see why Catharina should catch cold in the rain so you can have fresher bread. She was very useful with all these skins, and I dare say that her pumice work is finer than yours. If you must have the best meat, get up early and go buy it yourself."

Eager to avert any further arguments, Salomon suggested that his daughters could accompany Catharina to the food stalls and then go on home during this lull in the storm. "I'd like to stay a while longer and see the final steps." He attempted to mollify the son by appealing to his expertise. "Can you show me how you trim and fold the parchment?"

The youth took Salomon over to the worktable by the window. "We need good light for this part, folding the parchment into pages and cutting them perfectly straight." He glowered at his sister as she left, and she stuck her tongue out at him in return.

The three girls made their way to Rue de l'Epicerie, holding their skirts up out of the mud and trying to dodge puddles. The greengrocer and butcher shops were open, but to Catharina's dismay, the bakery was shuttered.

"Oh no, they must have sold all their bread this morning. Now what am I going to do?" She looked close to tears. "My father may put up with less than fresh bread for my sake, but he's going to be mad if I come home with no bread at all. And my brother will gloat over my failure for days."

Miriam took her hand and started pulling her toward the bridge. "Come with us to a bakery in the Jewish Quarter. The one near the castle is always open late."

"How do you know they won't be shut, too?" If this Jewish bakery were closed, Catharina would have gone all this distance for naught. But she soon received the answer to her question, for the mouth-watering smell of newly baked bread wafted toward them from the direction they were heading.

Joheved took a deep breath of the sweet odor and explained, "This bakery is a partnership, owned by both a Jew and a *Notzri*. On Sunday, your Sabbath, the Jewish partner bakes and sells bread, and on Saturday, our Sabbath, the *Notzri* bakes and sells bread. The same thing during Passover and your holy days. They're never closed, no matter what day it is."

"What's a *Notzri*?" Catharina's eyes narrowed with suspicion.

"*Notzrim* are those who worship the one from Nazareth, you know." Not eager to discuss what names the Jews had for the gentiles, Joheved urged her companions to hurry.

The sky had darkened alarmingly, but the bakery was in sight. Like other shops in Troyes, one of the bakery's windows had shutters that opened up and down rather than to the sides. The lower shutter was propped up parallel to the ground by posts, thus forming a large counter. The upper shutter was fastened halfway open to make a roof over the counter, sheltering its contents. Here the baker and his family served their customers. Catharina was not alone is her desire to buy bread during the storm's lull, so the three girls had to wait.

Miriam teased her sister. "Joheved's going to be a rich lady when she marries the sheep farmer's son. She'll have all the wool, parchment, and lamb roasts she wants."

Catharina joined the good-natured assault. "Did you hear my brother say the boy's father has a manor near Ramerupt? What a life. Bossing servants around and producing wheat, sheep, and babies! Lots and lots of servants." She elbowed Joheved suggestively. "And lots and lots of babies."

"I wonder what he looks like. Maybe he'll be tall, dark, and handsome." Miriam giggled. "But, if he's still not betrothed, he might be short and ugly."

"I bet he's a hunchback from spending all his time bent over books." Catharina covered her mouth with her hands, trying to repress her laughter.

"If he's a student, he's probably thin and pale. They spend all their time indoors and hardly ever eat." Miriam's tone became serious. "But if he's a scholar in Mayence, he'll be more learned than you, Joheved, just what Papa wants."

All this marriage talk was too much for Joheved. "I don't care if I have a thousand servants. I won't marry a scholar who spends all his time in Mayence and hardly ever comes home." She stared defiantly at Miriam. "I want a husband who lives in the same house as I do every day, not just on holidays."

She hadn't intended to reveal her fears to them, and until she'd spoken she hadn't realized what her fears were. But now she knew—she didn't want to sleep with a stranger. And a husband who only spent a few weeks a year at home would always be a stranger, no matter how long they'd been married.

Dismayed at her outburst, Catharina and Miriam tried to offer solace. But they both knew Joheved would have little say over whom she married. Miriam put an arm around her sister's shoulder. "Don't worry, Joheved. Most husbands don't stay away from home as much as Papa did."

Catharina had more practical advice, although it wasn't very comforting. "You're a Jew, which means you're either going to marry a merchant or scholar, and both of them are usually away from home a lot. Besides, maybe you won't like your husband much, and you'll be glad when he's away."

"It wasn't so bad having Papa gone, and I don't think Mama minded it as much as you think you will, Joheved," Miriam said. "Except for being poor, I liked living with just Mama, Grandmama, and you. Who needs a man around all the time anyway?"

Joheved had no answer for her, only questions jumping around inside her mind. Did Mama really prefer it when Papa wasn't home? And why didn't Grandmama Leah get married again after Grandpapa Isaac died? Aunt Sarah hadn't remarried either. Maybe there was something bad about marriage that nobody talked about. Yet Mama worried so desperately that her daughters wouldn't find husbands.

"At least you know that you will get married," Catharina said soberly, interrupting Joheved's musings. "All Jews get married, some more than once. No matter how poor you are, even if you're ugly, they make sure you get married. But if my father doesn't save enough money for my dowry, I'll never get a husband. I'll end up an old maid taking care of him forever."

Joheved and Miriam were shocked into silence at the thought of Catharina's not being allowed to marry. They knew about monks and nuns, but those people chose that life, and besides, they weren't Jewish. For Jews, to be fruitful and multiply was the Creator's first commandment, and anyone who refused to marry was considered selfish in the extreme, even sinful. Who knows what wonderful scholars would be denied life if their ordained parents didn't wed? Even old people beyond childbearing, like Isaac ha-Parnas, were supposed to marry. Didn't the Holy One create Eve because it was not good for Adam to be alone?

"But you're so pretty, Catharina," Joheved said, her own doubts dissolving into concern for her friend. "Even if your father doesn't leave you a dowry, you can still marry. Our maidservant, Marie, is saving her wages for her own dowry. She's engaged to a cobbler's apprentice, and by the time he's a journeyman, she'll have enough money for them to get married."

Miriam wanted to encourage Catharina, too. "Marie gets to marry whoever she wants. She earned her dowry herself and chose her own husband."

They reached the counter just as the first few drops of the renewed storm began falling. The baker's wife recognized the young rabbi's daughters and gave them a misshapen loaf to share on their way home. Joheved thanked her and tore off a piece for Catharina, who quickly took it and waved good-bye.

No sooner had Joheved divided the remaining bread in two, than Miriam whispered to her, "Look at those beggars. They're soaking wet. I bet they've been here all day."

Several paupers, sensing they were under discussion, stretched out their hands toward the girls. Miriam started to tear her bread into pieces, but Joheved stepped between her and the beggars.

"Surely you don't intend to give your bread away." Joheved's vehemence increased. "They're probably only pretending, to gain your sympathy."

The raindrops grew larger and more frequent, and Miriam pulled her cloak close around her. "What about those children?" She pointed to several skinny youngsters, dressed in sopping rags. "I don't care if they are fakers. I'm giving them bread anyway."

Joheved was hungry, but it was impossible to eat her own bread while watching the pathetic children wolf down Miriam's. With a sigh, she handed her bread to the small beggars and continued home with her sister in silence. A new worry assailed her and her appetite diminished.

At least Ramerupt was nearby. But what if Papa arranged a match with someone who lived far away and she had to move to another town, like Mama did when she married Papa? She might never see her family again. If she didn't live near Papa and Miriam, she'd never be able to study Talmud either.

She walked slowly, each foot suddenly heavy as lead, feeling increasingly pessimistic about her chances for a good marriage. There was nothing she could do about it either; her future was in her father's hands, and the Holy One's.

Also walking home from the parchment maker's, Salomon tried to remember the youngest students in Mayence. Was one of them from Ramerupt or had Salomon returned to Troyes before this particular boy began yeshivah? Parchment was scarce and expensive (and after today's work, he could see why), so Talmudic scholars were trained to develop prodigious memories. An advanced yeshivah student was expected to know Scripture by heart, plus all the major tractates of the Talmud. Salomon, who had learned many of the minor tractates as well, was justifiably proud of his memory, and knew if he had ever met such a boy at Mayence he would be able to recall it.

Voilà! He slapped his thigh in triumph. He had it. The more he considered the students whose first year at the yeshivah had coincided with his last, the more he knew he was right. The boy's name was Meir ben Samuel.

Older students like Salomon normally had little contact with their youngest colleagues. They all prayed together in synagogue and attended the same lectures, but contemporaries generally studied with each other. The first year was especially difficult, and boys at this level rarely did more than listen attentively and try to remember as much as possible. They rarely asked questions.

But Salomon remembered this one youth, mainly because they had traveled in the same merchant caravans to and from Mayence. He could picture Meir in his mind: small and thin, rather gangly actually, in the way boys are just before they start growing. Meir's trunk of books and new fur-lined cloak proclaimed him to be the son of a prosperous man. The boy never mentioned Ramerupt, but Salomon knew he lived nearby. Once, when he'd expressed concern about the youth's going on alone while the others stopped in Troyes, Meir had assured him that home was only a short ride away.

Their first trip together, they'd hardly spoken. Salomon utilized his time expanding the notes he'd taken during the recent session, and Meir was too intimidated to approach the *chacham*. By the following journey, Meir was so curious about the older man's journals that he couldn't resist asking about them. Salomon remembered that the youth had been both astonished and impressed. Talmud study was an oral tradition and an extensive *kuntres* such as Salomon's was unheard of.

Salomon smiled wistfully. He had explained to Meir that his yeshivah days were limited, that he'd been taking notes all these years so that when the time came, he'd be able to study Talmud by himself. Meir had been sympathetic and offered reassurance that anybody with such excellent records would never forget his studies. After that, the ice was broken and the boy had plied Salomon with questions.

The more Salomon recalled about the youth, the higher his opinion of him. Meir's questions had shown intelligence and enthusiasm for learning. It was possible . . . he might make a proper husband for Joheved. Then financial reality intruded into Salomon's pleasant reverie. The boy's father had an estate, which meant he was some sort of lord. He would expect his son to marry into an equally prominent family, to wed a girl with a substantial dowry. Salomon sighed heavily and continued home. He needed to concentrate on his new students and his grapes this summer; he'd worry about other matters later.

Eight

All summer, Joheved and Miriam tried to do as many of Mama's chores as possible so she could devote her attention to making the family's new *Shabbat bliauts*. The days were long, and between doing extra chores, working in the vineyard, and trying to find time to study Talmud, Joheved was so frustrated and exhausted that she didn't know whether to scream or cry. One night, after a difficult day when Mama had to redo nearly all of Joheved's embroidery, she couldn't wait for bedtime.

Making an effort to distribute the blanket evenly, Rivka tucked her daughters in and kissed them good night. She had no sooner gotten into her own bed, than the evening's quiet was broken by Joheved and Miriam quarreling.

"Ouch! You kicked me. When was the last time you trimmed your toenails?"

"Never mind my toenails. If you stayed on your side of the bed, you wouldn't get kicked."

"How can I stay on my side of the bed when you always grab all the covers?"

"That's not true. You're the one who hogs them all."

"No, I don't. You do."

As her daughters' disagreement degenerated into a litany of alternating accusations, Rivka sighed and pondered whether her intervention was necessary. She was so tired; taking care of Rachel and Leah, plus feeding all these guests and making her family's new clothes, kept her busy from dawn to dark, even with Marie to help. Joheved and Miriam tried to be useful, but they were more valuable in the vineyard than at home.

There was a sudden holler from Leah's bedroom. "You two girls keep quiet out there. I'm trying to sleep!" Silence resumed, and Salomon found his household asleep when he returned.

Soon the days grew shorter and the Troyes Hot Fair was but a memory. Salomon's family was busy with the grape harvest, but not his family alone. Most of the Troyes Jewish community was stomping on grapes, working the winepress, siphoning wine from one container to another, or sealing the casks—all jobs that had to be performed by Jews. Everyone worked furiously to transform the ripe grapes into kosher wine. Once that task was done, they could turn their attention to the spiritual arena. The holiest days of the year, Yom Kippur and Rosh Hashanah, were almost upon them. The wine would ferment in their casks until winter, when the final result of the year's labor would be known.

A few days before Rosh Hashanah, Johanna stayed a while after dropping her sons off for their studies. She had a package with her, a gift for the girls. Joheved and Miriam gathered around the dining table while Johanna unwrapped the most beautiful silk *bliaut* they had ever seen. It was such a vibrant blue that Joheved knew the color had to come from the rare dye, indigo. The embroidery around the neckline and sleeves, a pattern of leafless trees done in silver thread, shimmered in the light. How could such a present be for them? This was clothing for a princess.

"Johanna, thank you, but shouldn't this stay in your family?" Mama asked.

"My father-in-law gave it to me when I became betrothed to Joseph." Johanna smiled softly as she smoothed out the blue silk. "I was Joheved's size then, and, as you can see, it's been a long time since I've been able to wear it. I want to give your girls a Rosh Hashanah present, to bring them a good new year."

Joheved and Miriam stared at Johanna, amazed that she had once been small enough to fit into the beautiful *bliaut*.

Johanna laughed at their consternation and patted her broad belly. "You can see how much marriage has agreed with me." Then she became serious. "The twins' birth was so difficult that Sarah doubted I'd have any more children." She sighed. "So I thought I'd let Joheved wear it, and then Miriam after her."

"Very well, but we will have to return it if my husband doesn't approve." Rivka reached out to caress the *bliaut*'s softness. When Joheved wore this dress, she would also have to wear a red ribbon, to protect her from the Evil Eye.

On the afternoon before Rosh Hashanah, Joheved found herself dressed in blue silk with a red ribbon tied under each sleeve. It was important to start the year wearing one's best clothes and having eaten a lavish meal, since "He who has spent less is given less, and he who has spent more is given more." She could smell the traditional New Year's stew of squash, beets, and leeks cooking on the hearth. She wasn't fond of the dish, but because those vegetables grew rapidly, Jews ate them this time of year with hopes that their possessions would also multiply quickly.

This was the Day of Judgment, when the Almighty opened the Book of Life and decided whose names would be inscribed there for the coming year and whose would not. Joheved tried to meditate on her behavior of the previous year, to remember the good deeds and resolve to add to them, to regret the evil deeds and repent of them. For the whole month of Elul, she had not quarreled with Miriam over the bedclothes or whose turn it was to wash first.

For the most part, Joheved was excited and proud of her magnificent new holiday *bliaut*, but sometimes she felt fraudulent, at best like a little girl dressing up in her mother's clothing, and at worst like the small round pieces of mud mixed into black peppercorns by dishonest merchants. But Heaven forbid she should give Satan, the Accuser, an opening, so she tried to concentrate instead on how nice her family looked in their new outfits.

At first Mama insisted on tying the red ribbon around her neck, as protection from such envy, but Joheved had protested so vigorously against such a conspicuous splash of red that Mama finally agreed to let her wear the ribbons more discreetly. Miriam had no such worries. She was thrilled with her own soft wine-colored wool *bliaut*, expertly embroidered by Rivka with a pattern of vines and grapes, and she thought her sister looked positively royal.

"Joheved, the other girls will be fit to be tied when they see you all dressed up in indigo silk." She grinned as she sewed up the sleeves on her sister's chemise. "They don't dare be envious or covetous on Rosh Hashanah."

"At least we won't be envious or covetous this year," Joheved said seriously. With all their new clothes, she didn't feel quite so ashamed at services anymore.

Miriam was enjoying her musings too much to be serious. "Everyone will have to think generous thoughts, to compliment you on your new outfit and wish you a good year. And if they don't, that's why you're wearing red ribbons." She laughed out loud at Joheved's appalled expression.

If anyone was jealous of Salomon's family's sudden splendor, they hid it well. But Salomon was not the only one whose business had done well this year. The entire congregation seemed to be dressed in colorful new wear.

"May you be inscribed and sealed for a good year," they complimented each other. Cheerfulness and goodwill abounded, to assure the Holy Judge that they were worthy of another year of goodness and blessing.

In fact, the year had been so bountiful that the congregation didn't know what to do about *kapparah*. As long as anyone could remember, Jewish families slaughtered fowl on the eve of Yom Kippur, a cock for a man and a hen for a woman. Each person waved their bird overhead three times while reciting the following declaration: "This fowl is my substitute, this is my surrogate, this is my atonement. May it be designated for death, and I for life." The ritual was completed by presenting the bird to the poor, in accordance with the words from Proverbs, "Charity delivers from death."

As much as she enjoyed eating chicken, Joheved resented getting the rich man's sins along with his bird. Salomon may have felt the same, for when the community found itself with too few poor Jews willing to take its many fowl, he instituted an alternate procedure. This year, after the chickens made the usual progress around their proxies' heads, a family would give their monetary value to charity and then eat them themselves.

Yom Kippur dawned quietly in Salomon's courtyard. Much to Joheved's relief, she and Miriam only had to prompt Grandmama Leah occasionally during the lengthy services for Rosh Hashanah and Yom Kippur. But the best thing about the New Year was that, with the harvest finished, Papa had time to study Talmud with them every day.

Several miles north of Troyes, at his family's manor in Ramerupt, the New Year had not gotten off to a good start for Meir ben Samuel. His first year in Mayence, he had missed his family terribly, especially his sister, Hannah. The second year wasn't so bad. No longer overwhelmed by the change from child's schoolroom to scholars' yeshivah, he'd begun to enjoy his studies.

This year everything changed. He supposed that things had first become different in June, when he returned to celebrate the festival of Shavuot and his sister's wedding. For years after the marriage of their older brother, Meshullam, Meir and Hannah were the only children at home. Every evening in bed, they shared their day's activities with each other, and on *Shabbat* they took long walks in the fields around the manor.

He hadn't had time to be lonely during that previous visit, not with the house crowded with wedding guests. His visit was a whirlwind, and returning to his studies in Mayence was a relief. Meir knew he and Hannah wouldn't have the same relationship after her marriage, but he never imagined how different things would be. Of course, she would sleep in another room with her new husband, Simcha, but he didn't expect to be so bereft when he found himself alone at night.

Meir briefly considered asking his parents to let one of the servants share his room, but he already had enough of Marona, his mother, treating him like a little boy. So he nervously lay in bed the first few nights, noticing for the first time the myriad of sounds that disturbed the evening's silence. Sometimes he could hear Hannah and her new husband whispering in the next room and he missed her.

As he stayed longer at his childhood home, Meir realized that his relationship with his sister would never be the same. She spent as much time as she could with her husband and although she tried to spend time with her brother, it was clear that he was no longer her favorite. When his father suggested that they spend a few days in Troyes together before he returned to the yeshivah, Meir jumped at the idea of leaving Ramerupt early. He asked if he would have time to visit with a *chacham* who lived in Troyes, one whom he had known briefly at the yeshivah and greatly admired. Samuel smiled and said he didn't see why not.

The night before their departure finally arrived, and Meir was still packing when his parents joined him. This was a normal part of his leave-taking ritual, although his parents usually spoke to him individually. Samuel would say how proud he was of his scholarly son, encourage him in his studies, warn him to be careful on the road, and give him money for expenses. Marona echoed her husband's pride, hugged Meir, and told him how much she was going to miss him. In addition to slipping him money, she provided some treats to eat on the way.

This time his parents stood together in his room. Samuel shifted from one foot to the other, apparently reluctant to begin the conversation, and Marona looked back and forth from husband to son, nervously waiting to see who was going to speak first. Meir was trying to think of something to say that didn't mention their odd behavior when Samuel broke the silence.

"Meir, you're our youngest son, and we're proud of how well you're doing at the yeshivah." Samuel cleared his throat before continuing. "It has always been our dream that one of our sons should become a scholar. The Holy One has blessed us and given us sufficient affluence that you may remain in Mayence to study as long as you like."

So far this sounded like the speech Samuel always gave. What was going on? Then his father surprised him with a question about Salomon of Troyes.

"You mentioned wanting to visit a friend of yours in Troyes, a *chacham* you studied with at the yeshivah. Tell us about him."

"Salomon ben Isaac was one of the finest scholars I've ever known, and we used to travel together to and from Mayence." Meir spoke carefully, unsure what his father wanted to know. "He was very kind and would help me when I had trouble understanding something, even though he was older and I was just a beginner. He could explain the most complicated passages."

His parents seemed pleased with that, and Meir grew more voluble. "It was a terrible loss when he had to leave the yeshivah two years ago to support his family. I think his mother was ill. He had a wife and some children back in Troyes, who depended on him." Meir walked over and embraced his parents. "I'm glad that we're not poor. I mean I appreciate that I can study for as long as I want without it being a hardship for you."

Silence descended on the room again. Samuel cleared his throat a few more times, but Marona spoke first. "Now that Hannah is married and settled, we only have you to worry about. With you being such a good student, we think it would be splendid if we had grandsons who were scholars, too." She smiled and waited for this to sink in. "So the best thing would be for you to marry a *chacham*'s daughter."

As the implication of his parents' words dawned on Meir, a blush crept up his face. How wonderful if his parents could arrange a match between him and one of Salomon's daughters. But did Salomon have any daughters? Had he ever met them?

Samuel seemed to find Meir's reaction amusing. "I must say that I'm impressed with your devotion to your old colleague. Your mother and I have been doing some quiet investigating, and we've heard from both my cousin and the parchment maker of Troyes that your Salomon has two daughters, neither of whom is betrothed yet." He grinned fondly at his youngest son, now quite red in the face. "What do you think?"

Meir didn't know what to say. Things were happening so fast and his parents were waiting for an answer. "I would, of course, marry whomever you thought was best for me," he stammered. Then he realized that they probably wanted a more positive reaction. "I mean that I would like to marry one of Salomon's daughters, and I would appreciate it if you could make the arrangements."

"We can meet Salomon and his daughters while we're in Troyes," Samuel said. "If all goes well and you find one of them attractive, then we can open negotiations. If possible, I'd like to have the betrothal arranged before you return to Mayence."

"But I do think Meir must consider the older daughter as his potential bride," Marona added. "Salomon is unlikely to consider a match for a younger girl if the elder is still available."

Meir's heart beat faster. Once he joined Salomon's family, he would never lack a study partner, he would live in a home imbued with Torah, and he would be close to his family in Ramerupt. He had visions of his parents enjoying his and Hannah's children playing together. "I'm sure the older daughter will be best. Then we can get married sooner."

"Since we're all in agreement, we'd better get to bed." Samuel affectionately tousled his son's hair. "We'll need to have an early start tomorrow morning if we expect to arrive in Troyes before morning services are over."

Nine

The next morning Meir could scarcely hide his impatience as his parents consulted with the steward about what supplies the manor needed. Convinced they'd be late, he was greatly relieved when they entered the synagogue just as the Torah reading began.

Upstairs in the women's section, Joheved didn't take any special notice of the unfamiliar latecomer. She was completely engaged in preparing to translate the Hebrew Scriptures into French for the women's benefit. Leah had managed Rosh Hashanah without trouble, but the lengthy Yom Kippur service, done while fasting, had been too much for her, and she had asked her surprised granddaughter to translate the afternoon Torah portion in her stead. Since then, Leah had left the daily Torah translations for Joheved, much to the girl's consternation.

Johanna noticed the tall, slender newcomer immediately. This stranger had not been in Troyes for the holidays; Johanna would have remembered the aristocratic brunette. Her demeanor was happy, so she was not here for a funeral or illness, but nobody in town was celebrating a wedding or birth in the near future either.

Johanna moved closer, determined to engage the woman in conversation. "*Shalom aleikhem*, my good mistress, welcome to Troyes. What brings you to our fair city?"

"Johanna, peace be to you as well," the woman sitting next to the stranger answered for her. "Allow me to introduce Marona, the wife of my cousin Samuel. They have an estate near Ramerupt, and are in town to attend to some personal business." Marona's clothes were of excellent quality, a bit too fine for a weekday, and the longer she watched them, the more peculiar Johanna found the women's behavior. Their conversation seemed skittish, almost clandestine.

"In case your cousin has neglected to inform you," Johanna addressed Marona sternly, "I must remind you that all business conducted in Troyes requires a local agent."

Marona turned red, but her cousin giggled and quickly whispered, "They're not here to transact financial business, Johanna. They're here to negotiate a betrothal. Samuel and their son are downstairs right now."

"Will you be quiet!" Marona hushed her cousin through clenched teeth. "We haven't approached the girl's family yet and you're making announcements to total strangers."

Pleased at having discovered the newcomer's intentions, Johanna retreated. Was it her imagination or were they watching Joheved? When Joheved began translating the Torah portion, the women's interest and approval was so manifest that Johanna was convinced she had seen enough. She had to get to Rivka's house, to give her time to prepare for these potentially important guests.

When services concluded, Samuel and Meir made their way to where Salomon stood at the front of the synagogue, speaking earnestly with those who remained after the Talmud discussion. When Salomon saw Meir, his eyes opened wide and he hurried to embrace the boy. Meir was the first student he'd seen from Mayence since he'd left and the ache of nostalgia surprised him. He tried to refocus on Meir. How the boy had grown; he was as tall as Salomon now.

Meir saw the tears in Salomon's eyes and almost started crying himself. He quickly turned away to introduce his father and Salomon's expression became pensive. So here was Meir, and here also was his sheep-raising father, who was looking at Salomon the way he might appraise a ram at the livestock fair.

Salomon stroked his beard as he considered the situation. Joheved could certainly do worse than this young fellow. He had no trouble persuading them to return home with him, and was convinced that his suspicions were correct when Meir introduced his mother, waiting outside.

Sure enough, Samuel enthusiastically linked arms with him and announced, "Let's take the long route there, I have something important to discuss with you on the way."

The calm that Salomon projected was in direct contrast to the whirlwind of activity at his house. Rivka had just finished changing

Rachel's swaddling when Johanna rushed in, two servants weighted down with food in her wake. One servant produced several fat capons and had them roasting on the spit in Rivka's hearth before she could say anything. The other proceeded to furiously chop up a variety of vegetables.

Johanna burst into speech. "Rivka, we have to hurry. An out-of-town family is here today, and I'm almost certain that they intend to open negotiations for Joheved's hand. If I'm right, they will be here for *disner*, and we mustn't disappoint them."

"What?" Rivka gasped. "Who are these people . . . and how do you know they're here about Joheved?" She tried to resist being caught up in her friend's sense of urgency, but it was hopeless. "How much time do we have before they get here?"

Johanna told her what had transpired in synagogue. "I asked Joseph to investigate further. If he tells us it's a false alarm," and her tone of voice made it clear that this was unlikely, "then we'll just have a nice quiet meal here with our two families. By the way, the boy's parents are Samuel and Marona of Ramerupt. Do you have any idea who they are?"

"None at all. Nobody has approached us." Rivka was too shocked to think about such possibilities (Salomon had never mentioned the parchment maker's gossip to his wife, certain that she would only nag him more about planning for the girls' future).

Rivka went to the cupboard and took down her best linens, while Johanna got the wine cups and dishes. As they set the table, she said to Rivka, "Samuel has a cousin here in Troyes, who happened to mention that he has an estate nearby. And I must say that Marona's clothes were fine indeed." Johanna smiled conspiratorially. "I have a feeling that your daughter may do well for herself with this match."

"To see Joheved married into a wealthy family would be wonderful, of course, but I know my husband wants a learned son-in-law." Rivka shook her head. Only an ignorant rich man would want to marry a poor *chacham*'s daughter? A wealthy scholar would have his choice of brides.

After Rivka dropped a wooden bowl and knocked over two wine goblets, Johanna decided that talking about something else might calm her friend's anxiety. "Speaking of betrothals, I've heard that Count Thibault is planning to marry Adelaide de Bar. That will give him more land to the south as a buffer against the Duke of Burgundy."

Rivka walked over to the hearth and stirred several pots cooking in it. "Count Thibault is over fifty now. I wonder if he'll get any children from Adelaide." Somehow it was easier to discuss the count's marital prospects than her own daughter's.

"I don't see why not. I believe that she's still less than thirty years old."

"It will be exciting to have a big royal wedding in Troyes," Rivka said, pausing to taste a spoonful of liquid from one of the pots. "It's a good thing we had a big grape harvest this year."

Johanna frowned. "It's also a good thing the Hot Fair was so lucrative, since Thibault will certainly levy extra taxes on us Jews to pay his wedding expenses."

At that moment, the door opened and in came Grandmama Leah, followed by her granddaughters.

"Oh, what smells so good?" Joheved asked.

"Look, we're having capon, and Johanna's here, too," Miriam pointed out. "What's the party for?"

Rivka's panic returned and she didn't know what to say, but Johanna was eager to explain the situation. "Joheved, I don't have time to tell you everything now, but I believe some people will be here soon to discuss a betrothal between you and their son. So please go change into your blue silk *bliaut*."

Joheved was too stunned to speak, but Johanna continued giving instructions. "Miriam, why don't you help your sister dress? And you can wear your new *bliaut* too. Hurry up, now."

The two girls raced upstairs. Miriam insisted that Joheved take time to rebraid her hair. They said little besides the occasional *"Mon Dieu,"* and "I wonder who it could be." Miriam didn't have the heart to tease her sister. She'd never seen Joheved's face this white, and the poor girl's hands were shaking so badly that Miriam had to do her hair for her. If Johanna said people were coming to arrange Joheved's betrothal, then it must be so. But why hadn't Papa or Mama told them about it earlier?

They came downstairs to find that Isaac and Joseph had arrived with some delicacies for dessert. Joheved, her dread mounting, listened as the men confirmed that they had seen Salomon leave the synagogue with a well-dressed couple and a youth whose likeness proved him to be their son.

Joheved wanted to ask questions, but her mouth was too dry. It didn't help that the last thing Miriam said before they joined the company was, "Remember, they can't make you marry this fellow if you don't want to. You have to agree or there's no betrothal." Then Miriam disappeared outside to keep a lookout.

Rivka sensed her daughter's fear and tried to reassure her. "Don't worry, Joheved, you look lovely." She then added, as much to herself as to her daughter, "I'm sure everything will be fine," and gave Joheved a lengthy hug.

"Joheved will make an excellent impression," Isaac ha-Parnas said loudly. Then he turned and whispered to Johanna, "It's a good thing you got us invited, too. Salomon is a scholar with his head in his books, and now I can make sure any negotiations are done under my auspices."

Suddenly Miriam popped back into the room. "They're coming, they're coming," she squealed. "Papa, a gray-bearded man, a tall woman, and their son."

When Salomon arrived home with his guests, he was surprised, but not too surprised, to find Joheved and Miriam in their best clothes, a sumptuous meal prepared, and Isaac ha-Parnas's family visiting as though nothing extraordinary was happening.

As the guests were introduced, Joheved's heart was pounding so hard she was sure everyone in the room could hear it. The boy's name was Meir and he had apparently attended yeshivah in Mayence with Papa. Conversation avoided the subject of what these people were doing in Troyes, besides sending their son back to his studies. Salomon had Meir telling him all the latest news from the yeshivah, while Isaac questioned Samuel about his livelihood. Miriam couldn't resist poking her sister when Samuel replied that he had an estate in Ramerupt that produced wheat and sheep.

At the women's end of the table, Marona tried, with Johanna's help, to draw Joheved into conversation, but Leah dominated their discussion. Joheved didn't mind—her emotions were too jumbled for her to say anything worthwhile. Rivka, relieved beyond belief upon hearing that Meir had actually studied with her husband, hoped desperately that Leah wouldn't make up some improbable tale because she could no longer remember what had really happened.

The two young people, on whose account these strangers found themselves eating together, said nothing to each other. They knew better than to stare, but couldn't resist frequent glances in the other's direction. Joheved didn't find Meir especially handsome; he was too skinny and his skin was bad. But he wasn't ugly. His hair was nice, a warm shade of brown that was flattered by his deep gold *bliaut* and sunny yellow chemise, identical to his father's. He had a pleasant low-pitched voice, and when she caught him looking at her, he grinned and revealed a fine set of white teeth. She was glad he was taller than she was.

And he was a yeshivah student. She could study as much Talmud as she wanted now that Papa had found her a learned husband. Then her heart sank. If she married him, they would spend who knows how many years apart. Meir's father could probably afford to keep him studying in Mayence a long time. She tried to conquer her despair. Maybe his father would pay for both of them to live in Mayence, but then she'd never see her family.

All the grown-ups around the table seemed to be staring at her, and Joheved knew she was trapped. She didn't dare refuse the match, not with all the adults in agreement, not after Papa had made good on his promise to find a scholar for her to marry. Yet she didn't really want to refuse—for some reason this youth appealed to her. Enough! She must stop thinking about potential problems, problems that were out of her control, and start the New Year with an optimistic frame of mind.

The first thing Meir noticed about Joheved was that her eyes were exactly the same shade of blue as her *bliaut*. But she was so young, still only a child. He glanced at her chest and quickly looked away; she hadn't even grown breasts yet. An early marriage was out of the question and he tried to hide his disappointment. The girl wasn't bad looking—not that it mattered what she looked like, as long as she wasn't ugly. The important thing was, she was Rav Salomon's daughter. Their sons would be great scholars.

Gradually the meal came to a close. Grandmama Leah was having trouble sitting still, and Rivka suggested that the girls take her for a walk. To everyone's surprise, including his own, Meir jumped up and offered to accompany them.

But before they could leave, Salomon stood up and addressed his daughter. "Joheved, you know why all these people are here?" he asked gently. When she nodded, he continued, "I will not betroth you without your consent; you must see your bridegroom and accept him."

Salomon glanced back at Joheved, whose gaze was fixed on the plate in front on her. "So here he is, standing in front of you. Do you want Meir ben Samuel for your husband? Shall I work out an agreement with his father?"

Though she knew what her answer would be, what her answer had to be, Joheved made a point of looking at Meir from head to foot before speaking. Then she took a deep breath and tried to keep her voice from shaking. "*Oui*, Papa, I will have him. I give my consent." At least her future husband did not shy away, but returned her stare with an equally searching look.

Meir knew that he would be asked for his approval next and he didn't wait for the question, but said with what he hoped sounded like confidence, "I have seen your daughter and I agree to take her as my bride."

Salomon felt uncomfortable with magical incantations based on Scripture, but he had attended enough betrothals to know that it was expected. He stroked his beard and considered what mystic blessing he would invoke for the couple. Then he put his hands on Meir's and Joheved's shoulders, closed his eyes, and chanted in Aramaic:

How sweet is your love, my own, my bride. When the wind blows softly and the shadows flee, I will betake me to the mount of myrrh. You have captured my heart, my own, my bride. Drink deep of my love. How much more delightful is your love than wine. Every part of you is fair, my darling, and there is no blemish in you.

Although they had no idea what words Salomon had spoken, Rivka, Marona, and Johanna had tears in their eyes.

Isaac stood up, raised his wine goblet, and offered his congratulations. "So may joy be with you in the future."

Leah alone seemed unaffected. "We can celebrate when the agreements are signed. And with my granddaughter's *yichus*, you shouldn't need a large dowry. My brother was the *talmid chacham*, Simon ben Isaac ha-Zaken, may his merit protect us, and Rivka's brother, Isaac ben Judah of Mayence, is also a great scholar.

"Papa," Meir whispered urgently. "Isaac ben Judah is one of my teachers in Mayence. Some say he'll be the next *Rosh Yeshivah*."

Samuel nodded back with a grin. Content to be aligned with Salomon's family based on the *chacham*'s own worth, he now found that Joheved had a greater lineage. Isaac ha-Parnas was also smiling; this new information would make negotiations easier.

Leah, oblivious to the effect her announcement was having on the company, had sat long enough. "Right now I need to walk. Who's coming with me?"

The four walkers left the others to work out the financial details. They strolled along the Rû Cordé canal, which marked the western edge of both the old city and the Jewish Quarter, past the public baths and the castle at the north end of the canal, where it split off from the Seine. Then they walked south again toward Thibault's palace. Joheved's moment of boldness had passed and she left conversation to her grandmother and sister. Miriam proudly informed Meir that they knew how to make parchment, and he admitted his ignorance on the subject.

It was only as they approached Salomon's courtyard that Joheved found the courage to speak. "Meir, you understood what my father said?" It was more a statement than a question, but he nodded and she continued. "It sounded like the middle portion of Song of Songs, except the verses were out of order."

"You're right. I've been to several betrothals in Mayence and somebody always makes an Aramaic incantation from that chapter of Song of Songs. But they never say it like it's written." Meir hesitated a moment as his gaze met hers, and he stared into those incredibly blue eyes. "I mean, sometimes they transpose the words or recite a few of the verses three times. Once I heard it chanted backward."

"Thank you for explaining it to me," Joheved replied as they approached the house, and Meir felt a rush of pride at being able to demonstrate his esoteric knowledge to her.

It took several days, under Isaac's patient supervision, to negotiate the detailed betrothal agreement. Joheved found that spinning thread kept her nervous hands occupied, giving Marona plenty of opportunity to observe her future daughter-in-law's competence with spindle and distaff. Samuel, eager for scholarly grandsons, didn't quibble about the small dowry, one third of Salomon's vineyard and some jewelry from Leah. As a token of his esteem for the *chacham*, Samuel would begin providing any parchment Salomon needed. The *nisuin* (wedding) would take place as soon as Joheved was old enough. As was customary, Samuel would provide the wedding banquet, excepting the wine, of course, which would be Salomon's pleasure to supply.

With everything finally arranged, the congregation was invited to the *erusin* (betrothal) ceremony. Two young students called as witnesses were told to observe carefully as Meir betrothed Joheved by reciting the ancient formula, "Behold, you are consecrated unto me by this ring, according to the Law of Moses and Israel."

Now Joheved and Meir were married according to Jewish law. Only death or divorce could prevent *nisuin*, and the cohabitation that would finalize their marriage.

When Meir finally left Troyes, groggy and hungover from the previous night's raucous betrothal celebration, he could hardly believe how quickly his life had changed. When his fellows in Mayence asked about his holidays, and he acknowledged that he now had a fiancée waiting for him back home, several more nights of revel followed. By the time Meir was back at his studies, those days in Troyes seemed almost like a dream. It wasn't long before he couldn't quite remember what Joheved looked like, except that she had blue eyes. That she was learned enough to recognize Song of Songs recited at random in Aramaic had escaped him completely.

For Joheved, excepting that Rivka made her cover her hair in public now, life went on much as before. She worked on the vintage, studied Talmud, and helped Grandmama Leah lead the women's services. She didn't feel betrothed, whatever that ought to feel like—she didn't think she felt different at all. But in quiet moments, especially at night, she remembered that somewhere to the east was Meir ben Samuel, the young scholar who, *Le Bon Dieu* willing, would one day be the father of her children. And she wondered what he was studying.

Ten

Similar to its summer cousin, the Troyes Cold Fair began with cloth and finished with account settling. The winter livestock market was larger, because sellers hoped to avoid maintaining extra animals through the cold weather. Numerous knights looking to buy warhorses also ensured the presence of merchants selling armor and weapons. For Salomon's family, the Cold Fair was when the new vintage would be ready to taste and sell. The Parisian wine dealers would be there in force, needing only to load their barrels onto barges and float them downriver to market.

As during the Hot Fair, Salomon spent his mornings and evenings studying with the merchant scholars. Determined that all his vines would be properly cut back this year, he spent the short afternoons preparing to prune the vineyard. Joheved, Miriam, and Grandmama Leah's job was pulling out the vine-props and stacking them between the rows. As much as the girls disliked all the bending involved, they realized that their father had the truly backbreaking work.

Vineyards were planted on hillsides, and men had the task of transporting back up the slope earth that had gradually slipped downhill during the year. After several years of this, a vintner could truthfully claim to have carried his entire vineyard on his back. Thank Heaven Isaac ha-Parnas had found several strapping young fellows willing to work for meals and a few coins at the end of the week, reducing Salomon's toil considerably.

One afternoon, Grandmama Leah announced that she was too cold to continue in the vineyard. So Joheved, sure her grandmother would never be able to find her way back alone, volunteered to take her home.

Marie met them at the door with a look of relief. "Joheved, I'm so glad to see you. Mistress Rivka is out shopping, Rachel is napping, and Isaac ha-Parnas just arrived with a strange man to see Master Salomon."

"It's all right, Marie. Just help Grandmama get upstairs," Joheved said. "I'll see to Isaac ha-Parnas myself."

Isaac introduced the stranger as Hiyya ibn Ezra's agent.

"I hope that Hiyya is well," Joheved said in Hebrew, not sure how well the man spoke French. "And that he arrived home safely."

"Hiyya had an excellent voyage," the stranger replied, also in Hebrew. His gaze darted around the room. "Will your father be home soon?"

"I don't believe Papa was planning to leave the vineyard until sunset. Perhaps you should come back and see him later."

Isaac broke in before his companion could answer. "I don't think that will be necessary. It's nearly sunset now, and I'm sure he'll be home directly. In the meantime, you can show us the wine cellar and explain the different vintages."

Joheved lifted up the trapdoor and showed the two men the stairs going down into the cellar. The high windows brought daylight into the large room, and when Joheved reached the floor, she took a deep breath and sighed. The wine casks stood protectively around her and the wine cellar smelled pleasantly damp and fruity. Isaac was treating her like a knowledgeable adult. Was it because she was betrothed now, or did he still remember how she'd helped him convince Papa to buy new clothes?

"This year we'll have four different kinds of wine." Joheved hesitated when Hiyya's agent stared at her blankly. How could she make the wine process understandable?

"First," she began again, "or maybe I should say first and second, we have wine made with grapes from our vineyard and wine made with the abbey's grapes. That's two kinds."

The men were cautiously looking around the cellar, with Isaac pointing out identifying marks on the various barrels. He urged Joheved to continue.

"Then with the grapes from each vineyard, there's the free-run wine, which gets drawn off before we use the winepress, and then there's the additional amount the press produces. That's four kinds. The free-run wine is superior, so it costs more, but we won't know exactly how much more until Hanukkah."

The stranger's eyes narrowed in suspicion. "You don't have any idea what you'll charge until the dealers make their offers?"

Isaac put a reassuring arm around the man's shoulder. "During Hanukkah, after the Sabbath has ended, Salomon and Jewish wine-makers throughout France will taste their new vintages for the first time. He, and those of us lucky enough to be in his company, will toast the festival with his new wine." Isaac gave the man a knowing wink. "I expect quite a celebration this year."

"And, therefore, quite a profit for Hiyya." The merchant edged his way toward the outside door. "Could you please excuse me, I need to find the privy."

Isaac directed him to the back of the courtyard, but made no move to follow. "Joheved, you've impressed me once again." He grinned down at her. "A lord's son and a scholar—I think you have a worthy husband in Meir ben Samuel. Don't you agree?"

Joheved tried to control her emotions, but the sudden change of conversation took her by surprise. Everyone else had been so thrilled with her betrothal that she had kept her fears to herself. But Isaac looked at her with such concern that, tears rolling down her cheeks, she unburdened herself to him.

"Please don't think I'm being finicky or ungrateful," she concluded. "But I don't want to live in Troyes while Meir lives in Mayence, and I don't want to live in Mayence if the rest of my family lives in Troyes." It sounded so selfish; when she actually heard the words out loud, she felt ashamed.

But Isaac didn't admonish her. He smiled and said gently, "But one of the clauses in your betrothal agreement stipulates that part of your dowry will be Meir's board at Troyes from the beginning of the Hot Fair through the end of the Cold Fair. I reminded your father how busy he was last summer and suggested that Meir could help with the younger students."

Joheved blinked and looked at him without comprehension.

"It is one of my foremost goals that your father establish a yeshi-vah in Troyes," Isaac whispered.

Once they were married Meir would be living in Troyes at least half the year! Joheved couldn't believe her ears. "Does Papa know about your plans?"

"I haven't told him as directly as I've just told you," he admitted. "But he must realize that he can't go back to Germany. Even if he hired the best workers available, the vineyard still needs his supervision."

"That's true," Joheved said. How unhappy Papa must be, stuck here in Troyes teaching his daughters and little boys.

"Don't worry about your father," Isaac said as he helped Joheved close the cellar windows. "Already some of the best scholars in Europe are bringing their business to our fairs in order to study with him. I'm sure it won't be long before they want their sons to study with him as well."

Joheved wanted to believe him; he sounded so confident. She kissed his palm, the way children were taught to show gratitude to adults. "Thank you for telling me all this. I feel much better." Her fears melted away as she contemplated this wonderful new possibility.

"If only it were always this easy to change a woman's tears to smiles." Isaac chuckled and headed for the stairs. "Come along now, we'd better see what has become of our customer."

Joheved wiped her nose and followed Isaac up the stairs. She came into the kitchen and learned that her mother had invited the merchant to dine with them the first night of Hanukkah.

Because the Cold Fair began on All Saints' Day and didn't end until late December, Troyes was always full of Jewish travelers during the festival of Hanukkah. Each evening at sunset, Salomon's family squeezed into the crowded synagogue and watched as the holiday lamps were lit with blessings and songs during the service. Then, like other local Jews, Salomon's family shared their holiday *soupers* with guests. Before they ate he kindled the family's holiday lamp, a beautiful silver menorah that Leah had brought as part of her dowry. After the meal came more singing.

Women refrained from work while the lamp was lit, in memory of a woman's heroism. Salomon explained that, in those days, a virgin about to be married was required to first submit to the local sovereign. So when the high priest's daughter was betrothed, the Greek general demanded that she lie with him. She went to the general's tent, fed him cheese until he was thirsty, and then gave him enough wine to make him drunk. Once he'd fallen asleep, she severed his head, and when the enemy army saw their general beheaded the next morning, they fled.

Some women made the entire week a holiday, but Grandmama Leah regarded this as excessive and only allowed her granddaughters to rest on the first and last of the eight days. With all the pruning and digging that needed to be done in the vineyard, they couldn't afford a whole week of idleness. But for Joheved and Miriam, who had helped their father move vineyard soil uphill the previous winter, that the onerous job was being done by somebody else was vacation enough.

As wonderful as the weekdays were during the Festival of Lights, its Sabbath was better. During services, the Scroll of the Hasmoneans was read aloud, and the congregation listened raptly as the reader recounted the triumphs of Mattathias and his sons over the evil despot Antiochus, intent on destroying them. Grandmama Leah had read this part for so many years that she had no difficulty translating for the women, and Joheved thought she made it sound as if she'd lived through the time herself.

"When the enemy was defeated and the Hasmoneans entered the sanctuary in Jerusalem, they found only one flask of pure olive oil. Though its quantity seemed sufficient only for one day, it lasted eight days, owing to the blessing of the God of Heaven who established His Name there. Hence, the Jews instituted these eight days as a time of feasting and re-joicing, and of kindling lights to commemorate the victories the Holy One had given them."

On most Saturday nights, Jewish families prolonged their evening meal, reluctant to leave the Sabbath and reenter the regular week. But tonight Isaac's family joined them for a brief *souper*, and when they went outside to light the Hanukkah lamp at the doorway to the courtyard, Joheved was surprised to see over a dozen people waiting, covered dishes in their hands.

"I see the celebrants have already started to arrive." Isaac laugh-ingly nudged his host. "I wonder how many more we'll have by the time the Compline bells ring."

Salomon and Joseph made tables by laying boards on some of the benches outside as people continued to enter the courtyard. Salomon eyed the growing crowd with anxiety. "I hope there's still some of my wine left to sell tomorrow."

"You mean our wine," Isaac said, throwing his arm around Salomon's shoulder. "Consider it an advertising expense. If this vintage is as good as everyone seems to expect, merchants will be lining up at your door, making exorbitant offers."

Musicians soon arrived, and the strains of popular Hanukkah melodies filled the air. Joheved couldn't see who was performing, but she could make out the sounds of string and wind instruments, as well as drums. "We never used to have parties at our house before, and now we've had two in six months," she said in awe.

"Papa said we'd have a lot of people here to taste the new wine tonight, since so many of them helped make it"—Miriam had to shout to be heard—"but I never expected such a mob."

"Do we have to open up every barrel for tasting?" Joheved asked her father. "They won't drink it all, will they?"

"Don't worry," Salomon said. "Most will only fill their cups a couple of times. They know the wine is our livelihood."

"We'll only let them sample the pressed wine," Isaac declared. "The free-run wine casks remain sealed."

The menorah had nearly burned out, and torches were lit. Grandmama Leah took one look at the noisy bunch of strangers outside and announced that she was too tired to celebrate. Rivka jumped at the opportunity to withdraw, and asked Sarah to see to the guests so she could get Leah to bed. Joheved and Miriam held their breaths, afraid that Mama would make them come inside and miss this marvelous event. But she only admonished them not to make themselves sick by eating too many rich desserts.

The Hanukkah lamp's going out seemed to be a signal. Salomon and Isaac strode to the cellar doors where several men helped them lay down planks for ramps. Cheers rang out each time a cask was rolled out and righted. Then Isaac climbed atop a bench, and those nearby quieted. The hush spread like a ripple in a pond, and soon the courtyard was silent.

"Friends, my partner and I welcome you to our Hanukkah festivities," Isaac boomed, his arms extended wide, and many in the crowd yelled back encouragements.

"We have wine from both Salomon's and the abbey's vineyards. Be sure that you have tasted both." This comment drew more shouts of approval. "But please try to restrain your desire for seconds until everyone has had their first taste." His emphasis on the word *try* brought more guffaws from his listeners. "Now let us fill our cups with new wine and toast the Festival of Lights!"

He jumped down from the bench to loud applause and the musicians broke into spirited tunes. Circles of dancers moved in time, their shadows wheeling in the torchlight. Isaac and Joseph stationed themselves at the abbey's casks, while Salomon and his daughters stood behind those from their vineyard. Everyone waited for the owners and their families to have the first tastes.

Salomon took a few bites of bread. Then he filled his wine goblet and recited both the *Shehecheyanu* and the blessing over wine. When his daughters responded, "Amen," he handed the cup to them. He had waited so long for this moment, but now he couldn't bring himself to take the first taste.

Joheved took a sip and handed the cup to Miriam. The wine seemed quite good to her, but she knew she was no expert.

Miriam took her drink and passed it back to Salomon. It was now or never—Isaac and Joseph were waiting. He held up the goblet and proclaimed, "For life." Then he closed his eyes and took a mouthful.

Salomon kept the liquid on his palate and breathed in the bouquet. He could scarcely believe it. The Holy One had blessed him with an outstanding vintage, and this was the press wine! He savored the full-bodied flavor as he swallowed. The free-run wine must be truly sublime. He quickly took another taste to make sure he hadn't imagined that wonderful sensation.

Isaac saw the awe and pleasure in Salomon's eyes and quickly filled his own cup. "For a good life," he toasted his son.

Joseph returned the toast. "For a happy life." The wine from the abbey's grapes was excellent, but it did not merit the same exquisite expression as on Salomon's face. Salomon refilled his goblet and handed it to them, each of whom took a slow swallow and breathed out a contented "Ah."

The revelers in the courtyard whispered excitedly. They could see the pleasure and pride on the vintner's face and crushed forward to get their cups filled. A fine vintage was a blessing for the whole community. Everything Salomon's family bought would be paid for with this wine, and soon it would grace every Jewish table in Troyes.

Salomon had Miriam take some wine inside for Rivka and Leah, while Joseph refilled his cup and asked Joheved to bring it to his wife. She found Johanna deep in conversation with Aunt Sarah and offered them Joseph's cup. Like the others, Johanna tasted the wine slowly to savor it. Then she passed it to Aunt Sarah.

Suddenly Miriam ran up to them. "I need to talk to Papa and Isaac, but I can't get through the crowd." She was almost jumping up and down in her urgency to pull Johanna and Joheved toward the crush at the cellar door. She continued to talk rapidly, as if her speech could somehow propel them faster.

"I gave some wine to Mama and Grandmama, and she, that is Grandmama, got excited. She said that with wine this good, we have to hide it or sell it right away. She said that the count's men would be here any moment to take away his share, and we'd be left with nothing for all our work." Miriam was almost crying with frustration. "I've got to tell Papa what she said, but I can't see him."

"I doubt that tithes will be collected tonight," Johanna reassured her. Then she announced loudly, "We need to speak with Salomon and Isaac at once!" A path opened for them, and they soon reached the men, where Miriam poured out her story.

"Do you think we really need to move the best wine out tonight?" Salomon asked the small group surrounding him. He had thought his worries about the vintage were finally over.

"Did your grandmother tell you that the count's men had taken her best wine before?" Sarah asked Miriam. While Leah had become more distrustful as her memory declined, what she did remember was often accurate.

"*Oui.* She said that whenever she had a good vintage, the count's tax collectors came right away." In an aside to Joheved, Miriam whispered, "You wouldn't believe the curses Grandmama used when she talked about the count and his tax collectors."

Isaac was used to making decisions quickly when necessary. "I don't think we can take the risk. Let's at least remove as much of the free-run wine as possible tonight. We can leave the pressed wine in the cellar to avoid suspicion."

Salomon gave up all thoughts of celebration and considered the problem at hand. "We must find all the merchants who sold me goods in return for wine. They can take their shares tonight, and we'll tally accounts when the fair closes."

"That will be a perfect job for me and the girls," Johanna said. She took Joheved and Miriam by the hand and pointed them into the crowd. "First look for Nissim and Hiyya's agent, but if you recognize any of the others, send them over here too."

Sarah offered to take as many barrels as her small cellar would hold. Joseph made the same offer, and went off in search of his servants. Joheved found Nissim almost immediately; he had been one of the first in line and had not moved far after his cup was filled. Once he heard enough to understand the gist of the problem, he rushed off to the fairgrounds, promising that he would be right back with his cart and horses. Soon other buyers were located, and if anyone doubted the basis for Leah's fears, the merchants' hasty actions were all the confirmation they needed.

The night wore on. The revelers danced, sang, and ate and drank heartily, while against this festive background, men stealthily filled carts with wine barrels and slipped away into the darkness. Salomon instructed Joheved to keep a careful record of how much wine was taken away and by whom.

A few streets away in the palace, Count Thibault and his advisers crowded around one end of a long table. Warmed by fires blazing in the great hearth nearby, the men sat discussing His Grace's upcoming nuptials. Much planning was involved—after all, the uniting of two prominent noble houses was of great political importance: Who should be invited? Where should they be lodged? What foods should be served? Should he have hunts or a tourney for entertainment, or perhaps both? Soon their talk grew tedious, and during a lull in the proceedings, the merrymaking and music from Salomon's courtyard became noticeable.

"I'm glad to hear my fairgoers having a good time." Count Thibault's eyes took on a calculating look. "If they are happy, their business is profitable, which means that mine is as well."

"We can certainly use a successful fair this year, Your Grace," Guy, his chamberlain, said. "The wedding costs will make a large dent in your treasury." Thibault shot his chamberlain a dark look, and the man quickly replied, "I have been saving for the occasion for some time, and in any case, we can always tax the Jews if more is needed."

Girard, the seneschal, sat up and listened alertly, a frown on his face. "They certainly are loud down there. I hope I don't have to send my men over later to break up any fights."

Thibault rejected this idea with a wave of his hand. "As long as we hear music, I'm sure your intervention is unnecessary." He cupped his hand behind his ear. "It's quite loud to be coming from the fairgrounds. It sounds closer."

"Your Grace is correct about the closeness." Bernard, the cellarer, spoke in obsequious tones. "I believe the music is coming from the Jewish Quarter, where they are celebrating their winter festival."

"If it's the Jews making noise, I probably don't have to worry about fighting." Girard relaxed back into his chair.

"And if the Jews are celebrating with that much enthusiasm"—Guy rubbed his hands greedily—"then they are doing very well at the Cold Fair, and we can expect substantial tithes from them."

"Pardon me," Bernard interrupted politely. "One of the things they celebrate at this time of year is tasting the new wine. It has come to my attention that this year's vintage is expected to be one of the finest in years."

"If that's true, don't you worry that they will sell or hide the best of it before you can claim our share?" Guy asked.

Bernard stared at the chamberlain in disdain. "The Jews are His Grace's loyal subjects, who would undoubtedly be honored to provide wine for his table, particularly if it is superior wine and they are acknowledged as the vintners."

Girard was inclined to agree with the chamberlain and view the Jews as potential tax evaders. "I think it might be prudent for me to visit the Jewish winemaker first thing tomorrow morning and inventory his cellar."

"You shall do no such thing." The usually cool and civil cellarer was starting to show just a bit of pique. "If anybody is to go, it will be myself. And I am not going tomorrow!"

Count Thibault had heard enough. "None of my retainers is going to the Jewish Quarter tomorrow." He looked sternly at Girard and Guy. "The Jews take their Sabbath seriously, and I will not have them or anyone else thinking that my men do not observe our Sunday rest with proper reverence.

"However"—Thibault nodded in the cellarer's direction—"on Monday morning, Bernard will present himself at their winemaker's home to sample their new wine and decide how much to tithe for my use. I have no doubt that my Jews will cooperate with him fully."

Eleven

As Count Thibault ordered, his punctilious cellarer arrived at Salomon's door late Monday morning. Joheved answered it, and was not surprised to find the smartly dressed nobleman and his retainers waiting there. Upstairs tidying the bedrooms, Marie had seen the knights riding up the street and rushed to inform her mistress. The trapdoor to the cellar was open, and even with much of the free-run casks removed, the cellar looked well stocked. In fact, there was more than twice as much wine as the cellar had held last year.

Salomon was still at synagogue. He had announced earlier that his eldest daughter was perfectly capable of dealing with the count's cellarer, or whoever was sent in his place. Joheved had actually been in charge of the wine accounts for the last few years, ostensibly still learning the skill from her grandmother.

Rivka offered the visitors food and drink, but Bernard declined and asked to see the cellar. As the cellarer watched closely, Joheved identified the various casks and drew four small jugs of wine. Once back in the kitchen, the family observed him carefully as he tasted the wine.

Starting with the pressed wine, he chatted nonchalantly about the count's upcoming wedding and how a band of brigands had been caught in the western forest, lying in wait to attack the merchants returning to Paris from the Cold Fair. "The gallows at the city gates will soon be full," he announced.

Eventually he took a taste of Salomon's free-run wine, and his prattle stopped. Joheved had waited for this moment, and she was not disappointed. Like the other connoisseurs who had tasted Salomon's wine, Bernard could not hide his pleasure.

He saw them watching him and knew that they were equally aware of this wine's unique value. "His Grace will be pleased to serve such excellent wine at his wedding," the cellarer said. "I am not yet sure what his needs will require, so I must advise you not to sell over half your stock until he takes his tithe."

"Half the stock?" Joheved gulped. "But at least half the barrels come from Montier-la-Celle's grapes, and we haven't given the abbot his share yet."

Bernard's bland expression didn't change, but inwardly he was furious. The abbey's produce was their own, not subject to Thibault's authority. Leave it to their wily abbot to have the Jews make wine from his grapes, thus greatly increasing its value and Montier-la-Celle's revenue. The cellarer had no choice but to modify his initial demand.

"I mean, of course, that your father should not dispose of more than half the wine coming from his own vineyard until you hear from me again." Bernard abruptly rose from the table and bid the family "Bonjour." He was already trying to figure out some way to obtain the abbey's wine; it was nearly as good as the Jewish vineyard's product.

Rivka couldn't wait to report the morning's events to Salomon when he returned from services. "Joheved was wonderful. While I was nearly mute with fright, she stood her ground against Count Thibault's cellarer and outwitted him, too."

"But I was lucky," Joheved admitted, her face coloring. "I didn't realize the abbey's wine was exempt from their tithes. I only hoped to save a few barrels for the abbot's personal use."

"It doesn't matter how much Thibault wants." Filled with pride at his daughter's success, Salomon was philosophical about the loss. "Our creditors have been paid, we have enough for our own use, and I'm sure the Jewish community will not make our family bear more than our fair share of the wedding's cost."

He turned to Joheved and continued. "I want you to go with me to the fair this afternoon. We must settle our accounts now that the merchants are leaving, and we also need to buy a Hanukkah present for Meir."

"A present for Meir?"

"Isaac reminded me that it's customary for the bridegroom-elect and the father of a betrothed maiden to exchange gifts," Salomon explained. "A supply of parchment is waiting for me on Rue de Petit Tannerie, so I should reciprocate. I thought you could help pick out something appropriate."

"I'd love to go shopping with you, Papa." Everything with the wine had worked out so well, Joheved wanted to celebrate.

In a way, Meir's family had given her a Hanukkah present as well. After the betrothal, Marona had sent over so much raw wool that Mama had been able to weave a new blanket out of the thread that Joheved and Miriam had spun from it. That reminded her—"May Miriam come too?"

So the three of them spent the afternoon at the Cold Fair. "Maybe we could find Meir some silk hose, like the new ones Papa has," Miriam suggested.

"What about a wine goblet?" Joheved remembered the fine ones that Isaac and Joseph had given her parents.

"That would make an excellent gift, but probably more appropriate for a wedding present," Salomon replied, his gaze sweeping over the merchandise as they walked along.

They continued past the booths and listened to the merchants' extravagant descriptions of their wares. "You would think they're giving things away at the fair's closing, their prices are such bargains," Salomon said, clearly not impressed.

They passed a table with a few leather items left on it, including a beautifully worked belt. Joheved stopped to admire the intricate pattern.

The merchant started his litany. "This beautiful belt was made in Spain, of the finest Cordovan leather. Look at the workmanship." He thrust the belt at Salomon. "It's my mistake that I have not sold this excellent piece already—it's too small for most men. After all, the men who can afford this kind of merchandise are too plump to wear it. You can have it for a ridiculously low amount." He named a figure that was actually reasonable.

"Meir is rather skinny." Miriam tried the belt around her own tiny waist. "I bet it would fit him."

Once the merchant saw he had a potential customer, bargaining began in earnest, and the sale was quickly made. They would send the belt with some merchants going through Mayence after leaving the Cold Fair. Meir was not likely to expect a gift and shouldn't mind receiving it after Hanukkah was over.

When Salomon asked Joheved to procure fresh parchment a week later, she was reluctant to go. Yet if Miriam went in her place, her sister and Catharina would surely gossip about her betrothal. So Joheved set off for Rue de Petit Tannerie, determined to remain unaffected no matter how much her friend teased her.

Catharina was helping a bald brown-robed monk examine some parchment in the storage room, and her face lit up when she saw Joheved come in.

"Congratulations." She hurried over to give Joheved a hug. "I hear everything worked out between your father and Lord Samuel. My brother says we are to give you as much parchment as you want."

"*Merci.*" Joheved returned the hug. At least Catharina hadn't teased her immediately. "Samuel's betrothal gift was generous. For our part, my father only has to give him a cask of wine each year at Passover."

Before they could continue their conversation, the monk came over and, to their surprise, addressed Joheved. "Excuse me." His voice was gentle, yet he spoke with authority. "I couldn't help overhearing. You are the daughter of the Jewish winemaker?"

"I am." Joheved cast a questioning look at Catharina, who shrugged her shoulders in reply. But Joheved didn't want the strange monk to think that Papa was only a vintner. "My father is also a scholar. He needs parchment for the commentary he's writing on the Bible."

"I am Robert, prior of the Abbey of Montier-la-Celle." While his posture didn't change, he somehow gave the impression of bowing to them. "I owe your father a debt of gratitude for the excellent wine he produced from our grapes this year."

"Oh." Joheved relaxed at the monk's kind words. "Count Thibault's cellarer said the vintage is one of the best he's ever tasted. We are grateful to you as well, for sharing your grapes." She could see that Robert wasn't really bald; his hair was such a pale blond that his short tonsure made it appear that way.

"Your father is writing a commentary on the Hebrew Scriptures?" His pale brows furrowed in thought. "There are some passages that confound me, and perhaps he might spare a few moments to help me understand them better."

Joheved suspected that her father would rather not discuss Torah with the heretics who worshiped the Hanged One, but she merely suggested, "Perhaps you should ask him your questions when you come get the abbey's wine." After all, Papa wouldn't want to antagonize anyone important at Montier-la-Celle.

"Give your father my regards and tell him I'll be visiting him soon," Robert said. Then he turned to Catharina and added, "Give your father my regards as well, and inform him that the abbey needs six more folios. Count Thibault has commissioned an illuminated Psalter as a wedding present for his new bride." He left them with that delightful piece of news.

"It must be nice when somebody wants to marry you," Catharina said wistfully, thinking of Samuel's gift of parchment and Thibault's Psalter. "But then look at you, you have new clothes on, too. I'm glad things are going so well for you."

"You are a true friend to be happy in my good fortune." Joheved hugged her again and sighed. Now that Miriam was an apprentice midwife, all the Jewish girls wanted to be friends with her, but Catharina was still the only friend Joheved had.

"What's the matter?" Catharina could see the sadness in Joheved's face. "Is there something wrong with your fiancé?"

"*Non, non.*" Joheved made an effort to look more cheerful. "There's nothing the matter with Meir, that's his name, by the way. He's not handsome, but he's not ugly either, and he seems nice enough. He's a scholar, which is what Papa wanted, and his family is well off, which makes Mama happy. I just wish things could work out well for you too."

Catharina gathered up several sheaves of folded parchment and handed them to Joheved. "I do too."

"I'll pray for the Holy One to send you a good husband." Joheved took her parchment and walked home slowly, feeling guilty that her future looked so bright compared to Catharina's.

Her spirits brightened when Papa announced that it was time to resume their nightly Talmud sessions. Since the holiday was still fresh in their minds, they would study the section in Tractate *Shabbat* that explained the laws of Hanukkah.

As always, the sages Shammai and Hillel were arguing. This time the subject was lighting the Hanukkah lamp.

For those who fervently pursue mitzvot, Shammai says that on the first day of Hanukkah one kindles eight lights, and then continuously decreases the amount; but Hillel says to kindle one light on the first day and continuously increase . . . . Hillel's reason for a continual increase is that in sacred matters we elevate, not lower, the level of holiness.

Miriam and Joheved stared at their father in surprise. "That means Shammai starts with eight lights the first night, seven on the second night, and ends with just one light," Miriam said.

Salomon nodded. "That's right."

"But why light them backward like that?" Joheved asked. Who would have imagined that other Jews did things so differently?

"Shammai believes this publicizes the true nature of the miracle, the single flask of oil that gradually diminished over eight days," he said.

"Everybody here does it like Hillel . . . I think," Miriam said.

Salomon nodded. "That's true, no one follows Shammai anymore."

Joheved continued reading.

What is Hanukkah?

"Don't they know what Hanukkah is?" Miriam interrupted. "They've been discussing it for pages."

"Maybe they're asking how we know to celebrate Hanukkah," Joheved said. "It's not mentioned in Torah at all, not like our other holidays." She glowed with pride when her father said she was right.

Miriam continued reading and there was the story of the miraculous small flask of oil that burned for eight days. When she finished, Salomon asked if there was anything in the Gemara that puzzled them.

"Why did it take eight days to get new oil?" Miriam asked. "That seems like a long time."

"And why did the Sages make an eight-day festival?" Joheved frowned. "I mean, since the flask started with enough oil for one night, didn't the miracle really occur the next seven nights?"

"Those are both good questions." Salomon nodded in approval. "Miriam, some sages say the nearest pure oil was a four-day journey away. Others say that the Jews were impure due to contact with corpses, because of the fighting, and it took seven days for their purification. Then they needed one more day to press the olives into oil."

He turned to Joheved with a smile. "Many scholars have asked your question. Some answer that the flask of oil remained full after the lamp was filled, so it was evident on the very first night that a miracle was occurring. Others suggest that they divided the oil into eight parts and poured only that small amount into the menorah, yet the lamp burned the entire night. Thus a miracle did happen each day."

They continued studying Tractate *Shabbat* for weeks, the Gemara's debates over the minutiae of observance growing overwhelming. One night, after an arduous day working in the vineyard, Miriam refused to spend another moment reviewing Talmud with her sister.

"I'm too tired to study. Let's just go to sleep." Miriam yawned and pulled the covers over her head.

"But we have to review every day or we'll forget." Joheved pulled the covers back. "And we've worked so hard to learn it."

"But this Gemara is too hard. And it isn't as interesting as *Berachot* was."

"You don't want to study Talmud anymore because it's too difficult?" Joheved was stunned. If Miriam abandoned their nightly ritual, she'd never find out what was in all those other tractates. "But you mustn't give up. I can't do it alone."

"I didn't say that I wanted to stop altogether, but we never play hide-and-seek anymore, or make the kittens chase strings, or do something fun. Don't you want to do anything except talk about Talmud?"

"I like learning Talmud, and I thought you did, too." A cold fear gripped Joheved. It would be like going back to stirabout for every meal after eating meat. "Maybe we could tell Papa we want to study *Berachot* again."

Miriam might have been kinder if she hadn't been so tired. "Don't you realize that no matter how much Gemara we learn, Papa will still wish he had sons instead of daughters."

There was nothing Joheved could say to that. She put the pillow over her head and cried herself to sleep.

During their next session, Salomon was astute enough to see that his students' enthusiasm was flagging. He didn't fault them; it was his responsibility to make sure his lessons were challenging without being onerous.

Salomon praised them. "Joheved, did you know that Tractate *Shabbat* isn't usually studied until a student has been in yeshivah for several years? And Miriam, some of the boys are almost twice your age. You two are doing an excellent job learning such advanced material. I'm proud of you."

"*Merci*, Papa." They surreptitiously exchanged glances. Had he overheard their conversation last night?

Joheved looked back at him and quickly answered, "Tractate *Shabbat* isn't that hard, Papa, we can learn it."

"Even so, I intend to go back to *Berachot* after we finish this section on Hanukkah," Salomon said. "Be patient. There are only a few pages left about Hanukkah, and soon we will come to a part that you'll find particularly interesting."

It was Joheved's turn to read when they got to the discussion he meant.

A woman may certainly kindle the Hanukkah light. Rabbi Yehoshua ben Levi said: Women are obligated in the mitzvah of Hanukkah for they were involved in that miracle.

Joheved's voice rose with excitement. This was the first time she'd read about women's ritual observance in the Talmud.

Miriam leaned forward eagerly. "Papa, how were women involved in the Hanukkah miracle?"

"The Greek oppression affected Jewish women uniquely, since every bride had to submit to the local Greek commander," he replied. "In addition, as you know, a woman was an instrument of their deliverance, the high priest's daughter who killed the Greek general."

Thus they continued all winter long, studying Talmud at night and pruning the vineyard during the day. Joheved tried to learn pruning techniques with the same determination she applied to learning Gemara, because she doubted that Grandmama would be able to instruct them next year. Last winter Leah had confidently directed her granddaughters; every cut came with an explanation of why it was best for this particular vine.

"Cane-pruning requires the most skill, but spur-pruning is quicker," she had told them. "Remember that shoots farthest from the stock bear the most, and that sunlight on the woody parts, especially the new canes, makes a more fruitful vine. Cut short, leaving only two or three buds, if the plant appears weak, aiming for quality over quantity. Cut long, three or four buds to a branch, when the plant seems vigorous and you want a more plentiful harvest."

Leah used to be indefatigable when it came to such knowledge, but now she volunteered little. She answered questions the girls put to her, but the fountain of her knowledge was a well they had to bucket water from, not a gushing stream. Joheved and Miriam asked any question they could think of, to try to learn everything Leah knew and also because her silence so distressed them.

"Grandmama, why do we have to cut the vines so close to the ground?" Joheved was tall enough now that it hurt to stoop over the low vines all afternoon.

Leah might appear frail, but she chopped off the branch in front of her as easily as slicing a piece of cheese. "Here in the north, dear, the closer the grapes are to the ground, provided they do not actually touch it, the better they will mature."

"How do we know when to finish the pruning?" Miriam asked.

"You can tell that the vines have completed their winter rest when they start to discharge sap from the pruning wounds. Be careful, these 'tears of the vine' are sticky." Leah held up the cut branch for them to inspect, but it was still dry. "Some say the sap has medicinal properties, and I try to take a little each year as a spring tonic."

This year when the sap rose, it was raining heavily, and no one would brave the muddy vineyard to harvest it. For Joheved and Miriam, the continual downpour meant far too many days indoors keeping Grandmama Leah company. To pass the time they asked her about their father's childhood. To their disappointment, she told the same stories over and over again, mostly along the lines of what a prodigy he had been in school, instead of stories of his mischievous boyhood adventures. She also told them a bizarre tale.

"For years after I married your grandfather, I was barren. Then he acquired a valuable pearl that the bishop wanted for the cathedral. My pious husband, may his merit protect us, refused to allow such a jewel to be used for the heretic's idolatry, and he threw it into the Seine. Soon afterward, there was a solar eclipse and he dreamed of an angel, who told him that because of his sacrifice, he would be rewarded with a son who would become a great scholar," Leah said proudly. "Six months later, our little Salomon was born."

Joheved and Miriam didn't know what to make of such a story. Their grandmother did occasionally make up something rather than admit she didn't remember the answer to a question. At first it had been funny when she gave them different answers to the same query, but now her mental lapses were painful to hear.

When they asked Papa about his father's pearl and the angel dream, he shook his head and said, "She probably dreamed the thing herself. So now she thinks it's true." Yet Grandmama told them the strange story several times, and it never varied.

Twelve

Once the rain stopped, everyone was far too busy to think about family stories. Besides the vineyard, which required daily attention, both Leah and Rachel needed supervision. Rivka was sure the baby would toddle into the hearth or garbage pit the moment nobody was watching. The days when Rachel could spend hours sitting content-edly in Grandmama Leah's lap were but a pleasant memory. By necessity, Salomon began keeping his youngest daughter with him while he taught. She was satisfied to sit on his lap and watch as he dipped the long goose quill pen into the ink holder made of a cow's horn, and then wrote his letters or *kuntres*.

Salomon's time was increasingly spent writing. In addition to expounding the meaning of biblical texts to his students, he wrote down his explanations. Now anyone new could catch up with his other pupils. He continued to expand his Talmud notes, letting Joheved and Miriam read his writings whenever they wanted, partly for them to proofread and partly to make up for his having less time to study with them.

He also wrote regularly to Meir in Mayence. Meir had begun their correspondence with a letter of thanks after he received his Hanukkah present. He filled the rest of the parchment with news of the yeshivah, and included regards to Joheved. Salomon had responded in kind and encouraged his daughter to add a few lines of her own. Meir's letters kept the old yeshivah world alive for him, and he was thankful for that tenuous connection.

Until the most recent letter arrived. Meir wrote that Isaac ha-Levi had enacted an edict restricting how kosher cattle could be slaughtered. But the forbidden practice was used by French butchers and Salomon was expected to retract his approval of it.

Joheved was usually eager to read Meir's letters after Papa was done, but when she saw his clenched jaw and red face, she backed away. What had Meir said to cause such anger? She forced herself to wait for an explanation. It was not long in coming.

Salomon threw the letter down on the table and grabbed for parchment and ink. As he wrote, he put his wrath into speech as well. "Will our teacher please refrain from adding to the number of 'forbidden foods'? For it would be impossible to accept this; otherwise we in France would never be able to eat meat. We are unable to stop this practice—unless we are willing to pay for the entire cow, whether it is found fit to eat or not."

He took a deep breath to compose himself and continued writing. "If you wish to erect a 'fence around the Law'—yours is the great court and you are worthy to enact restrictive measures. We prefer, however, that our teacher stand by the accepted law and not forbid doubtful cases."

Salomon saw that Joheved was watching him. "That was a public letter for my teachers. This one is just for Meir." He took out a fresh piece of parchment.

"I, Salomon, your devoted, inform you that I have not retracted so far, and do not intend to retract in the future. I do not find the words of my teachers fully convincing; their arguments were but superficial, and I shall reveal my view to you, my very discreet student. Were it not for the calamity that overwhelmed my family, I would teach them my position in person, even if they would not abide by it, for I cannot adopt a view that would cause the loss of money to Jews in a matter that is so obviously permitted."

Now that Papa had written down his fury, he seemed calmer. Joheved didn't understand why he was so angry and took the risk of asking, "What do the butchers in Troyes do that your old teachers don't like?"

He stroked his beard for a moment before replying, "None of the butchers in Troyes are Jewish. We slaughter our meat in cooperation with them, so that if the animal is found to be not kosher, the butcher can still sell it. But of course, Edomites do not want to buy meat that Jews have rejected, so the butchers make it look like the animal was slaughtered in the usual way. Isaac ha-Levi forbids this, although he knows I permit it. He thinks I would not dare to contradict him, but I rely fully on my own judgment to advocate the more lenient view."

"Of course. Who would slaughter an animal if he couldn't eat or sell the meat?" It didn't seem right for the rabbis so far away to make eating meat difficult for Jews in Troyes. Then she thought of something else Papa had written.

"Papa, when you wrote to Meir about our family's calamity, did you mean Grandmama Leah, that she can't remember things anymore?"

Salomon nodded sadly. "I'm afraid that Potach has her firmly in his clutches." He sighed heavily and wiped away some tears. "My mother will never be able to run the vineyard without me."

He quickly added an incantation of protection against the demon. "I adjure you, Potach, Prince of Forgetfulness, that you remove from me a fool's heart, in the name of the holy names, Arimas, Arimimas, Anisisi'el, and Petah'el." He looked down at the letters he had written and sighed again. "I doubt that I will ever study with my old teachers again. My life is in Troyes now."

Had the idea of starting his own yeshivah first come to him after writing that letter to Meir? Or had it been there earlier? Salomon only knew that enough merchants had approached him about teaching their sons that he'd agreed to open a modest yeshivah. He insisted on taking only those candidates just starting to study Talmud, like Ephraim and Menachem.

The week after Passover, Salomon had four new students, beardless, bewildered youths just past their thirteenth birthdays. There was a vintner's son from Rheims, a pair of cousins from Provins, and a pudgy boy from Bar-sur-Aube with relatives in Troyes. The first three intended to lodge with Salomon, so Joheved and Miriam helped outfit the attic as quarters for them.

Marie and the girls swept the floors and covered them with fresh rushes. They brought up sweet hay for the boys' bedding, and a few benches as well. Getting things up to the top floor was difficult. The circular staircase inside the house only extended to the second floor; one reached the attic by means of a ladder in the courtyard.

The larger household consumed so many eggs that Rivka bought some hens of their own, and Miriam found that she enjoyed hunting for eggs in the courtyard grass. Joheved was still begging for a few more moments of sleep while Miriam was already outside, searching out the hens' secret nests. Benjamin ben Reuben, the new student from Rheims, was often there to help her.

Wavy hair was a common Jewish trait, but Benjamin's sandy hair was curlier than Rachel's. Miriam liked to toy with the baby's curls by stretching one to its complete length and then letting it bounce back, and she felt a strange desire to similarly play with Benjamin's light brown ringlets.

"*Merci*, Benjamin," she said as he handed her another egg. "You're a good egg hunter. You can find two eggs for every one of mine."

"I ought to be." He grinned back at her. "My mother keeps poultry too, and since I'm the youngest, collecting eggs is my job." Suddenly Benjamin's expression changed from cheerful to forlorn, and his hazel eyes filled with tears.

Miriam could see that he was fighting to control his sorrow. "What's the matter?"

He leaned against the apple tree and tried to shield his face with his arm. "I miss my family. I miss my mother."

Miriam watched helplessly as the tears rolled down the homesick boy's cheeks. "Do you want to go home?"

"I don't mean to complain," he said. "Your father is a wonderful teacher, and during the day, I'm usually fine. But it's different at night. I remember how far away my parents are and I feel so alone."

The poor fellow, no wonder he was unhappy. Miriam tried to think of something comforting to say. "Did you know that my father left his mother, his only relative, at the same age as you, and traveled all the way to Worms? At least you're still in France; you don't have to learn a new language."

"Thanks for your encouragement." He smiled wanly at her and started searching for eggs again. "I'll try to keep it in mind."

"I'm sorry you're so unhappy." What could she do to make him less miserable? "Maybe if you save some tidbits at meals and share them with one of the cats, you could entice it to sleep with you in the attic. Then you won't feel alone at night."

"I suppose that might help," he said skeptically.

Miriam knew that Benjamin was several years older than she was, but he hadn't started growing yet and still looked more like a boy than a youth on the verge of manhood. It didn't occur to her that they shouldn't be alone together; to Miriam they were both still children.

She ran over to him, scattering the chickens. "I know, let's pretend that I'm your sister. Then it won't be like you're separated from all your family. What do you think?"

Benjamin's demeanor brightened immediately. He grabbed her hand and gave it a quick kiss, exactly as he had done with his parents hundreds of times. Miriam had kissed her share of palms, especially her grandmother's, but nobody had ever kissed hers before. In the nights that followed, she remembered the sensation of Benjamin's lips on her hand and marveled at the feeling.

In the sunny spring days that followed, Miriam and Joheved tried to be wherever their father was teaching, which often turned out to be in the vineyard. There Salomon's pupils learned simple vineyard skills along with Mishnah and Gemara. Once Salomon was confident of Benjamin's skills in the vineyard, he allowed the youth to work there without supervision. And it wasn't long before Miriam was trying to cajole her older sister into joining him there.

Joheved suspected that Miriam was more interested in Benjamin's company than in improving her vineyard techniques, but she kept those thoughts to herself. She hadn't liked being teased about Meir and resolved not to turn the tables on her sister—at least not without extreme provocation.

But after spending hours with Benjamin and Miriam in the vineyard, Joheved wasn't sure about her sister's intentions. Mama had been so adamant that no potential suitor would be interested in such learned girls that Joheved never mentioned her studies in her letters to Meir and she tried not to let Papa's students catch her studying.

Yet it was clear that her sister didn't care what Benjamin thought, because when he stumbled and improperly chanted some Mishnah, Miriam jumped right in to correct him. To Joheved's amazement, he didn't appear offended, not even surprised, and they were soon reciting the week's lesson together in the vineyard. But Joheved couldn't bring herself to join them, though she knew the text perfectly.

It never occurred to Benjamin that Miriam wouldn't know the Mishnah. After all, she attended her father's classes nearly as often as the male students. Benjamin was the first in his family to attend yeshivah, so he hadn't been taught who could study Talmud and who couldn't. His father and his two brothers had started working when they reached their majority, but they were now sufficiently prosperous to delay his own entry into the workforce.

When Benjamin returned home for Shavuot in the middle of May, his parents were pleased to hear how wise and patient his teacher was, and how he studied in the *maître's* vineyard. For Benjamin to learn both Talmud and viticulture at the Troyes yeshivah was an unexpected bonus. When he innocently mentioned that he worked closely with Salomon's daughter in the vineyard, his parents decided to delay their search for his bride until he'd spent more time in Troyes.

After the festival, Benjamin took solace in knowing that, with more students beginning their studies during the Hot Fair, he would no longer be the newest. To celebrate, he decided to lead them on a beehive hunt when the vines flowered. The blossoms attracted thousands of bees from the surrounding countryside, and if a fellow were lucky, he could follow one of them back to its hive and plunder their supply of honey.

Soon the weather warmed, and morning found the vineyard shrouded in a soft haze. Salomon and his students were in the vineyard every day, tying up the branches and keeping the tendrils from entangling each other. There was a sense of urgency in their efforts; all work on the vines would halt when the buds flowered. During the delicate time of flowering and pollination, nobody was allowed in the vineyard.

When the first yellowish blossoms began to open at the base of the vine, the children's eagerness to search for beehives reached a fever pitch. Salomon wasn't optimistic about their finding a beehive, but as long as they stayed out of the vineyard, he had no objection. The days were long and there was time enough for both lessons and games. He even agreed to let Joheved and Miriam join the hunt.

Salomon would put his extra time to good use by answering some legal questions that had arrived with the good traveling weather. Asking him to decide their difficult judicial issues was a sign that local communities recognized his scholarship. This question-and-answer process was called responsa, and the more renowned a rabbi became, the more time he spent on it.

Salomon also spent hours conversing with Robert of Montier-la-Celle, both of them using their forced rest from vineyard duties to study Scripture. Some of the students were surprised to find a monk calling on their teacher, but Joheved and Miriam were used to Robert's visits and didn't give the two men a second glance. They couldn't wait to start looking for beehives.

The first afternoon the children alternated between enjoying the grape blossoms' perfume as they waited to sight a bee and running around helter-skelter chasing the bees they saw. Soon they became familiar enough with the location of the peasants' hives that they could quit following a bee as soon as its route veered in that direction. After a few days, they were consistently ending up in the forest, but it was harder to follow a bee among the trees.

On *Shabbat* of the second week of flowering, they knew there wasn't much time left. The blossoms at the end of the branches had opened and pollination would soon be complete. They ran from the vineyard into the forest, through the trees, and then, once the bee was lost, back to the vineyard again, getting more discouraged as the afternoon wore on. Perhaps the beehive was further into the woods than they could go on *Shabbat*.

When Benjamin and Miriam managed to follow a bee so closely that they were sure the hive couldn't be far away, only to lose sight of it among the fluttering branches, they sat down on the ground in dismay instead of running back to the vineyard to start over. That's when Miriam heard it, or rather, them.

"Listen," she whispered with an urgency that grabbed her companion's attention. "I hear buzzing."

They focused all their attention on their powers of hearing. "You're right," Benjamin whispered back. "I hear it too."

They silently made their way toward what was obviously going to be the hive. The humming was getting so loud that the number of bees involved must be enormous, but they couldn't see any.

Finally, when it seemed like they must be right on top of the hive, Benjamin looked up and pointed. Miriam gazed skyward and there were more bees than she had ever seen, flying in and out of the top of a tall, dead tree. They stood and stared in awe.

They had found the hive.

By the time Joheved and the other students reached the dead tree, their enthusiasm had faded. Nobody could reach the honey without cutting down the tree and that meant adults would have to be consulted.

But when they returned, Salomon wouldn't plan any work on this day of rest. "We'll discuss it later, after *Shabbat* has ended, after we make *Havdalah*."

In June the Sabbath ends late, and by the time three stars appeared in the sky, Rachel and Grandmama Leah had already gone to bed. Everyone involved in the frantic beehive hunt was nearing exhaustion as they gathered in Salomon's courtyard for *Havdalah*, the ceremony that marks the close of *Shabbat*. Even if she had been awake, Rachel was too little to hold the ritual braided candle, so the honor fell to Miriam, the next youngest daughter.

"Hold the candle high," Rivka urged her, "so you'll have a tall husband."

But Miriam kept it close to her, refusing to lift it above her own head. She kept her eyes on the candle's flame, which flared brightly with its three wicks, while Joheved surveyed the circle of students. Did anyone else find it significant that Benjamin was the shortest boy in the group?

Any woman who drank from the *Havdalah* cup would grow a beard, so Joheved passed the wine on for the boys to bless and taste. Rivka handed around the container of fragrant spices, whose purpose was to mask the stench of Gehenna's fires when they were relit after being extinguished for the Sabbath. Joheved recognized cinnamon and cloves, but there were more.

In the Talmud, the Rabbis taught that wine and spices restored one's learning, so the scholars' *Havdalah* ceremony came to include the incantation against Potach, Demon Prince of Forgetfulness. Salomon made his students recite the incantation together with him, to protect them from forgetting their Torah learning during the coming week. Miriam said it out loud as well, but Joheved murmured it under her breath.

Finally, with many in the group stifling yawns, it was time to chant the final blessing. The candlelight cast strange shadows behind the circle of students, their faces distorted as the flame grew and danced about. There was a liminal moment of sadness as the candle was poised about the wine cup and then a soft communal sigh along with the hiss of the extinguishing flame.

Everyone wished each other, "A good week, *shavua tov*." The moon had risen, allowing Salomon to watch as the boys climbed up to the attic. Downstairs, Joheved and Miriam were waiting for him.

"Papa"—Miriam had a worried look on her face—"what will happen to the poor bees when their tree is chopped down? Where will they go?

How can they live if we take away their honey?"

"Don't worry, *ma fille*, the bees will be fine." He smiled down at her. Sarah was right, she would make a good midwife; she was even concerned about hurting insects. "Robert told me that the monks of Montier-la-Celle would send someone to move our bees into a new hive at the abbey. So we can't go for the honey until Monday; we have to wait until their Sabbath is over."

"You and Robert planned all this before you knew that we'd found the beehive." Joheved was more convinced than ever that her father was the wisest man in France.

As the three of them climbed the stairs, Salomon seemed to be thinking out loud. "It's interesting . . . I've read about honey so often in Torah, but I've never seen the inside of a beehive."

Once in bed, Miriam stayed awake only long enough for the implication of her father's words to reach her. "Joheved"—she nudged her drowsy sister—"maybe Papa will let us come too."

"That would be nice," Joheved mumbled, and she drifted off to sleep wondering how they could possibly arrange it.

As it turned out, Aunt Sarah made all the arrangements they needed by announcing that as long as everyone was spending an afternoon in the forest, she could use help gathering her special midwife's herbs. Now was the perfect time for Miriam to begin her education on the subject, and it wouldn't hurt for Joheved to become familiar with these things as well. They could watch Rachel at the same time.

The sun was high in the sky as Sarah and her three nieces accompanied Salomon and his students, Joseph and two strong servants, plus the beekeeper and a couple of novices from the abbey. When they reached the forest, the groups divided according to gender, the males swiftly heading for the bee tree, their eyes fixed skyward, while the females meandered slowly in no particular direction, their concentration focused on the ground.

Aunt Sarah directed most of her instruction at Miriam, pointing out the various herbs and explaining how each was used. "See these columbines' large downward-hanging violet flowers? An infusion of ragwort and columbine seeds helps speed the birth, so we'll come back in the fall to collect them."

They walked a bit farther and came to a small bush whose felt-like leaves were green on top and white underneath. "This plant has two names, artemisia and wormwood. Tea made from its leaves helps the anxious mother relax, while its seeds bring on a woman's menses when it's delayed."

Sarah talked on, explaining the properties of each herb as they came upon it. Miriam was fascinated with Aunt Sarah's lessons, but Joheved grew bored and directed her attention toward entertaining Rachel. Together they chased butterflies, stopping occasionally to help Sarah dig up a special root or pick some unusual leaves. In the distance, they could hear the sounds of men wielding axes.

Suddenly Joheved thought of something she'd never considered before. Sarah was Mama's older sister, which meant she ought to know about Mama's youth. All they knew was that she'd grown up in Germany and that her parents were dead. They came to a grove of black alder trees and stopped to peel off the bark.

"Aunt Sarah"—Joheved made her move—"how did Mama end up marrying Papa?"

Sarah picked up the alder bark that had fallen around the base of the tree. "After our father died, it fell to our brother Isaac to arrange her marriage. Salomon was his study partner at the yeshivah in Mayence and Leah didn't care about a big dowry; she wanted a daughter-in-law from a learned family. So it seemed a good match. Your mama only met your papa once before their wedding in Troyes."

"So how did you come to live here, Aunt Sarah?" Miriam asked. "Did you stay with Mama after her wedding or did you move to Troyes later?"

Sarah paused a moment. "You may as well know that in-laws don't always get along. My brother and I stayed in Troyes for the celebratory wedding week, and what I saw of Leah's domineering ways convinced me that I should move to Troyes to help my lonely and frightened sister. I'm ashamed to say that I thought Leah would treat her badly."

Joheved had suspected there was some problem between Aunt Sarah and Grandmama Leah because their aunt didn't seem to visit anymore. She'd never dared to ask about it, but now she'd hear Aunt Sarah's side of the story.

"When I found out that Troyes's Jewish midwife had recently died, I bought a house here, in the same courtyard as Leah's. She was immediately suspicious."

Joheved and Miriam stared at each in amazement. Rachel was squirming to get down, and distracted, Joheved almost set her down in a stand of nettles. Who would have imagined her aunt and grandmother being jealous of Mama's affection?

"But there was no battle for Rivka's loyalty." Sarah shook her head wanly. "My sister was relieved, happy even, to be the dutiful daughter-in-law under Leah's overprotective wing."

They stopped to inventory the herbs they'd collected so far. "After Rivka had the two of you, Leah became a doting grandmother," Sarah said. "And now I have to admit that she did an excellent job of teaching her granddaughters."

Sarah paused to let her nieces enjoy the memory of their grandmother in her better days. "But then Leah's illness started. She imagined that I was plotting behind her back and she accused me of putting a curse on Rivka, my own sister, so she wouldn't have more children.

"It was too much for me." There was hurt and anger in her eyes. "I didn't want to cause any more grief than Rivka already had with Leah, so I tried to avoid her whenever Leah was home."

Joheved and Miriam stood in pained silence. Each struggled to find something suitable to say, but could think of nothing that might begin to address the years of estrangement between their mother and her sister. In desperation, Joheved said the first thing that came into her mind.

"Aunt Sarah, what's a wandering womb?"

The older woman turned to her in surprise. "Where did you hear about wandering wombs?"

"Somebody told me that girls who study too much will get it."

Aunt Sarah smiled and shook her head. "Girls don't get wandering wombs, only grown women do. And the proper term is hysteria, which is caused by a wandering womb."

"What are the symptoms?" Miriam asked eagerly.

"It depends on where the womb wanders to. If goes to her head, the woman suffers from headaches. When it presses against her lungs, she has trouble breathing, and if lodges near her stomach, she experiences indigestion. But only the *Notzrim* get hysteria."

Observing her nieces' puzzled expressions, Sarah explained. "Not all the *Notzrim*, of course, just women who don't marry, like nuns and ladies-in-waiting. Married women, Jewish or not, are not susceptible to hysteria."

Before Joheved could ask why not, the men's enthusiastic shouts interrupted their conversation. They picked up Rachel and the herbs they'd collected, and arrived in time to see the men carefully lowering the top of the honey tree, now severed from its trunk, to the ground with a contraption of ropes.

The hollow tree was almost completely filled with honeycombs. It took every container they had plus Salomon's empty wine barrels to hold it all. Benjamin immediately became a hero to his fellows, and his popularity grew when Salomon sold the excess honey at the Hot Fair and divided the proceeds among the students. His pupils couldn't believe their good fortune; here they were, at the largest fair in France, their purses full of spending money.

Thirteen

One morning in mid-August, Joheved was awakened by Leah's shrill voice, insisting that she needed to go on a walk. Joheved listened as Marie soothingly told her to be patient, to wait until her hair was done. Soon Leah complained again that she wanted to go out now, and again Marie calmed her, assuring her that Master Salomon was almost done with his prayers and then he'd be happy to walk with her. It was early Elul, the month preceding the Days of Awe, when Papa got up before dawn to add *Selichot*, special penitential prayers and supplications, to his morning litany.

Joheved, sure she would have to lead Rosh Hashanah and Yom Kippur services for the women, wanted to prays *Selichot* herself in preparation, but it was difficult waking up early. But now she was awake with time enough for the longest prayer. When she heard her father join Grandmama Leah downstairs, Joheved stepped into the hall. Mama was downstairs preparing the morning meal. She tiptoed toward her parents' room, peeked in, and saw that Rachel was still asleep in her cradle. *Another late sleeper like me.*

Then she noticed that Papa had forgotten to put his tefillin away. Joheved stared at the worn black leather straps and boxes that made up the tefillin, one box for the hand and the other for the forehead, as it was written in Deuteronomy, following the Shema.

Bind them as a sign on your hand and let them serve as a symbol on your forehead.

Before they were Papa's, they had belonged to Grandpapa Isaac. It didn't seem right for such holy objects to be left out on the bed, exposed and vulnerable. What if a mouse gnawed on the leather?

With every intention of returning the tefillin to their storage bag, Joheved silently entered her parents' room. She picked up the arm box first; its long straps were in disarray and she tried to gather them up quickly. She couldn't help but caress the lengths of black leather, supple from years of handling. Papa, and all Jewish men, wore tefillin when they said their morning prayers, as a sign of accepting the commandments. Tefillin were also powerful protection—Papa had hung them on the bed frame when Mama was in labor.

Joheved had almost finished folding up the straps when a shocking thought struck her. She accepted the commandments. Why shouldn't she pray with tefillin? Nobody would see her if she closed the door. She'd just try it once, to see what it was like.

Shaking with fear and excitement, she rolled up the sleeves of her chemise, unwrapped the tefillin's arm straps, and started putting them on. When she finished winding them around her hand, a sense of holiness enveloped her that obliterated any feeling of wrongdoing. The sacred leather, pressing tightly against her skin, gave her a constant awareness of the Holy One's presence. Before, it had been hard to shut out the world and concentrate on her prayers. Wearing tefillin, she had no difficulty devoting herself to her *Selichot*.

When her morning blessings were done, she reluctantly removed the tefillin and carefully replaced them on the bed, just as she had found them. As much as she regretted leaving them exposed, she didn't dare put them away and have Papa wonder who had disturbed his things. Then, heart pounding, she slipped back to her room, leaving Rachel still asleep and nobody the wiser. The rest of the morning Joheved could feel where the tefillin straps had left their mark on her arm, and she was careful to keep her chemise sleeves lowered.

The next day, overcome with remorse, she fought the temptation to wear Papa's tefillin again. But she kept thinking how the tight tefillin straps made her feel as if the Holy One was holding her arm Himself, and she was unable to focus on her prayers. So the following morning, terrified but helpless to stop herself, she stole into Papa's bedroom and prayed with his tefillin. Again she felt the Holy One's strength fill her, and she knew she couldn't be committing a sin.

Except for *Shabbat*, when tefillin weren't worn because the holiday itself is the sign of devotion, Joheved urged Miriam to wake her early. Then, as soon as Papa took Grandmama Leah on their walk, she quickly put on his tefillin and prayed.

It wasn't long before Mama, not Papa, discovered her, after coming upstairs to wake her sleepyhead daughter. As Rivka watched in appalled silence, she couldn't help but observe the look of awe and concentration on Joheved's face. She shook her head, sighed heavily, and waited for her daughter to finish, all the while trying to decide what to say.

It was her inability to give Salomon sons that had made him teach the girls Talmud in the first place, Rivka thought bitterly. She had hoped that once the yeshivah was thriving he would concentrate on his male students and forget about educating his daughters, but no, he had encouraged the girls to listen to his lessons. Perhaps he had sanctioned them to lay tefillin too.

Rivka groaned inwardly. This could only lead to marital problems for her daughters. Salomon had made good on his promise to find Joheved a *talmid chacham* for a husband and would likely find matches for the other girls among his students. But what would they think when their wives acted more like men than women? Rivka wrung her hands in frustration. How could she prevent her husband from raising the girls however he wished, particularly when they were willing accomplices?

The surprise and fear on Joheved's face when she turned and saw her mother convinced Rivka that Salomon knew nothing of his daughter's actions. Joheved had tried to think of what she would say when she was finally caught, as she knew she would be, but she was speechless. She quietly put the tefillin away while waiting for her mother's angry lecture, one she knew she deserved.

But Rivka couldn't bring herself to chastise her daughter. The girl had only been praying, after all. Besides, this was Salomon's problem. He had Joheved studying Talmud like a boy—how would he react when he found that she wanted to pray like one too? Rivka felt a surge of satisfaction at her husband's dilemma.

She addressed Joheved simply. "If your father allows you to pray with tefillin, then any objections I have are meaningless. You are a betrothed maiden, no longer a child, so I have no intention of running to your father with this tale of misbehavior. You must speak to him yourself, and not use his things again until he gives you permission."

Tears of remorse and shame filled Joheved's eyes; she had not expected to be treated with such respect. "I'll talk to Papa soon, I promise." Unable to face her mother, she slowly walked past her, eyes fixed on the floor. "I'm sorry, Mama, I should have asked him first."

But Joheved couldn't find the right time or the right way to ask her father about the tefillin, although morning prayers no longer felt right without them.

"It's too bad he's not still in Mayence," Miriam said as they took turns braiding each other's hair. "Then you could write him, and not have to actually face him with your question."

Her sister's offhand comment was just what Joheved needed. "I will write to him. I'll send him a query just like other people do when they have a difficult ritual question."

"A betrothed maiden (thus she is an adult) who studies Talmud (therefore she is learned) wishes to observe the commandment of tefillin. Is this permitted?" Joheved read the letter out loud for Miriam's approval. "There, what do you think?"

"Short and to the point. It sounds fine to me." Miriam gave Joheved a hug. "Good luck."

That evening Joheved paced the salon waiting for her father to come home. She wanted to give him the letter in private, and she hoped he would be in a pleasant mood after studying with other scholars at the Hot Fair. She tried to compose herself, to be ready to defend her position against any objections he might offer. But when she heard the door open, her heart began to pound.

Salomon, tired but satisfied after a long day in the yeshivah, slowly set down his manuscripts. He was taken aback when Joheved handed him the query; surely it hadn't arrived at this late hour. His daughter seemed unusually quiet. Normally she was full of questions if he returned while she was still awake. He started to tell her about his studies, but she stopped him and asked him to read the letter first.

Salomon read it twice, then surveyed his visibly nervous daughter and weighed how to respond. She couldn't know that, in Worms, the prayer leader in the women's section of the synagogue reputedly wore tefillin, or that the Talmud reported that King Saul's daughter, Michal, did so as well. In fact, a woman praying with tefillin wasn't nearly as scandalous as a woman studying Talmud.

"According to the Talmud, women are exempt from tefillin and certain other mitzvot performed at a specific time because a woman's time belongs to her husband," he said.

"Does exempt mean 'forbidden,' Papa?"

He shook his head and smiled. "No, *ma fille*, a woman may do them if she wants to."

Joheved thought about how wonderful it felt to pray with tefillin. "Then I want to."

"You realize that once you take on this mitzvah of wearing tefillin, you are committed to it?" he asked with a sigh. At least she wouldn't be wearing tefillin in public, like the woman in Worms. Here in Troyes, they were only worn at home.

"*Oui*, Papa."

"You are betrothed now." He paused and stroked his beard. "Perhaps we should write to Meir about this.

Joheved's heart sank. Did her time belong to Meir already? What if he didn't approve? And if he did, it could still take months before they'd find out.

"But as long as you live in my house and not your husband's, my permission is all you need," he decided.

Joheved's belly relaxed and she gave a sigh of relief.

"And I suppose my permission is meaningless unless you have tefillin to pray with"—Salomon continued to the logical conclusion—"which means we must buy you some."

"*Merci*, Papa." Joheved hadn't thought that far. But Papa was right; she couldn't expect to borrow his every morning.

Even so, Joheved was surprised when Salomon presented her with her own set of tefillin the following Sunday, just before she went to bed. Miriam stroked black leather and looked hopefully at her father, who responded that she was not yet old enough to take on the responsibility of tefillin. Yet as much as Joheved basked in her sister's admiration, her pride was tinged with trepidation at how Mama would react.

Walking downstairs the next morning, Joheved steeled herself to face her mother's wrath. But there were no clanging pots or words of recrimination; Rivka served breakfast and *disner* in a sullen silence. Overcome with guilt, Joheved had to say something to heal the breach. Rosh Hashanah was less than a week away.

Joheved finally found her mother alone, weeding the herb garden. "Mama," she said, stooping to help her. "I can't explain it, but tefillin make me pray better. Please don't be angry."

Rivka shook her head sadly and sighed. "Just as the Holy One created roosters to crow and hens to lay eggs, so too it is with people. It's not natural for girls to study Talmud and pray with tefillin; it's not right."

"But Papa found me a husband more learned than I am," Joheved cried out. Wasn't that what Mama cared about?

"If your father wishes to indulge you and pretend he has a son, that is his affair. But Meir may prefer that his wife pursue more feminine pursuits." Rivka's voice softened and she said, "Joheved, dear, think about what I'm telling you. I don't want you to be unhappy when you're living with your husband."

Would Meir really object to her praying with tefillin? Joheved didn't want to know if her mother was right. She and Meir were married now, so her time belonged to him . . . except he didn't know about her tefillin. That was the answer; somehow she'd find a way to pray privately. Then he'd never know she wore tefillin.

Summer was drawing to a close, and just when vintners thought they'd managed to get through the season successfully, they were denied the fair weather they'd anticipated. The last week in August brought such a drop in temperature that Bernard the cellarer briefly considered delaying the grape picking. But cool, damp weather inevitably brought a gray woolly fungus, *pourriture grise*, which quickly ruined a vineyard full of grapes.

Many believed the ripening process was like pregnancy, that *Le Bon Dieu* decrees that a grape will be ripe one hundred days after flowering, just as a child will be born ten lunar months after conception. The weather only affected the flavor of the ripe grape, not the time to reach ripeness. Having originally set the harvest for the hundred-day mark, Bernard declared that it would be prudent not to change it.

Salomon held to a middle ground. "Just as most babies are born after ten months in the womb, with some early and some late, so most grapes ripen about one hundred days after flowering. But it seems to me that heat tends to speed the process while the cold delays it."

He explained that cool weather had both a good side and a bad side for the winemaker. "The wine's flavor may suffer because the grapes cannot reach optimum sweetness, but fermentation will be slower, and thus easier to control."

A few days later, when carts full of grapes began to arrive at Salomon's courtyard, Ephraim declared to Menachem, "If this is a slow fermentation, may the Holy One save us from a fast one."

For the next three weeks, except for prayers and meals, Salomon's household and students spent every waking hour on the vintage. First the grapes were piled into vats in the courtyard, the last job performed by non-Jews. Then Salomon's people took over. Wearing linen boots and their oldest chemises, they trod the grapes vigorously.

Then they waited for the stinging smell of fermentation to fill the courtyard. From then on they labored in shifts, both day and night. Morning and afternoon, Joheved and Miriam carefully climbed into one of the vats. Their combined weight was barely enough, with a bit of bouncing, to break the thick raft of skins and grapes buoyed on the surface by the fizzling fermentation below.

Once into the warm half-wine, they used blunt wooden spades to turn the raft fragments upside down and tread them back in, all under the watchful gaze of Grandmama Leah. Leah no longer needed walks to soothe her agitation. She circled the courtyard like a hawk, intently observing the treaders, every so often dipping a finger in the vats and taking a taste. At night, the courtyard lit by torches, Salomon and the older students took their turn.

Everyone was relieved when the stormy first phase of the fermentation, *bouillage*, was over in time for the Days of Awe. Thereafter the fermentation would proceed calmly for another ten to twenty days, allowing time for the intense contemplation and prayer that the holiday period demanded. Joheved and Miriam successfully took turns leading the women for Rosh Hashanah and Yom Kippur, although it took every bit of concentration they had to stay awake and follow the service.

As soon as the contents of the vats needed only one daily treading, the workers returned to their normal lives. One arduous task remained, that of removing the heavy stems, now free of grapes, from the vats and discarding them. Joheved listened carefully as Grandmama Leah and Salomon tasted the half-wine and considered whether to leave all or part of the stalks in the vats, and for how long. In a good vintage these gave the wine more astringent tannins, greater flavor and bite. But in a cold, damp year they merely diluted it.

Ephraim was working in one of the vats with Menachem when Leah came over, took a taste, and suddenly prodded him with a large wooden rake. Before he could reply, Joheved rushed over to see what her grand-mother wanted with him and to intercede if necessary.

Leah poked Ephraim again and demanded, "Young man, take this rake and pull it through the crushed grapes, from bottom to top. Then dump out any stems that cling to it outside the vat."

Joheved stared in astonishment; her grandmother rarely spoke to the students. He raked out several large stalks and said, "Mistress, do you want me to take out all the stems?"

Leah took another taste and made a sour face. "Bah, this stuff has no flavor, the grapes were picked before they were properly ripe. You two may as well take out all the stems before what little quality this wine has is lost altogether."

Ephraim and Menachem each took a drink, not wanting to miss the subtlety Leah had discerned, but the liquid tasted sweet and syrupy. "How can anybody call this flavorless?" Menachem whispered to Joheved.

Leah chuckled at his puzzled look. "When you've been making wine for as long as I have, young man, then maybe you'll know what I'm talking about."

Joheved had a taste, too, and Leah looked at her expectantly. "It's sweet, but not as sweet as other years, I think." Joheved hesitated, but her grandmother's smile of approval emboldened her to continue. "It's definitely not as sweet as two years ago, when everyone said the vintage was superb."

Of course Leah didn't remember what the vintage was like that year, but she did know how sweet an excellent wine should taste at this stage in its formation. "Joheved is going to be a great winemaker someday, just like her grandmother," she announced.

Once the stalks were removed from the vats, their contents would sit undisturbed until the grape skins and other solid debris settled to the bottom. Then it was just a matter of running the wine into the casks and storing them in the cellar. When that final job was done, it would be time for the Cold Fair with its return of merchants and students to Salomon's yeshivah.

But winter also brought the pox to Troyes, and Rachel was among those stricken. An endemic childhood disease, smallpox swept through a community about once a decade, sometimes so severely that a third of its children died. Worried about his youngest daughter, Salomon spent a week unable to study properly, although Rivka assured him that Rachel wasn't nearly as ill as Joheved and Miriam had been during the previous epidemic. Indeed, this outbreak was milder than usual, with most of Troyes's children surviving it. Rachel recovered with no visible scars, and like others who survived the pox, she now enjoyed immunity for life.

With the smallpox epidemic behind them, the rest of winter passed uneventfully, and when springtime arrived, Joheved and Miriam were once again busy in the vineyard. Miriam spent more time than usual among the vines, especially after Benjamin returned from celebrating Passover with his family. He proudly reported that he was almost as tall as his oldest brother.

Benjamin wasn't the only boy who'd grown. When they returned for the Hot Fair, several yeshivah students' fathers barely recognized their sons, many of whom were half a head taller than when they'd parted company at the end of the Cold Fair.

Salomon's family wasn't exempt from the growth process either. In the past year, Joheved seemed to have made the progression from girlhood to young womanhood, a development most apparent on a late Friday afternoon when Rivka and her two older daughters visited the bathhouse in readiness for the Sabbath.

It had been hot and sticky all week, so when Rivka prepared to go to the stews, Joheved and Miriam asked if they could join her. The bathhouse was located on the Rû Cordé canal, near the edge of the Jewish Quarter. Rivka gave the attendant a small coin and received three towels in exchange. Encountering Johanna there was a pleasant surprise and Rivka settled in for a leisurely soak.

Joheved and Miriam couldn't bear sitting in the hot water so long and amused themselves by perching at the edge of the large tub and gently splashing each other. It was only when they accidentally splashed the older women, causing Rivka to look up from her conversation and scold them, that the physical difference between her two daughters was evident. Joheved's body was rounded, with full breasts, and her waist a definite indentation above abundant hips. In contrast, Miriam's shape was slim and childlike. They were only a few years apart in age, but it was evident that Joheved had crossed the threshold that Miriam was just approaching.

Johanna observed the naked girls as well. "My goodness. Joheved looks so grown up now. Have you set her wedding date?"

"*Non.* not yet." Rivka was embarrassed to admit that she'd been caught unaware by her daughter's maturity. "We wanted to wait until she started her flowers, so there'd be no doubt about her ability to bear children." A woman's menses were commonly called her "flowers," be-cause, just as an apple tree without flowers will not bear fruit, so too women without their "flowers" were not fruitful.

Her daughter's maturity was still in Rivka's mind when she and Salomon went to bed. "Salomon," she whispered. "Joheved and Miriam came with me to the bathhouse this afternoon, and I don't think we should wait much longer to set Joheved's wedding date. She's not a little girl anymore."

Salomon had to accept his wife's expertise in this matter. "Very well, I will suggest to Samuel that our children marry next fall, after the harvest. It will give Meir a year to finish his studies." That would work well, he thought. More merchants had approached him about sending their sons to the yeshivah, and he would need someone to assist the new, younger students while he continued teaching the older ones.

Fourteen

Two months later, when the weather was trying to decide if it was fall or winter, Leah was outside in the courtyard and noticed some apples still hanging on the tree. Marie, digging onions in the garden, saw the old woman swinging her cane among the apple tree's branches and ran to stop her. But she was too late. Leah lunged at one of the remaining apples, lost her balance, and crashed to the ground. When Marie tried to help her up, Leah groaned with such pain that Rivka sent for the doctor.

It took only a few prods here and there, with resulting yelps from his patient, before the physician announced his diagnosis. "Her left hip is most likely broken, although it may only be a bad bruise. If the latter, and *Le Bon Dieu* wills it, she might be up and about after some bed rest." He didn't need to describe the consequences of the former.

The doctor wrote out instructions for a painkiller and Joheved ran off to the apothecary's. Leah's moans only grew louder as Salomon and Rivka gently carried her upstairs to bed. When Joheved returned, Aunt Sarah was preparing one of her own remedies for pain. They gave Leah both medicines, and to everyone's relief, she quieted down and slept.

Now Joheved led all the women's services at synagogue, but she was too distraught to notice that the other girls looked at her with awe instead of disdain. Rachel continued to sit downstairs with Salomon, although most small children, and certainly all girls, joined their mothers in the women's gallery. She sat patiently on his lap during the study session after services as well, and Salomon became convinced that she could understand both Hebrew and Aramaic, so keenly did she appear to follow the scholarly discussions.

When the Cold Fair ended and the merchant scholars went home, Salomon was left with just his students and daughters to teach again.

One afternoon as they were pruning the vineyard, he took the girls aside.

"My mother will likely remain bedridden for some time, so your Mama will need all the help you two can give her in the upcoming months." He looked around to make sure none of the students were close enough to hear. "For we are expecting another child."

Joheved and Miriam exchanged anxious glances and nodded. Miriam wanted to ask when the baby was due, but Papa had already put Mama and the baby in danger of the Evil Eye just by mentioning her pregnancy aloud. Joheved sighed with relief that at least her grandmother's condition had stabilized. Leah's pain had diminished considerably, but what little intellect she had previously possessed now deserted her altogether. She allowed Marie to feed, bathe, and swaddle her like a baby, reacting only if somebody inadvertently jostled her sore hip.

For her part, Joheved found her grandmother's degeneration so distressing that she avoided her as much as possible. Filled with shame each time she passed Leah's door, Joheved threw herself into doing chores that Rivka, as her pregnancy advanced, was unable to perform. Nobody complained about her neglecting Leah, but Joheved still felt she was stealing time to study. Not that she stopped studying Talmud; she just felt guilty doing it. She also felt guilty for hoping that Mama would have another girl.

The household's mood brightened when Rivka easily gave birth to a fourth daughter in early spring, her labor so rapid that Miriam learned little from it. This time Salomon had a full cadre of students praying with him, and when Joheved woke the next morning, she had a baby sister. Two weeks later, when Papa was called to bless the Torah in honor of his youngest daughter's naming, she learned that her new sister was called Leah.

Spring brought two changes for Joheved. Her flowers started and Papa told her that he and Meir's father had confirmed her fall wedding date. Mama taught her how to use a *sinar*, the special article of clothing women wore when they had their flowers. Shaped like an apron, it held absorbent rags in place to catch the menstrual flow. Joheved, however, received a quantity of soft raw wool from Marona, stuff that was usually used for baby's swaddling. Yet Joheved disliked wearing her *sinar* so continuously; the material rubbed against the inside of her thighs, chafing her skin.

She was also annoyed that Miriam kept asking for the two of them to walk to the vineyard when Benjamin was working there. Joheved didn't like being an accomplice to these clandestine rendezvous, but she wouldn't tattle on Miriam, who at least worked on the vines while visiting her friend. But her sister became more persistent about sneaking off to see Benjamin as the season progressed.

"I can't explain it," Miriam told her. "But it's frustrating to spend all this time in public with Benjamin, at meals or in the salon during Papa's lessons, yet we never have time together without Papa's supervision."

Joheved nodded, though she didn't understand. What difference did it make whether Papa was there or not?

"Maybe we could take Rachel on a walk along the Seine tomorrow afternoon?" Miriam asked, her expression not as innocent as she hoped. "Then once we're outside the city walls, I'll meet Benjamin and the two of us can go to the vineyard together."

Joheved's jaw dropped. "Have you lost your mind? You know that nobody is allowed in the vineyard now—the grape blossoms are beginning to flower." How could her sister be so reckless?

"We aren't going inside the vineyard." Miriam fidgeted with her skirts. "Just near enough along the road to smell the flowers."

Joheved's concern heightened. Both girls had been repeatedly warned not to disturb the vineyard during the delicate pollination process. But Miriam obviously didn't care, and when Joheved tried to look her in the eye, Miriam blushed and avoided her gaze.

That's when Joheved remembered hearing that the blossoms' perfume was reputed to be an aphrodisiac. "Miriam, don't go there alone with him, not now," she pleaded, but to no avail.

"We'll be on a public road in broad daylight. Don't you remember last summer when we found the honey? We all smelled the grape blossoms then and nothing terrible happened."

Miriam too had heard tales of the grape flowers' effect on men and women, and it was exciting to imagine her and Benjamin enjoying the fragrance together. She had no idea how they might be affected, but that was part of the attraction.

Joheved realized that her sister might go off with Benjamin even if she refused to be an accomplice to their scheme. "All right, we can go on a walk along the river tomorrow, but promise me you'll be home well before sunset. And please be careful."

Miriam gave her older sister a grateful hug. She didn't know how she was going to wait until the next day. For her part, Joheved couldn't imagine any man being so compelling, but at least Miriam had promised to tell her everything that happened.

The following afternoon, all went as planned. As the bells chimed Vespers, Miriam saw Benjamin waiting for her just outside the Preize Gate, the one closest to the vineyard. At first they walked the familiar road in silence. Miriam could sense that Benjamin was nervous, but she was too shy to ask what was bothering him. She tried to think of a subject they could discuss and remembered the Gemara they had been learning.

"Benjamin, could you help me remember what we studied today from Tractate *Pesachim*? You know, the disagreement between Hillel and Shammai about which blessing is said first at the seder, the one for the wine or the one for the holiday."

He easily recalled the beginning of the Gemara. The class had been studying this tractate ever since the students returned from celebrating Passover with their families.

Miriam was in the middle of reciting why Hillel said to bless the wine first, when she paused for a moment. Did she actually smell something pleasant or was she imagining it?

When Benjamin first noticed the faint sweet scent on the breeze, he missed a few of Miriam's words. He forced himself to calm down and listen to what she was saying. "Thus, because the holiday arrives before the wine, its blessing should come first." There was another reason, but he couldn't seem to remember it.

Miriam no longer cared about Hillel and Shammai. As soon as she became aware of the vineyard's lovely fragrance, she happily reflected on why Benjamin had wanted to get her under its influence. "Oh, I can smell the grape flowers." She tried not to sound too excited. "We probably shouldn't get much closer."

Benjamin stopped. The perfume was already powerful enough; they didn't need to go farther. "Miriam, I . . ."

He began to speak, but when she turned around to look at him, he couldn't think of anything to say. Had it only been a year ago that they had ignored this wonderful smell and followed bees instead? Somehow in that time, he had left childhood behind. He stood staring at her, inhaling the wonderful fragrance that surrounded them. Were her eyes blue, green, or gray, or some of each?

Miriam tried to continue their discussion, but the look in Benjamin's eyes flustered her. To avoid his compelling gaze and concentrate on the beautiful scent, Miriam closed her eyes.

Benjamin, interpreting her actions as an invitation, leaned forward to kiss her. She momentarily gloried in his embrace, but then she noticed the rough beginnings of his beard against her skin and came to her senses.

What on earth was she doing, allowing herself to be kissed in the middle of a public road, where anyone could see them? What could have possessed her to act so shamelessly? She spun out of his grasp and vented her outrage.

"You must be in league with demons! You've cast a spell on me. I can't believe I followed you up here and let you kiss me in front of the world. We aren't married, or even betrothed."

Benjamin was stunned by her sudden wrath, but he had to say something to overcome her distrust. "But, Miriam, I do want to marry you, more than anything. I've wanted to marry you for over a year. I've already talked to my parents about it.

"Try to understand," he pleaded with her. "You're the daughter of a *talmid chacham* with his own yeshivah, your older sister already has a great match arranged for her, and your parents probably hope to do better for you. I know they can find you a greater scholar than I am, and a richer one, too. My only hope is to make you want me."

His confession washed away Miriam's anger. He wanted to marry her! And he worried that he wasn't good enough. She threw her arms around him and kissed him, not caring who saw them.

This time he broke their embrace. "If you want, I'll ask my father to speak to yours just as soon as I get home for Shavuot." Despite her apparent pleasure in his company, Benjamin still wasn't sure that she wanted to marry him.

She took his hands in hers. "Please make your parents hurry. Our *erusin* must be complete before the merchants return for the Hot Fair, before somebody else approaches Papa about me."

"I'll have them come back with me immediately after the festival," he assured her. "Your father wouldn't make another arrangement without your knowing, would he?"

Miriam shook her head. "I don't think so. He made Joheved consent to her betrothal, in front of witnesses." She quickly looked up and down the road. "And speaking of witnesses, if we don't want any to our behavior today, we'd better get home."

"We're safe enough." He was so happy; he couldn't help but laugh. "Everybody knows that they should stay away from a vineyard while it's flowering. And by the way, weren't you saying something about Hillel and wine?"

After *souper*, when the sisters had gone to bed, Joheved insisted on finding out exactly what had transpired outside the vineyard. Miriam shyly told her that she had never smelled anything as wonderful as the grape flowers . . . and that Benjamin was bringing his parents back to Troyes as soon as Shavuot was over to arrange their betrothal.

More relieved than disappointed when Miriam became reticent about sharing the romantic details, Joheved gave her younger sister a happy embrace. "It's about time."

Miriam wanted to lie back and reflect on her wonderful afternoon, but she couldn't let Joheved have the last word. "You should take Meir to smell the blossoms next year."

"When the time comes, I'll try to remember." Joheved didn't want to spoil Miriam's happiness by arguing. But by this time next year, she'd be married, hopefully pregnant even, and therefore not likely to be interested in smelling any aphrodisiac flowers.

The days passed, and eventually Salomon looked up from his studies and Rivka from her new baby, and they became aware of the mutual satisfaction emanating from Miriam and Benjamin. There didn't seem to be much else to do except ask Benjamin to invite his parents to return with him when Shavuot was over, to which he shyly answered that he had already planned to do so.

Under the guiding hand of Isaac ha-Parnas, negotiations went smoothly. Benjamin's parents easily agreed that their son would live in Troyes and help manage Salomon's vineyard so Miriam could remain there as the community's midwife. Salomon hosted his daughter's *erusin* feast just as the Hot Fair began, disappointing several merchants who had hoped to negotiate on behalf of their own sons that summer. It was a good thing that Rivka still had a substantial supply of honey down in the cellar, because the quantity of honey cake she was obliged to serve in honor of the happy couple was so great that she was forced to utilize the baker's large ovens for two days.

And a happy couple they were. Sitting next to Benjamin at their betrothal banquet, Miriam reveled in her good fortune. Love matches were the exception, not the rule, and she squeezed Benjamin's hand under the table as she reflected on the difference between her *erusin* and Joheved's. Now that Papa had made good on his promise to find them both learned husbands, Mama was beaming.

The musicians began playing a dance for pairs and Joheved beckoned her to join them. When Benjamin applauded as the two sisters performed the dance's intricate steps, Miriam started feeling sorry for Joheved. Her older sister hadn't seen Meir in nearly a year, and when he did stop by on his twice-yearly return to Germany, he spent most of his time with Papa.

"Oh, Joheved." Miriam gave her an extra hug as they twirled each other. "I hope you and Meir will be as happy as Benjamin and me when you're married."

"Happy?" Joheved gave a snort of disbelief. "Marriage is to have children, not for happiness."

Miriam was in too good a mood to be intimidated. "Then I hope you and Meir have lots of children and a happy marriage."

Joheved gave a quick glance to Leah's upstairs window. "It's too bad Grandmama can't enjoy these good times with us."

But even that thought dampened Miriam's joy only for a moment.

Leah's sad condition was the only taint on that otherwise happy summer. Her situation was stable; she did not regain her former health, but neither did she get worse. She seemed to appreciate her family's company, that is to say, she smiled at whoever sat and talked to her, and held fast to their hands. Rivka warned the invalid's visitors to be sure her limbs were kept well inside the bed, so demons couldn't grab them.

Hopeful that Leah might remain this way indefinitely, Joheved and her family turned their attention to her nuptial preparations. At the Hot

Fair, they bought material for wedding clothes and bed linens, plus a chest and cabinet to house the new couple's possessions. Aunt Sarah had graciously offered one of her bedrooms to the newlyweds, and Rivka decided to outfit it with new wall hangings as well.

The fair was in its second month when Grandmama Leah began to fail. She had difficulty breathing and was often so drowsy that they could barely wake her for meals. The doctor came regularly and bled her, but to no avail. Salomon and his students spent hours praying and reciting psalms on her behalf, but her condition continued to deteriorate.

One morning a worried Marie confessed that she had not been able to give Leah breakfast. The old woman had clenched her teeth tightly together and refused to swallow any food. At midday, Rivka attempted to feed Leah herself, with the same unhappy result. In late afternoon, Miriam had success getting her grandmother to drink some well-diluted wine, but no one could persuade her to eat the evening meal.

The next day, Rivka directed Marie to prepare a chicken stew with garlic for *disner*, and to set aside a portion of the rich broth for Leah. But despite encouragement by both granddaughters, this delicacy failed to tempt her, and Rivka tearfully brought the untouched dish downstairs later. Salomon's household, which had so recently been joyfully anticipating the future, now viewed it with dread.

Joheved sadly packed away her new fabrics. Clutching the amulet she always wore, Rivka lit candles near Leah's bed and removed the chicken-feather pillow, hoping to lure away any demons who would prolong her death-agony. The family avoided wearing new clothes, knowing that they would have to rend them at news of her demise. Bowls of water were set out as traps for demons, to be dumped outside immediately after the death was discovered, and Rivka sternly warned the household never to drink from them.

Thus it was that Miriam, awake early and gathering eggs in the courtyard, learned of Leah's passing when she saw Rivka tearfully pouring a dish of water into the dirt outside the kitchen door. One by one, the other members of her household appeared, each emptying a container of water outside. Joheved went all the way to the courtyard gate and spilled hers in the road, just in time to meet a neighbor on her way to the bakery.

Instantly recognizing the significance of these events, the woman crossed to the other side of the street. The dead woman's ghost was surely nearby and perhaps the Angel of Death was still in the vicinity as well. But Joheved knew the neighbor would inform the community of Leah's passing. Now somebody would be sure to prepare food for the mourners before midday, and people could arrange their affairs to free them for an afternoon funeral.

One of the most rigid rules of Judaism is that a funeral must take place at the earliest possible moment after death. If Leah had died on the first day of a festival, non-Jews would have carried out her burial. But her early morning demise left plenty of time to attend to all of the funeral minutiae and still have her body under the earth before nightfall.

While Benjamin and the other students were at the riverbank, cutting fresh rushes for the floors where the mourners would sit during the next week, the women of Salomon's family focused their attention on *tahara*, ritually preparing Grandmama Leah's body for burial. Joheved dreaded the next few hours, but she had to do it. *Tahara* was one of the most important mitzvot a woman could fulfill, an act of unselfish kindness whose recipient could not possibly return any favors. It was performed for the sake of the mitzvah, knowing that one day it would to be done for her.

Joheved steeled herself as she helped Miriam, Mama, and Aunt Sarah lift Grandmama Leah's corpse onto a wide board. But it wasn't as bad as she feared. Mama encouraged them to recall Leah in her prime as they washed and salted the body. During the occasional silences, Joheved could hear Papa praying outside the door, performing his watchman's duty. The body had not been left alone since the moment of death and would be accompanied constantly until burial.

Mama made sure that the corpse was wrapped in a new linen shroud; Leah had been a proud woman and they wouldn't want her shamed by appearing in Gan Eden poorly dressed. Joheved shivered as she remembered tales of ghosts who refused to leave their former homes because their shrouds were too shabby to be seen in.

She knew that some of Salomon's students were finding an appropriate coffin, while others were in the cemetery, digging the grave. Mama had given strict instructions to prevent them from choosing a plot next to any of Leah's old adversaries, lest the two ghosts return and make their displeasure known.

By midday, when Johanna had laid out a small repast in the kitchen for the family, Leah's covered body had been placed in the coffin and all was ready for the procession to the cemetery. Before they left, Mama marked the side of the board on which the corpse had lain; Heaven forbid it be turned over and incite the deceased's ire, resulting in an untimely death for another in the household.

Benjamin and several of Salomon's bravest students carried the coffin down the stairs and out of the house, followed by the immediate family and then the rest of the mourning congregation. As they walked beside Salomon, Joheved and Miriam recited the antidemonic 91st Psalm to prevent the spirits awaiting the corpse from seizing a living victim instead.

The heart of the funeral service was the Justification of the Judgment, a short prayer that affirmed the rightness of the Creator's disposition of humanity. Here, and as part of every service prayed during the seven days of mourning, the congregation would proclaim verses from Deuteronomy:

He is our Rock, His work is perfect; for all His ways judgment;
are a God of truth and without iniquity, just and right is He.

The Hot Fair had not ended, so there was no lack of pious and learned men to repeat the 91st Psalm seven times as Grandmama Leah's coffin was lowered into her grave.

He will cover you with His pinions, you will find refuge under His wings, His fidelity is an encircling shield. You need not fear the terror by night or the arrow that flies by day, the plague that stalks in darkness or the scourge that ravages at noon.

They continued reciting as the body was buried, until the grave was full of earth, but Joheved could barely hear them; she was crying too hard.

Next Papa and Mama, followed by the congregation, reached down to tear up and smell a portion of grass and dirt, which they then threw over their shoulders while reciting the verses from Psalms, "They shall flourish as the grass of the field" and "Remember that we are dust." Now Leah's soul had permission to leave her grave, and the prayer also prevented her ghost from following the mourners home. A double line of people formed for her family to walk between, and the entire company escorted them to Salomon's house.

Upon entering the courtyard, Joheved found that washing utensils and water had been prepared for them. Everyone bathed their hands, and some, including Mama and Papa, their eyes and face as well. On the dining table, the traditional mourners' meal of boiled eggs and lentil stew was laid out. Even the breads were round, to remind the mourners that bereavement is like a wheel, ever recurring. But though she'd barely eaten anything since yesterday, Joheved had no appetite.

For the next seven days, her family would sit on the ground, abstain from meat and strong wine, and not leave the house except on the Sabbath. Daily prayers, each including the Justification of the Judgment, would be recited at home, as the community joined the mourners to share their anguish and console them.

Although Salomon was the legal mourner and tradition demanded these strict rituals for his benefit, Rivka, Joheved, and Miriam felt greater grief than he did. The woman who died was a stranger, not the mother he remembered from childhood. As far as Salomon was concerned, he had lost his mother long ago.

Rivka had mixed feelings. She loved Leah as another mother, yet she couldn't help but feel relief when Leah died. The old woman had lain in a bed of pain for six months and hadn't been able to function in dignity for several years. In addition, the burden of Leah's care had become increasingly onerous with the new baby's arrival. Rivka grieved over Leah's demise, but she knew that it was time.

Joheved and Miriam had their own fond memories of Leah that they were glad to share with those who came to console their family. More than their own mother, who seemed rather like an older sister, their grandmother had raised them. She'd provided their food, clothing, and shelter, and she made sure they acquired the skills necessary to run a Jewish household and make Jewish wine.

"She was the one who taught us how to read Scripture," Joheved said, recalling how they used to sit in front of the hearth and recite the text together. "And she taught us all the prayers, too."

"When we were little, she helped Mama bathe us and get us dressed," Miriam added, a tear rolling down her cheek. "She loved to braid ribbons into our hair."

"She tucked us in bed and kissed us good night . . ." Now Joheved was crying too.

"And she gave us hugs each morning when we came down to breakfast," Miriam said, finishing for her. With Leah gone, it was easy to forget the recent past and remember the good times.

For Salomon, a new picture of his mother emerged as seen through his daughters' loving eyes, and he realized that his only chance of receiving such a fond eulogy lay in being a devoted father to Rachel and little Leah. He would have to make sure that they grew up with equally warm and affectionate memories of him.

Fifteen

As shivah, those first seven days of intense mourning after the funeral, drew to a close, Rivka sadly suggested that perhaps they should write to Meir. With Salomon in mourning, wouldn't the wedding be postponed?

"Oy, I forgot about Meir completely." Salomon shook his head. "He's probably already on his way by now."

"What are you going to do with him?" Rivka asked. "Send him back to Mayence or to his parents' house?"

"My mother's death doesn't change my need to have Meir help with the younger students." Salomon stroked his beard. "He may as well stay here. He and Joheved can wait a few months."

Joheved almost cried with relief at Papa's announcement. Now she wouldn't be wed to a stranger. She and Meir would see each other every day, share meals, get a chance to know each other. Joheved would never admit, even to herself, how much she envied Miriam's love match.

At first Joheved kept a sharp eye out for any young strangers at synagogue. She wasn't sure she'd recognize her fiancé when he arrived; she hadn't seen him for almost a year, and during their brief times together she'd been careful not to stare at him. After a week went by without Meir's appearance, Joheved grew less vigilant, and three weeks later, she gave the men's section only a cursory glance as she climbed the synagogue stairs.

Thus she didn't give a second thought to the young man who stood hesitantly at the cellar entrance one afternoon. She was occupied with a wine buyer who could not decide which cask's contents to purchase. Papa and the others were in the vineyard, stringing up netting to keep the ripening grapes safe from hungry birds, and Joheved would much rather have been outdoors listening to her father's lessons than in the cellar drawing unending wine samples for this merchant who was drinking more wine than he'd likely end up buying.

Her impatience grew. The only reason they had such a choice of wine to sell this late in the season was because Salomon no longer needed it for her wedding. So when she noticed the second man coming into the cellar, she sighed in resignation. Another customer—she'd never get out to the vineyard now.

She forced herself to greet the stranger politely. Tall and brown-haired with a full beard, his lanky frame proclaimed his youth. He seemed ill at ease, probably a new junior partner, one who undertook the risky journeys to distant markets while the senior partner provided the capital and stayed safely at home. His dark green *cote* was of excellent quality, somewhat dusty from travel, and rather handsome with his deep yellow chemise and hose. At least it seemed likely he could afford their prices.

She was drawing him a cup of wine when Rivka called to her from the kitchen. "Joheved, are you still in the cellar?"

"*Oui*, Mama. I have two buyers down here with me. Do you need me for anything?"

"Nothing that can't wait," the voice from upstairs replied. "Don't let me keep you from the customers."

Meir's suspicions were confirmed. The young woman handing him a cup of wine was his betrothed, but she had no idea who he was! And after all he'd endured to get here to marry her.

It had never been difficult to find companions traveling home for holidays, but any merchant going to the Troyes Hot Fair had left long ago. Meir had nearly despaired of finding anyone going west, when word came of a party of knights attending the fair. They were likely to be poor company, but he would get to Troyes in safety. The journey had been as irritating as he had anticipated, and this morning, when he knew he could make Troyes's gates before dark if he rode hard, Meir gladly bid his comrades adieu.

Meir's annoyance evaporated as he surreptitiously watched Joheved. The wine was excellent, and after downing the contents of his mug, he decided to conceal his identity a while longer. In Mayence, Meir always drank his wine well diluted, so he was unprepared for the effect of a full cup of strong wine on his empty stomach. His mood lightened considerably as he continued observing his fiancée.

She had certainly grown up to be an attractive woman. Her skin looked soft and creamy next to her dark braids, which ended below her waist. He briefly wondered what all that hair would look like, loose and flowing against a pillow, and then chided himself for harboring such unseemly thoughts.

Her *bliaut* was a deep rose color, and her pale blue chemise was embroidered with flowers in shades of blue, pink, and burgundy. Meir couldn't help but notice that the figure under her *bliaut* was definitely not that of a young girl, and when she lifted her skirts to climb upstairs to bring them more bread, he openly savored her exposed ankles and calves, instead of modestly looking away as he normally would have done. Why shouldn't he admire her? In less than a month they'd be sharing a bed.

Upstairs in the kitchen, as she tried to relax and slow her racing heartbeat, Joheved was also having a silent conversation with herself. For shame, she scolded herself, getting flustered just because a handsome stranger couldn't keep his eyes off her. *Don't encourage him, you're a betrothed woman! Don't waste the fresh bread on him; give him some from yesterday.*

Joheved knew she should listen to her conscience, even as she knew she was going to ignore it. She resolutely cut the source of her consternation a large piece of the freshest bread and brought it downstairs. As he ate, she silently refilled the young man's cup from a different cask, feeling flattered yet annoyed that he was staring at her so brazenly. Did he think his fine looks and clothes gave him such license? She felt her face growing warm and was mortified that he might notice her blushing. This was definitely going to be a trying afternoon.

The older merchant finally made up his mind, so she tried to ignore the impertinent young one's interest in her and concentrate on negotiating a price. But both tasks proved difficult. Implying that there must be something wrong with the wine because it hadn't sold earlier, the first merchant made a ridiculously low offer.

Joheved expected bargaining, but this was outrageous. Her eyes narrowed in anger, and Meir, emboldened by his second cup of wine, entered the fray by loudly remarking that this fine vintage was certainly worth more than such a paltry amount. Perhaps the good mistress should deal with him first. The older man, furious at his competitor's interference, turned to Meir and ordered him outside to discuss the matter.

Meir gallantly agreed, and after suggesting that Joheved might bring down some more of her excellent bread, followed him into the courtyard. Joheved returned to the kitchen, sure that there was something familiar about the young merchant's voice. But she couldn't seem to place it.

"What do you mean by meddling in my business?" The older man kept his voice low but the anger was unmistakable. "If you keep quiet we may both profit well."

"*Shalom aleikhem*, Master . . . ?" Meir said.

"Simon ha-Levi." The merchant rudely ignored Meir's greeting.

"Meir ben Samuel, at your service." He bowed deeply. "Now Master Simon, perhaps you aren't aware that the vintner in question here is the town's rabbi, their *Rosh Yeshivah*. What are a few *deniers* to you when the Day of Judgment is nigh and the Holy One is about to weigh your deeds?" Meir held out his hands as if balancing something invisible. "Which do you want written by your name in the Book of Life, that you generously supported a Torah scholar or that you deprived one of sustenance?"

Simon's face blanched. He reached over and clasped Meir's shoulders. "You are absolutely right, my friend, and I thank you." This young man's warning may have just saved his life.

He turned and walked back down into the cellar, thanking his lucky stars that there was still time for such a good deed to be inscribed onto his heavenly ledger.

Joheved was waiting for them with some cheese as well as bread, and Meir forced himself not to wolf down his share, no matter how great his hunger. Before she could say anything, Simon surprised her by agreeing to match whatever price the previous customer had paid. Joheved looked back and forth at the two men, who seemed on the most amicable of terms. What on earth had transpired between them?

As they marked the casks his carter would collect later, Simon made friendly conversation. "Mistress, I must admit it is unusual to have so much wine available this late in the season. You must have had a fruitful harvest last year."

"I'm afraid not." Her face clouded and she fought back tears. "My father had saved this wine for my wedding, but a few weeks ago his mother died. So we are in mourning and there will be no wedding."

No wedding! Meir sat down hard; it was as though he had just been punched in the gut. He listened in shock as Simon offered Joheved condolences on the loss of her grandmother. By this time, Meir's head was swimming so badly that he was unable to stand and wave good-bye when Simon took his leave.

"Farewell, and *shalom aleikhem*, Meir ben Samuel," the older man said to him. "I will offer a toast for your good fortune in the coming year whenever I drink this wine."

"*Shalom aleikhem*, indeed, Meir ben Samuel." Joheved's voice was slow and controlled as she approached him.

Meir couldn't tell if she was hiding anger or amusement. He didn't dare look at her.

Joheved was more astonished than anything else. She had been looking for him in vain for weeks, and now he appeared out of no-where in her own cellar, just in time to hear from her own mouth that their wedding was off. Any annoyance she felt at being misled vanished when she saw how forlorn he looked, lying on the bench, arms crossed over his belly, face to the wall.

"Are you all right?" Had he really gotten so upset when he'd heard that they weren't getting married? How flattering.

"Am I all right?!" He turned to face her. "I haven't had anything to eat since dawn, my stomach feels like a horse just kicked it, and my bride, who doesn't even recognize me, just informed me that our wedding is canceled. And you ask me if I'm all right?" He tried to sit up, but his head hurt too much. With a grimace of pain, he reached out to support himself.

"Don't move." She helped him lie back down on the bench. "I'll get you some food."

Meir closed his eyes and berated himself for staring at her legs when he should have been noticing the tear at the neck of her chemise. How could he have missed that obvious sign of recent bereavement? And now what was going to happen to him?

His pessimistic thoughts were interrupted by the sensation of being watched, and he turned to see an orange striped cat staring at him, less than an arm's length away. To his surprise, the cat walked over to him and pushed its head under his hand. His horse liked its ears scratched, so he proceeded to do the same for the cat. He was rewarded with a loud purr and was soon so engrossed in petting the cat that he almost forgot his miserable situation.

Joheved heard Meir's stomach growl as she came down the stairs with a large bowl of stew and two loaves of bread, and she tried not to smile. She was sure he hadn't had such a nice beard the last time she'd seen him. No wonder she hadn't recognized him. She sighed with relief. Thank Heaven this attractive man had turned out to be not such a stranger after all.

Meir finished his stew so quickly that Joheved insisted on bringing him a second helping. Ashamed at how he'd openly scrutinized her legs on the stairs earlier, he made a point of looking at her face as she returned to the kitchen. She smiled down at him in return.

He ate more slowly this time, while Joheved enlightened him about what her family had suffered recently. When he heard Joheved say that Salomon intended for him to live in Troyes despite their postponed nuptials, Meir was feeling almost happy. His bride-to-be had proved to be kind and forgiving of his less than admirable behavior. And she had good-looking legs. In a rush of generosity, he left the last of his stew for the cat.

In the weeks that followed, Meir decided that, in spite of remaining unwed, life in Troyes was good. He enjoyed giving his young students their first taste of Talmud, watching their eyes light up with understanding and their faces shine with the pride that comes from mastering difficult material.

The grape harvest and winemaking went by in a blur, and then Rosh Hashanah was upon them. Meir's family came to Troyes to worship, and he listened proudly as his female relatives praised Joheved's skill in leading the complicated Yom Kippur service. Salomon and his father didn't set a new wedding date, but Meir hoped he would not have to wait a full year of mourning.

Next came Sukkot, the Festival of Booths, commemorating the temporary shelters the Israelites lived in as they wandered in the desert after leaving Egypt. The yeshivah students took great pleasure in building a sukkah in their *maître's* courtyard. For seven days they would eat, study, and, if the weather was decent, sleep in the rickety structure, thus fulfilling the commandment to "dwell in the sukkah."

Besides dwelling in the sukkah, Jews celebrated Sukkot with special blessings made while holding four varieties of plants, as it said in Leviticus:

Take the fruit of goodly trees, branches of palms, boughs of thick trees and willows of the brook, and you hall rejoice before your God seven days.

The fruit traditionally used for Sukkot was the *etrog*, or citron, considered "goodly" because it was both fragrant and flavorful. Thanks to the generosity of Hiyya ibn Ezra, who brought them all the way from Cairo, Salomon's family was assured one of the beautiful fruits.

Joheved and Miriam couldn't believe their good fortune at having their own *etrog*. Even their pious grandmother had never been able to obtain one. For the whole week, it sat in its special dish, bright and yellow like a miniature sun. Any time they wanted, they could pick it up and inhale its sweet, citrusy perfume. Everyone who came to their house couldn't help but stop and smell the *etrog* when they saw it.

Boys had a great time during the week of Sukkot. They held competitions, played ball games, and, when no adults were watching, gambled with nuts or dice. Meir was constantly being asked to lend out his horse. It was difficult to refuse, though he knew the boys intended to race her. It was Sukkot—the Season of *Simcha* (Joy).

It wasn't all fun and games for the girls. While the resident students were gone, Rivka had Joheved, Miriam, and Marie replace the attic's dirty straw. Sweeping up the old stalks and dumping them into the courtyard was easy. But the next part, carrying clean straw up a rickety ladder into the attic, was both awkward and a bit scary.

They were busy with carrying and spreading the stuff on the attic floor when Meir, having interrupted his studies to use the privy, stopped at the well to wash his hands. At this particular moment, Joheved was starting up the ladder with a load of straw while Miriam was waiting at the top to take it from her. Remembering what a prude her sister had been when she wanted to be alone with Benjamin, Miriam was struck with a mischievous idea. Joheved had indignantly told her how Meir had enjoyed watching her on the cellar stairs, and she couldn't resist this opportunity to tease them.

After assuring herself that Marie was occupied at the rear of the attic, Miriam called out, "Meir, can you give us a hand and hold the ladder steady for Joheved?"

Meir couldn't refuse, not that he wanted to, and Miriam chortled with glee at the furious look on her sister's blushing face as Meir took hold of the ladder. Her initial notion was to tempt Meir with a view of Joheved's legs as she climbed higher, but Miriam soon concocted a more devilish idea. She waited until Joheved's hips were level with Meir's shoulders, then gave the ladder an abrupt shake. When she peeked over the ledge, what she saw surpassed her wildest expectations.

Miriam had imagined her sister stopped with Meir's upper body pressed against her legs as he steadied the ladder. But instead, Joheved lost her balance entirely. Miriam watched openmouthed as Joheved, falling backward off the ladder, managed to knock Meir down as he attempted to catch her. They landed in a pile of debris from the attic, both covered with straw.

For a moment they were too dazed to move. Then Meir gently rolled Joheved off him and helped her up. "You're not hurt, are you?" he asked, trying to brush the stems off his clothes.

Joheved shook her head. She ought to ask how he was, but she was too flustered to speak. Physically unharmed, she had never felt more embarrassed in her life. She glanced around the courtyard and thanked Heaven that nobody was outside to see her and Meir lying in the straw together. Up in the attic, Miriam howled with laughter as she watched the couple awkwardly trying to remove the stalks from each other's hair and clothes.

As much as she wanted to contain her mirth, Miriam was still giggling when Meir, insisting that Joheved rest a bit while he carried the straw upstairs, reached the attic and dropped his load at her feet. His inquisitive look made Miriam giggle more, until it occurred to her that he might tell her father what had happened. Her smile froze and then disappeared as she returned his gaze. But he only winked at her, then climbed down to get more straw.

That night, it took great willpower on Miriam's part not to laugh as she helped Joheved remove the final pieces of straw from her hair. And it took more willpower on Joheved's part not to accuse her sister of orchestrating the incident that neither one dared acknowledge. But discomfited as she felt, Joheved had to admit that falling on top of Meir had not been a completely unpleasant experience.

✑

Early the next morning, Salomon made his way to the courtyard sukkah and began prodding the bundles of cloaks and blankets containing Meir and the students to wake them for morning prayers. Meir was still trying to recapture the pleasant feeling of Joheved's body on top of his, when his reverie was interrupted by a woman's screams coming from the house.

Salomon had already closed half the distance between the sukkah and his house by the time Meir threw off his bedding and took off after him. Meir reached the open door, hesitated about whether to go in or not, and nearly collided with Joheved's aunt Sarah as she bolted past him and on up the stairs. Now there were more female voices wailing above. Behind him, the small band of frightened students congregated in the pale dawn, some of them shivering in their light chemises. He motioned them near the hearth and tried to compose himself enough to lead them in psalms.

Just then Salomon stumbled down the stairs, tears streaming down his cheeks, and Meir hurried to support his teacher. Salomon buried his head in the young man's shoulder and wept loudly. "My baby, my poor little girl. She was perfectly fine when Rivka put her to bed, we never heard a peep from her during the night, and now she's dead."

Meir's response was automatic. "*Baruch Dayyan Emet* (Blessed is the True Judge)." Since Talmudic times this was the prayer Jews said when first informed of a death.

As the significance of Meir's words reached him, Salomon's wild weeping ceased, and he looked down at his clothing for a place to tear. He was wearing a new outfit for the festival, one originally made for Joheved's wedding. Meir could see him hesitate and knew Salomon didn't want to ruin his fine holiday *cote*. But his chemise had already been rent at his mother's death. As Meir and the other students watched in trepidation, Salomon grabbed the beautiful embroidery and tore the neckline open nearly to his waist.

Sixteen

For Joheved and Miriam, the next few days seemed almost a repetition of Grandmama Leah's death. Yet some things were different. Their grandmother was the rabbi's mother, thus deserving of honor for his sake, but she was also a respected elder of the community, their vintner and women's prayer leader. Nearly every Jew in Troyes had attended her funeral and visited their house during the week of mourning.

But baby Leah's demise went almost unacknowledged. Babies died regularly in their first year, and usually another child came along soon enough to console the parents. Besides, it was still Sukkot, and it was forbidden to mourn or lament during the joyous festival. Only Salomon's students and a few of the men who studied with him regularly attended the funeral.

The family members' need for consolation was the opposite of when Grandmama Leah had died. Joheved and Miriam, who had deeply mourned their grandmother's loss, felt little grief for the baby sister they had barely known. Rachel was almost relieved at the disappearance of this competitor for her parents' attention, although she was old enough to know that she shouldn't show it.

Rivka, who had discovered baby Leah dead in her cradle, had recovered from her initial hysterics only to become terrified that this second death, so soon after Grandmama Leah's, portended an imminent third visit from the Angel of Death. Sure that some lapse during her mother-in-law's bereavement had brought this misfortune upon them, she clung tightly to her amulet and turned her efforts toward ensuring that all mourning rituals were carried out punctiliously.

When Rivka was a child, her mother insisted that she cut her nails starting with the first finger, explaining that starting with the third finger caused the death of one's children, with the fifth, poverty, and with the second, a bad reputation. Rivka was always careful to cut her thumb-nail first, even if a different one needed paring, but maybe Salomon hadn't been so meticulous. When she got up the nerve to ask him, he assured her that he invariably trimmed his nails in the same order: left hand, 4, 2, 5, 3, 1; right hand, 1, 3, 5, 2, 4. Scholars were taught to never pare any two nails in sequence because it caused forgetfulness. So Rivka become resigned to her fate. She had lost babies before, and this one was only a girl.

Strangely, while Salomon had been the least bereft by his mother's passing, he now suffered the most. Once he got over the initial disap-pointment at not producing a son, little Leah had been a joy to him. Rachel was starting to prefer the company of her sisters, and just as he was looking forward to cuddling another toddler on his lap as he studied, she was suddenly taken from him.

It had to be his fault. Baby Leah couldn't have committed any sins during her short lifetime. Was there some sin he'd forgotten to atone for at Yom Kippur, some person he had wounded yet neglected to ask for forgiveness, a vow unfulfilled? He searched his memory in vain for such a lapse, yet he knew it must exist. How many mourning fathers came to his *beit din*, begging the court to release them from a careless oath before another child died? At least those men knew what they'd done wrong.

Sitting on the rushes that covered the floor of his house, he sur-veyed his three remaining daughters and felt a stab of regret that he would never know the little girl or young woman that baby Leah might have been. The infant had died sometime during the night, yet he'd gotten up and gone outside without noticing anything was amiss. A sudden terror seized him—*what if another of my daughters dies in her sleep tonight?*

Emotions in turmoil, he surveyed the small group who had come to his house of mourning so he'd have nine men to pray with. Meir prayed with the family every day, but the other students had been encouraged to enjoy their Sukkot holiday. Today Hiyya ibn Ezra, in addition to a couple of other foreign merchants and a few local men, sat in silence until services started. Because of the holiday, it was inappropriate for them to offer words of consolation.

When they reached the place when one would usually say the Justification of the Judgment, Salomon paused, and Joheved sensed the distinguished visitors' uneasiness. This bereavement prayer was never recited on *Shabbat* or during a festival, yet at the appointed time, Salomon stood up and said it alone. None of the men challenged him, but they didn't join him either.

Once the service was over, she could tell that the men stayed only long enough to be polite. Hiyya motioned to Meir to walk with him, and she followed at a distance.

"I don't understand why Salomon is so distressed that he laments during the festival." The Egyptian looked more puzzled than angry. "After all, he only lost a baby girl, and he already has three daughters. Now if the infant had been male . . ."

"Perhaps this daughter wasn't destined to be fruitful and build something great for him in this world," another man suggested.

Meir shook his head. He didn't want to criticize Salomon, but he couldn't explain such a blatant disregard for accepted mourning practice. Meir no sooner closed the gate behind the men than Joheved and Miriam approached him. They, too, were upset with their father's breach.

Joheved lifted her hands toward the heavens. "What was there to grieve over? Baby Leah died peacefully in her sleep and is surely in *Gan Eden* now."

Meir had had no answer for her. None of them dared ask Salomon directly, and he never offered an explanation.

Gloom enveloped Salomon all winter. Pupils returning after the fall holidays noticed that their *maître* no longer began study sessions with a joke or funny story. Despite a successful wine harvest, the new vintage celebration at Hanukkah was subdued, and Salomon left the festivities early, pleading a headache.

That night he dreamed that he was back in Mayence, attending synagogue with his mother. Dressed in her new violet silk *bliaut*, she looked younger, like when he first left home to study with her brother, Simon ha-Zaken. The expression on her face was fearsome, and she proceeded to denounce him to the scholars.

"Look how he ignores me, how little he mourns for me," she screamed. "And after all I sacrificed for him. So I gave him something to mourn about. If he wouldn't grieve for one Leah, he can grieve for another!"

Then Uncle Simon stood up and pointed a finger at him. "Have you forgotten everything we've taught you?"

Salomon woke up in a sweat, his heart pounding. How could he have forgotten the Talmudic discussion that began:

Why do a man's children die when they are young? Because he did not weep and mourn over a kosher person.

The answer was a sword in his breast. Only fear of demons kept him from rushing to the cemetery immediately, and when the roosters crowed at dawn's first light, he was dressed and ready to visit his mother's grave.

"Please forgive me, Mama!" He threw himself down on the few tufts of grass that had grown since the funeral. "Have mercy on me and your granddaughters, pardon my iniquity, I beg you." But he could not bring himself to weep.

That day he was so visibly disturbed that Rachel, the only one not intimidated, finally asked him, "Papa, why are you so upset?" She inquired with the self-centeredness of childhood, "Did I do something wrong?"

Salomon, ashamed that his emotions were so obvious, assured Rachel that she had done nothing to anger him.

She was not deterred. "Then who did make you mad?"

"It's not something anyone did." He had no intention of revealing his nightmare, so he stroked his beard and finally thought of something else he could tell her.

"You remember Robert, the monk from Montier-la-Celle, who comes to visit me and ask questions from time to time?"

"The one who gives us grapes to make wine from?"

"*Oui*, and for one of the *Notzrim*, he's not so bad." Robert's naive interest in Torah had forced Salomon to formulate plain, simple explanations to deceptively deep questions. The process had honed Salomon's intellect in a way that was different from teaching Talmud, and he'd come to relish their meetings.

"He is leaving Montier-la-Celle to found an abbey at Collan."

Joheved couldn't restrain herself. "But what about the wine?" Without the abbey's grapes, their household income would drop considerably.

"Don't worry, the abbot at Montier-la-Celle has no intention of changing our current business agreement." He was quiet for a moment, then sighed. "I will probably never see Robert again, and we had an argument the last time he was here. He asked me about the creation of man, and I should have been able to answer him without getting angry."

The students around the table came to attention. Creation was only taught to the most advanced pupils.

"You see," he said. "Robert brought up the subject of original sin and wanted to know what we Jews believed." The confusion on Rachel's face told Salomon that he needed to back up.

"Original sin is what the *Notzrim* heretics believe is the nature of man. They say anyone not baptized, even babies, cannot enter *Gan Eden* and must spend eternity in the flames of Gehenna." His voice, which had begun with mild derision, rose into fury. "How can they possibly think the Creator would condemn innocent babes to such torment?"

Whether it was this horrible concept or her father's angry voice, tears formed in Rachel's eyes. Salomon fought to contain his outrage, and decided that somebody else should speak until he calmed down.

He turned to Meir and asked, "In the last chapter of Tractate *Berachot*, what does Rav Huna say about the creation of man?"

Joheved knew the quote and felt relieved that she had not been forced to display her Talmud learning in front of Meir. He was sitting next to her, and she felt him tense in response. Lately she'd noticed that Benjamin and Miriam's adjacent hands often vanished together beneath the table, and she suspected that Meir had launched a campaign to similarly take hold of her hand.

He had begun by keeping his nearer hand on his lap, and each day he moved it closer to her, apparently waiting for her to bring hers down as well. Today, with a decision that had her pulse racing, Joheved was slowly moving her hand toward the table's edge when Papa suddenly spoke to him.

Meir snatched his hand back and rested it on the table. "Pardon me, Master Salomon, could you repeat your question?"

Salomon did so, and Meir responded with alacrity.

Rav Huna said: What is the meaning of the verse "And God formed man," the word formed being spelled with two yuds?

Of course Meir knew the reason why *formed* was spelled with two *yuds* in Genesis, instead of its usual one, and he immediately provided it. "The Holy One, Blessed be He, created man with two *yetzers*, two inclinations, one good and one evil, the *yetzer tov* and the *yetzer ha-ra*."

Salomon had Miriam bring them the Bible. "See." He showed the words to Rachel. "The Hebrew word for 'to form' is *yotzar* and for 'inclination' is *yetzer*. It's a pun, a play on words." Hebrew is written without vowels, so the two words looked exactly the same. "This teaches that we are not condemned at birth, because man can choose between his good and evil urges," he concluded, this time keeping his voice steady.

While waiting for Salomon's reply, Meir sensed an almost imperceptible movement at his thigh, and with a quick intake of breath, he saw that Joheved's hand had vanished from the table. His heart beating wildly, he reached down and captured her hand with his own. She flinched slightly in response, but didn't pull away. His spirit was suddenly soaring, and he hoped his surge of happiness wasn't obvious. But everyone except Joheved, whose concentration was focused on how strong and warm Meir's hand felt on hers, had been intent on hearing Salomon's explanation.

Every day for the next two months, ignoring both rain and snow, Salomon went to the cemetery and begged his mother's forgiveness for not crying over her death. If it hadn't been unlucky to visit the same grave twice on the same day, he would have gone more often. When February came and went without his mood improving, his family wondered if his good humor would return in time for the raucous holiday of Purim in late March.

In previous years Rachel had been too young to take much notice of Purim, and last year her family had been too busy ministering to Grandmama Leah. But when she saw how eagerly everyone anticipated the holiday, she approached Joheved and Miriam for an explanation.

"Purim celebrates how Queen Esther and her cousin, Mordecai, saved the Persian Jews from Prime Minister Haman's evil plan to exterminate them," Joheved explained succinctly. "His scheme was thwarted when Esther convinced the king to nullify the decree."

"That's enough history," Miriam interrupted. "At Purim we read Megillat Esther (Book of Esther) in synagogue, send gifts of food to friends and relatives, and give charity to the poor. But best of all, we feast, eat, and drink to our heart's content, and then some."

Joheved continued with a grin,

The Talmudic sage, Rava, said that on Purim a man must drink wine until he can't tell the difference between "blessed is Mordecai" and "cursed is Haman."

With their love of food and wine, French Jews excelled in Purim revelry. After a day of fasting before the holiday, there was one banquet in the evening, followed by another the next day after services. Because Queen Esther's position as a new wife enabled her to influence the king, betrothed and newlywed couples celebrated Purim with special enthusiasm.

No one was sure how the decision was made, but it became common knowledge that Salomon, with two betrothed daughters, would host this year's midday Purim celebration in his courtyard. After all, where better to observe a holiday that required excess drinking than at a winemaker's? Salomon accepted the fait accompli reluctantly. At least he only needed to provide the place and the wine; the community would supply the rest.

Recruiting the requisite jongleurs and musicians would be easy. Two years after presenting her husband with their first son, Eudes, Countess Adelaide had recently given birth to another boy, Philippe, and the entertainers hired for his christening were still wintering in the palace.

As March approached its close, the Jewish community filled with nervous anticipation. For days the weather had been overcast. Rain on Purim would be a disaster, and if the day before were wet, the courtyard would be too muddy for dancing. But drizzles did not hamper the children.

They ran through the streets, eager to deliver Purim gifts and take others in exchange. Rachel was beside herself with glee as she waited for Rivka to decide which sweets she and Marie would deliver to whom. Someone seemed to be continually knocking at the door, and the dining table was piled high with dishes. Joheved and Miriam helped sort the gifts, trying to keep track of what they received and sent out again. Heaven forbid they should accidentally give an item back to the family who had originally sent it. But with all the coming and going, mix-ups were inevitable and a source of much amusement in the community.

With great relief Joheved had stopped delivering Purim presents once she was betrothed. She could still see the looks of pity on the faces of the prosperous women who had condescendingly taken her small offerings and replaced them with much larger ones containing more staples than luxuries. Mama made Miriam stay home this year too, but even so, Miriam had no intention of missing the Purim frivolity. She and Benjamin concocted a scheme that was sure to fluster both Meir and Joheved. First, they moved Meir's bedding next to Benjamin's, directly above the girls' bedroom. Then they waited impatiently until evening.

"Who moved my things?" Meir carefully checked his possessions, sure that some Purim trick was being played on him.

Benjamin allowed himself a slight smile. "Miriam and I did. She told me that Joheved would rather you slept over here now."

"What's the difference between this spot and where I used to sleep? Why should Joheved want me to sleep next to you?"

"If you can't figure it out, I'll show you."

"I'm not interested in games, just tell me." Meir was in no mood to talk. Though Joheved continued to hold hands with him at meals, she seemed unable to carry on a conversation with him. As soon as he tried to speak to her, she blushed and stammered and found an excuse to flee. Everyone said she was intelligent and articulate; why wouldn't she talk to him?

"There's no need to act so touchy." Benjamin grabbed some pieces of straw and arranged them in a layout of Salomon's house. "Here's the chimney; it goes up through our teacher's mother's old bedroom and out the middle of the attic. To the right is his room, and here on the left is where Joheved and Miriam sleep."

"How do you know where everyone's bedrooms are?" Meir asked. Had Benjamin been in Miriam's room?

"When Miriam's grandmother died, I helped carry the coffin downstairs." He waited as Meir surveyed the diagram, then the attic, and then the diagram again.

Meir's face reddened as understanding dawned on him. "You've got us lying right on top of them!"

Benjamin grinned. "An appropriate arrangement, don't you agree?"

In the room below, Miriam was setting up her side of the prank. "Joheved, why don't you want to speak to Meir? You don't even say bonjour to him in the morning."

"It's not that I don't want to talk to him, it's just that somehow I get shy and flustered whenever I try." She couldn't talk to Meir without looking at him, but as soon as her eyes met his, she became tongue-tied. "I can't explain it."

"Shy and flustered! You, who can speak at least four languages, who lead services and negotiate with wine merchants all the time, who outwitted Count Thibault's cellarer. I don't believe it. I tell you what. You just start slowly," Miriam said slyly. "Tomorrow morning, when you first see him, wish him 'bonjour' and ask him if he slept well."

The next morning, after Meir's sputtering response to her question sent Miriam and Benjamin into gales of laughter, Joheved pulled her sister aside and demanded to hear the joke. In between giggles, Miriam told her what they'd done.

Joheved slammed her hand against the wall. "That's your idea of a Purim prank? How could you disgrace me like that?" She was going to die of humiliation the next time she saw Meir. "Meir's going to believe I deliberately set him up for embarrassment this morning. I can't imagine what he thinks of me for enticing him to move his bedding above mine and then asking him how he slept!"

"It was only a joke for Purim." Joheved looked exactly like a feminine version of their father when he lost his temper, and Miriam realized that she had gone too far. "Do want Benjamin and me to apologize and have Meir put his bedding back where it was?"

"I don't want either of you telling him anything," Joheved hissed. "You've said enough already. I'll talk to him myself."

But she had no opportunity that day or the next. Meir was taking his meals at his cousins' house, where his parents were staying, and he spent the rest of his time with the students. Joheved found that she missed holding his hand at the table and she worried how displeased he might be with her. Tomorrow was Purim; maybe all the wine she'd drink would help her find a way to speak with him.

Seventeen

The Purim gift exchanges were finally finished the day before the festival. The congregation observed the Fast of Esther under gray skies, but when the day ended and they prepared to exchange fasting for feasting, the weather cleared. Before Meir left to attend the evening banquet with his parents, he presented Joheved with the present he had carefully saved until last. It was a miniature pair of men's boots, sculpted completely out of sugar.

Meir had heard about this Provençal Purim custom, the special confection a bridegroom gave his intended. Made of sugar, it represented a common item belonging to his gender, and Meir had hired a baker to make one of the simpler designs.

Relieved that he wasn't upset with her, Joheved managed to whisper, "Merci." But she could never eat anything so beautiful, so she placed the sugar shoes on a shelf in the pantry before joining everyone at the dining table. It was covered with nearly every dish and bowl her family owned, each one filled with such savory fare that she didn't know what to eat first.

The evening Purim feast finished, a sated community gathered in the synagogue. Before the service started, a tray was passed around, and each man gave a small donation. This was a symbolic offering; the community leaders had already collected for widows, orphans, and others in distress. As the tray progressed through the room, the sounds of adults trying to hush restless children increased. Finally the blessings were said and the congregation's most recent bridegroom opened the megillah scroll and began to chant.

In the women's gallery, Joheved translated his words into French. Everyone listened quietly, at least until the villain's name, Haman, was read, at which time pandemonium broke out. The congregation stamped their feet, clapped their hands, and made as much a clamor as possible to drown out the hateful word. With Haman mentioned more than fifty times in the Scroll of Esther, the reading was continually interrupted by shouts, screams, and every other noise a person could make.

Those who wished to fulfill their religious obligation and actually hear each word, crowded close around the reader. Room was made for Salomon near the stand holding the scroll and he motioned for Meir to squeeze in next to him. Rachel perched on her father's shoulders with a saucepan in one hand and a spoon in the other, and Meir couldn't imagine how Salomon could tolerate such a din so close to his ears.

This was the first time Meir had been near enough to see the Megillah read, and when he turned his attention to the words written before him, he was astonished. The scribe, in order to make up for the absence of the name of God in the Book of Esther, had written its constituent letters larger whenever they occurred close together, so that those reading might see the Holy Name emerge, as it were, out of the text.

It seemed as though the cacophonous recitation would never end, but finally Haman's name was chanted for the last time, as he was hanged on the very gallows he had built for the Jews. Families reunited downstairs, exhausted children slung over their parents' shoulders, and friends bid each other "Bon soir."

The next morning, Salomon's household was up early as Rivka and Sarah prepared for a busy day. Soon women would be arriving with dishes of every kind of delicacy. Poultry was preferred above all else at Purim, so there was sure to be a large selection of chicken and goose. Meir's family provided a lamb, usually in short supply this early in the season. Roasting on a spit, it took up the entire hearth in Sarah's kitchen.

The baker's helper had delivered so many loaves of bread that he needed a cart to carry them all, and he would return later with savory pies containing pigeon and quail. Finally he would bring the sweet cakes and pastries, more varieties than can be imagined, giving him a short respite before another batch of bread was needed for the evening meal.

Rivka wanted both Joheved and Miriam to stay home and help, but they argued that at least one of them should be at services to translate for the women. Not that many women would be there, most of them being just as busy in their kitchens as Rivka was. Still, she sent Miriam with Rachel and Salomon.

Salomon had planned to dress in his regular festival attire, but his daughters insisted that he wear something unusual, especially since he was hosting the feast. Not in a jolly Purim mood, he finally agreed to wear mismatched hose, one leg red and the other yellow, to give his children pleasure. Then they joined the other Purim revelers in the street, boisterously making their way to the synagogue.

Last year Miriam had been one of the pot-banging children downstairs on Purim morning, so she was disappointed to see that her mother was right, the women's section was nearly deserted. Miriam recognized the few elderly ladies sitting down, but not the three young women looking over the railing. Maybe they were visiting Troyes for the holiday.

"*Shalom aleikhem*, ladies." Miriam felt proud for offering hospitality to strangers, but to her dismay, the women ignored her. Perhaps they couldn't hear her over the din.

She came closer, but they avoided her. Determined to be heard, she maneuvered herself directly in front of the nearest one, only to discover that it was Menachem in women's clothes. She let out a shriek of astonishment and then dissolved in giggles. The "lady" next to him was quickly revealed to be his twin brother.

They each had a veil, fancy headpiece, and matching girdle. Neither had a beard yet, so the disguise was quite good. One would have sworn they were young women, just past puberty.

"What are you doing up here?" Miriam scanned the older women for signs of ire, but they smiled back benignly.

"How do you like our masquerade?" Menachem gave her a wink. "We must look pretty good if we fooled you for so long."

Ephraim looked around nervously. "You won't tell anyone, will you?"

"I suppose not." The women here probably wouldn't recognize them, and even if they did, the boys weren't likely to get in trouble on Purim. "But why come up here? It's more fun downstairs."

"It was all his idea." Ephraim pointed to what looked like another young woman, heavily veiled. "Everyone was treating us like women, so he suggested we come up here and have a look. I told him it was nothing special, that we used to spend lots of time up here with Mama, but he still wanted to see it."

"Who is 'him,' and how many of them are you?" Miriam looked suspiciously at the old ladies in the back.

"Just the three of us." Menachem motioned for their veiled companion to come over.

His/her familiar gait filled Miriam with apprehension and she could barely bring herself to watch as his veil came down to reveal her fiancé standing in front of her. His scraggly bearded face grinned back at her, looking ludicrous in the feminine head covering.

"You are the ugliest woman I have ever seen," she teased. "You'll need a large dowry to attract a decent-looking husband."

"For your information, I am engaged already," Benjamin retorted truthfully, but in falsetto. "And my betrothed is so fair that the sun pales in comparison."

Miriam blushed at his compliment, but before she could say anything clever in return, the noise level rose below. "The Megillah reading is starting. I have to go translate for the real ladies," she said. "You fellows stay out of trouble."

The students amused themselves for the duration of services by watching to see which men winced the most when Haman's name was read. Benjamin told Miriam later that while it was more fun to be in the middle of the crowd below, the view from the women's gallery was better.

As Miriam walked home with her three new "girlfriends," they could hear the music playing blocks away. Inside the courtyard, musicians with lutes, violins, and cymbals played so loudly that normal conversation was impossible. Many of the guests were sitting at long tables set up in a square, while others danced in the empty area formed in its center. Concentric circles, each of men or women, danced in opposite directions from one another, slowing and speeding up as the tunes varied.

Youngsters preferred to watch the jugglers and jesters. Miriam was heading toward a man who seemed to have no difficulty producing coins from people's ears, when she passed Joheved and Meir speaking seriously under the apple tree. Meir was wearing his fur-lined cloak inside out and, with the hood drawn tight around his head, he looked like a large hairy animal. Miriam got near enough to overhear the word *bedding* and quickly turned back toward the dancers.

"Meir," Joheved began, her face growing warm. He turned to face her and she had to force herself to keep speaking. "I'm sorry for what I said the other morning, I mean I apologize if I embarrassed you, I didn't realize . . ." Why was it so difficult to talk to him? Even several cups of wine weren't helping.

"You have nothing to apologize for. Benjamin told me about their Purim joke."

"You weren't angry? I was so mad at Miriam that I wanted to break something." She smiled ruefully. "And I nearly did break my hand."

"I was angry at first, but when I saw how upset you were, I knew that you had to be a victim as well."

Maybe the wine was affecting her, because she then asked him, "Did you return your bedding to its old spot?"

He moved closer to her. "I left it exactly where Benjamin put it. I didn't want the students to think we'd had an argument."

"I'm glad it's still there." The wine was definitely affecting her. "It comforts me to know you're up there."

Comfortable was not how Meir would describe his feelings about their sleeping arrangement, but at least she didn't object. "I like knowing you're down there, too."

"What are you thinking when you look at me like that?"

She was looking at him so earnestly, those big blue eyes staring up at him. "I was admiring your eyes," he replied. "They're exactly the same color as the sky today."

"Really? I'm not sure what color my eyes are."

"You've never seen yourself in a mirror?"

"Not that I can remember. My family doesn't own one."

They had been gazing into each other's eyes too long. Meir was slowly leaning toward her and she realized that he was going to kiss her, no matter how many people were watching.

Joheved had just closed her eyes and tilted her face up when Miriam called out from the crowd, "Joheved, come and dance with me. They're playing our favorite tune." The spell was broken, and with mingled relief and regret, she ran to her sister's side.

Meir watched the dancers for a while. A gentle melody provided the backdrop for pairs to turn and sway in intricate patterns, all the while gracefully swirling their skirts. The sky deepened, and the clouds parted to reveal the full moon rising. He was about to head for the dining tables when the music grew lively again. Recognizing the tune, a young man jumped up and challenged him. Immediately another pair joined them, then another, the crowd cheering as the men performed an athletic dance involving jumps, spins, and fancy footwork. Two by two, each pair kept up the frantic pace until one of them dropped in exhaustion and his partner was declared the winner. Joheved applauded proudly at how vigorously Meir danced.

Once it was dark and the torches lit, the merrymakers separated into two groups, one of each gender. Outside, the men recited various Purim parodies that imitated famous Talmudic passages, their themes usually the praise of wine and those who drink it to excess. The women, who found these mystifying rather than clever, gathered indoors at Sarah's, where a female jongleur was strumming a lyre and singing riddle songs. When she saw Joheved come in, the musician announced that the next riddle was for the learned among them.

> *A man sat at wine with his two wives*
> *And his two sons and his two daughters,*
> *Beloved sisters and their two sons, noble, firstborn.*
> *The father of each noble one was with them as well,*
> *Uncle and nephew. Altogether there were five*
> *Men and women sitting together.*

The room was silent as the women, heads dizzy with wine, tried to count on their fingers and otherwise solve the mystery. Hopeful faces turned toward Miriam and Joheved, expecting them to uphold the town's honor and provide the answer. Joheved was deep in thought, but Miriam was too drunk to figure out any more than that the man was married to sisters. She looked around the *salle*, and there was Benjamin. *Mon Dieu, how long has he been there?*

Suddenly it felt as if all the wine she'd consumed had gone straight to her bladder, and she hurried out to the privy. Luckily Joheved was less intoxicated and was able to provide the riddle's key: the five were Lot, his two daughters, and their sons, Moab and Ammon. Murmurs of praise for her knowledge of Scripture filled the room. Nobody noticed that Benjamin had infiltrated their group, or that he left as soon as Miriam did.

Outside, the moon's brilliance illuminated several women waiting near the privy. Miriam impatiently went upstairs to use her own chamber pot, only to find Rachel asleep in bed and Salomon snoring there with her. Miriam smiled at the familial scene. He must have been telling her a story when they both nodded off.

Benjamin was waiting for her below. Fearful of waking her father, Miriam had hurried her business and been inattentive in tidying up. An admiring Benjamin couldn't help but notice that her skirt was stuck in her girdle, exposing her calves and thighs. He pointed out her carelessness, and as she struggled to straighten her *bliaut*, he offered his assistance and guided her under the stairs where they were unlikely to be disturbed.

Sometime later, Meir tired of the men's scholarly humor, and he wondered what the women were finding so hilarious. None too steady on his feet, he headed toward Sarah's house, but his trip was interrupted when he noticed Salomon's open front door. The noises within drew him to investigate, and what he discovered there staggered him.

At first he thought it was two women having a tête-a-tête, but as he watched, he could see they were embracing, their hands busy under each other's clothes. He shook his muddled head, trying to make sense out of what he was witnessing, when a shaft of moonlight played on the pair long enough for him to identify them. One of the women was his fiancée's sister, and the other was no woman at all, but Benjamin in feminine dress.

Meir backed away, intending to find Salomon, but once outside, he remembered seeing the man carrying his sleepy young daughter upstairs, not to return. By now the moon was low in the sky and most of the guests had gone. He noticed Joheved at one of the far tables, collecting dirty dishes. This was perfect—he would help her bring things into the kitchen and make sure she saw what her supposedly innocent sister was doing. His plan worked, except that Joheved didn't seem to be as upset as he was.

Thanking him for bringing the matter to her attention, she shooed him outside and told her she'd deal with her errant sibling herself. Moments later she appeared in the doorway, supporting a pasty-looking Miriam, and the two of them walked hurriedly to a nearby wall, where Joheved offered comfort as her sister's stomach rejected its contents. Then she helped the sick girl upstairs to bed. But this was complicated by their father's presence, and she needed Meir's help to move Salomon to his own bedroom. When that was accomplished Joheved was nearly exhausted, but she felt an irrational determination to continue cleaning up.

Meir waited until they were out of earshot and vented his displeasure. "What are you doing? Let your servants do this tomorrow."

Why is he so mad about my trying to tidy up? "You mean today, not tomorrow," she said as a rooster crowed nearby. "I believe it's nearly dawn."

His anger increased when she ignored his question, and he brought up the true source of his indignation. "I can't believe the depravity I witnessed tonight. Your sister embraces her lover with impunity in your own house and your father lies upstairs in a drunken stupor, oblivious to everything." Meir had consumed so much wine that any shred of discretion was gone.

Intoxication loosened Joheved's tongue. "How dare you accuse my family of immorality! And on Purim yet, when we're supposed to drink and celebrate."

She continued to berate him. After all, he had practically called Miriam a harlot. "And you have the self-righteousness to complain about immorality on Purim. The entire holiday encourages excess. Why do you think the rabbis in Tractate *Megillah* complain so much about licentiousness at Purim if it didn't happen to them all the time?"

"I suppose you've studied Tractate *Megillah*?" Meir's voice dripped sarcasm.

"I certainly have! And Tractates *Berachot*, *Shabbat*, and *Pesachim* too." Joheved immediately covered her mouth in horror.

Meir stared at her in stunned silence, trying to process the indictment he had heard from her own mouth. He couldn't resist challenging her learning with his own from Tractate *Sotah* (the suspected adulteress). "Since you're such a *talmid chacham*"—his tone was icy—"I'm sure you'll understand when I say that I agree when Rabbi Eliezer says that teaching a woman Torah is teaching her lechery. I suppose your sister studies with you, and we can see where it's gotten her."

"Adultery!" Joheved's eyes blazed and she would have screamed except for fear of waking everyone up. "I have never even looked at another man. As for my sister, the man she was kissing was consecrated to her in *erusin* and I won't have you accusing her of adultery either." She turned and stalked away, terrified that he intended to put an end to her studies.

But before she'd turned away completely, Meir had seen the tears in her eyes. Overcome with remorse, he condemned himself for his drunken rage, for letting his *yetzer ha-ra* ruin six months of exemplary conduct. So what if she knew Talmud? What did he expect with her growing up in her father's yeshivah? Wasn't a learned wife what he wanted, to make sure his sons became scholars? He took off his mantle and replaced it right side out. He'd been enough of an animal tonight.

The next morning, Joheved slept through services. She didn't want to face Meir and she suspected, correctly, that there wouldn't be many other women in synagogue. She woke in time for the midday meal, and as she prepared to put on tefillin, she wondered if he would forbid her that.

Meir had gotten up early, hoping to apologize to Joheved on their way to services. Once it became obvious that she wasn't coming, he accompanied Salomon, who was in a surprisingly good mood. Under the influence of much wine, Salomon had experienced a catharsis. After depositing a drowsy Rachel in her bed, he had sat down and observed her innocent beauty as she slept. Drink loosened his inhibitions and he began to sob, first for his poor baby Leah, taken from him so young, and eventually for his mother too. The next thing he knew, it was morning and he was lying in bed next to Rivka, feeling as if a great weight he'd been carrying was gone.

At services, Salomon prayed with joyful thanks, while Meir prayed for forgiveness for desecrating the Creator's festival with ugly words. He also prayed that the Merciful One would open Joheved's heart and allow her to forgive him. Maybe he'd be lucky and find that she had consumed so much wine the previous night that she'd forgotten their argument altogether.

When Joheved finally came down to eat, her first thought was to sit as far away from Meir as possible. But even the students who'd slept through services were on time for *disner*, so the only place available was her customary one next to him. Not wanting to publicize their quarrel by squeezing in next to Miriam, Joheved took her usual seat, but she kept her hands resolutely on the tabletop. The sadness on her face was enough to convince Meir that their argument was neither forgotten nor forgiven. She avoided him the rest of the day, and he grew determined to speak with her.

After *souper*, he discreetly lingered in the courtyard until she finished in the privy. The orange striped cat seemed to know Meir needed support and twined companionably around his legs.

"Joheved, please wait." He stepped in front of her and nearly tripped over the cat. "I have to talk with you."

"Didn't you say enough last night?" She nearly bit her tongue in shame at her harsh words. She hoped he wanted to apologize, but maybe he intended to break their engagement and wanted to tell her first.

"I am terribly sorry for what I said last night." He corrected himself. "I mean this morning. It was the wine talking. I've been thinking about it all day and I swear to you that . . ."

"Don't make any oaths." Joheved covered his mouth with her hand, but before he could fully appreciate the feel of her skin against his lips, she pulled away as though burned.

"Let me rephrase that," he said carefully. Taking oaths was a serious matter that Jews avoided whenever possible. Children died young as the result of their parents' broken vows. "When we're married, *Le Bon Dieu* willing, I will hire as many servants as you need so you have time to study." His eyes pleaded with her. "Now that I have repented, will you forgive me?"

"I forgive you," she replied, her heart bursting with happiness. "And I, in turn, will try not to get upset over anything you say on Purim."

The relief of her forgiveness felt so good that he decided to open his heart to her. "I must also confess that when I got mad at your sister and Benjamin, part of my anger was because it was them embracing so openly, not you and me." There, he had said it. He nervously waited for her response.

"*Moi aussi*," she said softly and went back indoors, leaving him standing there in elation. The cat, realizing that there was no food in Meir's direction, turned and followed Joheved into the kitchen.

Eighteen

"Miriam, Joheved!" Rivka called to her daughters on Friday. "Please take my keys and take out some jewelry for *Shabbat*."

Rivka's position as mistress of the house entitled her to custody of the keys, which she wore pinned to her bodice like a brooch. She locked the doors at night and unlocked them again at dawn. She kept a key to every chest and cupboard in the house, excepting Meir's. If pepper or cloves were needed from the spice cabinet, she opened it, and it was she who unlocked the jewelry box before *Shabbat* or a festival, to take out what she and her daughters would wear on the holiday.

Rivka handed a key to Joheved, and the three sisters climbed down to the cellar. The jewelry box should have been hidden behind a wine cask, but Miriam couldn't feel it there.

"Are you sure you put it back behind this cask, Joheved?" Her sister had been the last one to bed on Purim.

"I thought it was this one," she replied sheepishly. She had consumed a large quantity of wine.

"I guess we'll have to search behind all the casks," Miriam said

They started from where Joheved thought she had put the box. Rachel was too little to reach behind the casks, but she could look underneath them. "I see it," Rachel squealed suddenly. "But I can't reach it. It's behind this barrel."

It took Joheved's entire arm's length to reach the object. But it was a leather-bound volume, not the missing jewel box. "It's in Hebrew and it's mostly numbers," Joheved announced after reading silently for a while. "I think it's Grandmama Leah's old ledger, but there's more here than just accounts. Some of the pages are about things that happened to her, like a diary."

"Are there dates in it? Can you tell when it was written?" Miriam squeezed around to get a better look.

"I think the first date is 4700-something. Goodness, that's before Papa was born." Joheved thumbed through a few pages. "We certainly get a higher price now than she did back then."

Rachel didn't try to hide her impatience. "Never mind what wine cost then. Read some of the diary part, something about Papa when he was little or when he got married."

But there was no mention of Papa, or of Mama. In between the pages of numbers, there were sporadic complaints about high taxes or that bad weather or disease had nearly ruined the crop, but there were also many years when she wrote nothing except the accounting. Much to her granddaughters' disappointment, it appeared that Leah wrote only about winemaking.

"Wait, listen to this final entry," Joheved said suddenly. "It's dated 4825, that's three years before Papa came home."

Leah had written: "I have had some distressing symptoms that I have not told anyone. New instructions do not penetrate; I hear them, but I can't retain them. A thick fog begins to descend after a few sentences. I make the appropriate responses, but I am aware that I am not understanding. It is driving me mad."

Joheved fought back tears. "Even when I make a notation to trigger my memory, I have no idea to what the notes are referring. Instructions on how to get to someone's house or a new recipe—these are old skills at which I excelled and now I cannot believe how this curtain always comes down.

"I am reluctant to try anything new for fear I will come off as an idiot, and people will notice. There are parts of the city I know nothing about and I do not go there. I do not go out at night anymore. Everyone is always talking to me and giving me instructions, but I cannot seem to assimilate new procedures or ideas. My thinking process frightens me—my mind is spent."

Joheved stood stone silent. That was the last thing her grandmother had written. How terrible for Leah to know that her intellect was failing, how painful to suffer such a thing in secret. Leah had always been so proud of her learning; the shame and fear of losing it must have been unbearable, not to mention the humiliation of people thinking she was crazy.

Tears were running down Miriam's cheeks. "Why didn't she tell us?"

she asked helplessly. "We would have helped her. Poor Grandmama, so afraid and so alone."

Even Rachel, who barely remembered her grandmother, was sad. When they finally found the jewelry box, Joheved put the old ledger back behind its cask too. She suspected that Leah herself had been the last one to read it, and had never intended for anyone else to do so. The sisters couldn't bring themselves to speak of what they'd found. Their grandmother had agonized so long over her secret, and now they had exposed it. It seemed best to leave well enough alone.

Leah's secret receded in importance as Passover approached. Rachel grew increasingly excited because this year she would finally join her sisters in making matzah, the unleavened bread that Jews are commanded to eat during the festival. For the eight days of Passover, it was forbidden to eat, or even possess, bread, cake, or any kind of pastry. Consequently, the Jews of Troyes had to make enough matzah to last the entire community a week.

For Joheved and Miriam, making matzah was the most pleasurable part of the festival preparations, and they volunteered to help at the bakery nearly every day. Rivka spent a few afternoons there as well, for both the camaraderie of her peers and to participate in the holy work.

Rachel, and all the town's children, wanted to help too, for part of their fun in baking matzah came from watching the adults working in such great haste. To eliminate any contamination by leaven, the women moved as quickly as they could. Those who mixed the flour with water, those who poured the dough and those who kneaded it, those who cut it into cakes and those who smoothed it, those who shoved the cakes into the oven, not to mention those who carried the dough from one worker to the next—they all raced through their tasks at lightning speed, taking care to ensure that the dough never stood for a moment.

One special task was delegated to the children, that of using the little cogwheels to perforate the dough and prevent it from rising in the oven. The children tried to make perfect pointed lines across the round cakes, and, for them, it was more play than work. Even for the adults, it was equally merry and pious labor. The women sang as they whisked the dough from one station to the next, songs as lively as their pace.

Salomon accompanied Rachel on her first day of matzah baking.

The most learned Jew in Troyes, it was his responsibility to supervise the workers and admonish them to remain diligent. But no one, not even Salomon, stood around and watched. Speed was unnecessary when it came to removing the baked unleavened cakes from the oven, and from this warm vantage point, he could make sure the dough was not delayed before it reached the oven.

Rachel was so excited that she found it impossible to concentrate on making quick straight lines with her little cogwheel. People hurrying about, circles of dough practically flying from one hand to the next, these were far more fascinating to watch. It seemed as though collisions would be unavoidable, yet the workers always managed to move out of one another's way in time. Then Rachel would let out her breath and return to her task, inevitably too late. But this learning period was expected; in time she would master making the perfect lines.

Joheved and Miriam were experienced dough rollers, and, sitting next to each other at the large table, they rapidly yet calmly smoothed their balls of dough into flat circles. When it came time to bake the last batch, the baker's wife took out decorative molds for the workers to make fancy-shaped matzah for their own seders. Joheved used a bird-shaped form, and Miriam chose one shaped like a flower. Salomon made sure nobody took longer making the special matzah than the regular ones. Finally, the matzah was sorted and stored in tall stacks. As the festival week progressed, each family would come and take what they needed.

Springtime filled Meir with pent-up energy and he took to swimming in the Seine, where the amused fishermen regarded him as a crazy penitent bathing in the chilly river for some kind of Lenten sacrifice. Joheved was also growing restless. At night, she knew it was only a few planks of wood that separated her from Meir, and she wondered if he was thinking of her too. Sometimes she could almost pretend that he was lying next to her snoring, not Miriam. It's only four months until the anniversary of Grandmama Leah's death. *When is Papa going to set a new wedding date?*

Home in Ramerupt for Passover, Meir spent more time thinking about Joheved than enjoying the seder with his family. To make matters worse, it had been unseasonably warm all week and he was having trouble sleeping. He awoke Friday before dawn, keenly missing the pleasure he usually felt as he imagined Joheved waking up below, and decided to return to Troyes.

The next day he asked Salomon to help him with Song of Songs, traditionally read during Passover, but the scholar wanted to take his nap first. Perhaps Meir could find a study partner at the synagogue. But the place was empty, forcing Meir to study alone.

Salomon taught his students that the Song of Songs should be read as an allegory, a duet of longing between God and Israel. Meir knew this, but the literal meaning of the words assailed him.

Let him kiss me with the kisses of his mouth, for your love is better than wine.

Meir savored the line and forced himself to recall that Salomon taught this meant that Israel longed for God to teach her Torah, "mouth to mouth," as at Sinai. But in that sweltering room, Meir could only think about real kissing.

The fourth chapter contained a litany of verses describing the bride's beauty: her eyes, hair, teeth, lips, mouth, neck, and finally,

Breasts like two fawns, twins of a gazelle, which feed among the lilies.

Salomon taught that this referred to the Two Tablets of the Covenant, which nourish Israel, but Meir couldn't help but visualize a real woman. He gave up and closed the book.

His damp hair clung to his skin; sweat trickled down his face and through his beard. He mopped his brow with his sleeve and decided to take a swim. He set off down the street, but somehow his feet led him, not to the Seine, but to Salomon's courtyard gate.

Inside Salomon's wine cellar, attempting to avoid the heat, Joheved was also reading Song of Songs. Salomon, Rachel, and the servants were sleeping, while Rivka and Miriam had gone to Johanna's to relax now that the ordeal of preparing for the leaven-free eight days of Passover had ended. They had urged Joheved to join them, but she had begged off.

As a child, she hated going to other women's houses during the festival week. She'd never learned chess properly, nor any of the nut games the other girls liked to play, and they laughed at her when she lost. She couldn't remember ever enjoying Passover; it was so much work to clean everything, and then Papa came home for such a short amount of time that it was mostly a disruption.

Joheved knew things were different, but the old feelings still surfaced this time of year. Miriam was an apprentice midwife now and friendly with all the young women, but Joheved only felt comfortable with women if she was leading them in prayer. Their talk of husbands, children, clothes, and where to find the freshest meat was not the least bit interesting.

Joheved sighed and focused her attention on the text. Some time ago she had heard Papa discussing Song of Songs with the monk, Robert. The prior declared it an allegory about love between God and the Church, while Papa countered that the Song told of God's relationship with Israel through time. After Robert left, Papa had muttered angrily about the *Notzrim* appropriating the holy Song for their heresy, when it was obviously a message of consolation to the Jews.

Now Joheved was determined to study the Song herself, to see if she could find the historical verses Papa said were there. It wasn't difficult. There in the first chapter was:

I have compared you, my own, to a mare in Pharaoh's chariots,

an obvious reference to Egypt. In the second chapter, she found,

My beloved among the young men . . . his fruit was sweet
to my lips. He brought me to the banquet house and his banner
over me was love,

which was about God's giving Israel the Torah. Solving this riddle was more entertaining than visiting with a bunch of gossipy women, Joheved thought, and she eagerly began chapter three. She was deep into chapter seven when Meir discovered her reading by the light of the clerestory windows. Dressed only in her chemise, her silhouette was clearly outlined beneath it.

Meir's body responded like lightning coursing through him and a gasp escaped his lips. Joheved looked up, smiled in recognition, and any hope he had of leaving unnoticed vanished.

"Meir, what perfect timing." She jumped up and showed him the book. "Papa told me that the verses in Song of Songs teach the history of Israel. Here, let me show you."

Excited to share her knowledge, Joheved was oblivious to the effect her nearness and thin clothing were having upon Meir. "See all the verses that mention wine or vineyards. Papa says that a vineyard often means, study hall, in the Gemara, so that these lines symbolize the progress from Mishnah to Talmud:

> Come my beloved ... let us see if the vine has budded, if its blossoms have opened.

Meir automatically continued with the line that followed,

> If the pomegranates are in flower, there I will give you my love.

Joheved remembered how smelling grape blossoms had affected Miriam, and was suddenly aware of the words she and Meir had just recited, as well as his proximity.

In the weeks that followed, whenever Joheved thought about that sultry afternoon in the cellar, which was often, she could never recollect exactly how it had happened. One moment she and Meir were quoting Song of Songs, and the next, he was kissing her with the hunger of a starving man presented with a banquet. And she was responding just as ardently. Time seemed suspended and Joheved had no idea how long they were lost in each other's arms. She also had no idea that her father, standing at the top of the cellar stairs, had discovered them and was trying to restrain his outrage.

Salomon had awakened, hot and thirsty. He was about to descend into the cellar for a cool cup of wine when he heard the unmistakable sounds below, and a glance was all he needed to identify the lovers. At first his anger blazed at how Meir had taken advantage of his hospitality and at how enthusiastically his daughter had abandoned her modesty. But by force of habit, Salomon's intellect began to temper his emotions.

The sound of a polite cough shattered the lovers' private world, and disoriented, they looked up at Salomon's furious disapproval. They sprang apart immediately, and he angrily demanded an explanation for their disgraceful behavior.

"*Rabbeinu*"—Meir used the honorific title, intending to say whatever was necessary to protect Joheved's reputation—"I apologize for subjecting you to this display. It was entirely my fault. Joheved did nothing to entice me." He seemed to be groveling, but Salomon noticed that Meir hadn't said he was sorry for his actions, only for exposing his teacher to them.

Joheved was humiliated beyond belief by her father catching her in such a compromising position. Her *yetzer ha-ra*, coupled with years of resentment and adolescent rebellion, fanned her anger. She stepped forward and challenged her father.

"Don't blame Meir, it's not his fault." Her voice rose. "This wouldn't have happened if you'd arranged for us to be married already!"

Salomon took a step to close the distance between them. How dare his daughter address him in such an insolent tone. In a voice of barely controlled fury, he lectured Joheved about showing proper respect for parents, reminding her that, according to Scripture, a rebellious youth forfeits his life.

"What do you expect?" she retorted. "You were never here to teach me appropriate behavior."

Salomon's eyes blazed as he shushed her. "Keep your voice down. People are trying to sleep upstairs." He had better end this confrontation before his daughter said anything more she'd regret. "Joheved, go to your room and think about the Fifth Commandment and repentance until you come to your senses."

Then he turned to Meir, who was frozen with shock. "Come with me. Let's take a walk."

They mutely trod the city streets. Most people were either indoors or at the river, and while Meir felt relieved that they weren't likely to encounter anyone he knew, he waited in dread for Salomon's chastisement.

His future father-in-law finally broke the silence. "If it weren't the Sabbath, we'd be on our way to Ramerupt."

Meir gulped. Surely Salomon didn't intend to inform his parents of the afternoon's debacle. He summoned his courage. "I apologize for being unable to control my *yetzer ha-ra*. I beg you to forgive me." He ought to have promised that it would never happen again, but he didn't dare make such a vow.

Suddenly Salomon started to chuckle. "The *yetzer ha-ra* certainly took control of you and Joheved today. Are you sure you want to marry my daughter now that you've experienced her temper?"

There was nothing Meir wanted more than to marry the woman who had kissed him with such fervor, but he said merely, "I do."

Salomon sighed at the young man's glum tone. Then, to Meir's amazement, Salomon told him that in a way, Joheved was right. "We do need to set a wedding date, and the sooner the better."

Meir's heart soared as his future father-in-law teasingly scolded him about their poor timing. "Instead of marrying quickly next week, you two must now wait a month until Lag ba-Omer."

Since Talmudic times, when a plague among Rabbi Akiva's students lasted thirty-three days from Passover until Lag ba-Omer, those days have been ones of semi-mourning when no weddings are held.

"As soon as the Sabbath is over," Salomon said, "we will ride to Ramerupt and confirm the wedding date with your parents."

Miriam had come home early, hoping to study Song of Songs with Joheved. But she found the house silent, all the bedroom doors closed. Sure that everyone was enjoying the traditional Sabbath nap, she tiptoed up the stairs and quietly entered the room she shared with her sisters.

Joheved, who had been lying facedown on the bed, snapped to a sitting position. She had obviously been crying.

"*Mon Dieu*. What's wrong?" It couldn't be a death or injury; somebody would have gotten Mama and her earlier.

Reluctantly, and with great embarrassment, Joheved related her story. Miriam didn't know what to say. She couldn't imagine which was more unlikely, Joheved speaking so rudely to their father or him catching her and Meir kissing.

"It's not fair," Joheved said between sobs. "You and Benjamin steal kisses all the time and never get caught, but the first time it happens to me, Papa has to walk in on us."

"Do you think Papa is more angry about you and Meir kissing, or your talking back to him?" Miriam longed to know how they had come to be embracing in the cellar, but that would have to wait.

"I don't know. What difference does it make?"

"The difference is that you'd better come up with an appropriate apology before Papa gets home."

They were still trying to compose one when they heard voices below. Joheved paced the room. "I can't face them yet. Please, Miriam, tell Mama that I'm not well, that I'm not coming down to eat." She was shaking with fright.

But it was too late. Salomon stuck his head in the door, and in a voice that brooked no excuses, said he expected them both to join the family for the final *Shabbat* meal. At the table, he and Meir discussed the historical allegory of the Song of Songs, with Miriam adding a few comments of her own. Joheved said nothing—her gaze fixed firmly downward, her face blazing with shame, both hands clearly visible on the tablecloth. Papa obviously intended her discipline to wait until the festive day had ended.

ꭱineteeꞃ

After *Havdalah*, when Salomon announced that he and Meir were riding to Ramerupt that night, Rivka expressed her alarm. "Can't it wait until tomorrow? You know how dangerous it is to go out tonight." Saturday night was particularly perilous because the evil spirits released from Gehenna for the Sabbath were angry at being forced back to their eternal punishment.

"Don't worry, Rivka, we'll be safe. The moon is nearly full and we'll stay out of the shadows." Salomon reassured her though he knew from Tractate *Pesachim* that Wednesday and Saturday were the nights the demon Agrath went abroad with eighteen myriads of destroying angels. "I need a ride in the cool evening air after such a warm day."

They would also be protected because they were on their way to perform the mitzvah of arranging a wedding, but Salomon wasn't ready to make that announcement yet. He had Joheved walk them to the gate, where he sternly told her that he'd hear what she had to say when he returned. As soon as they left, she ran upstairs, threw herself on the bed, and burst into fresh tears.

Was he sending Meir away? She couldn't imagine a single good reason for them to see Meir's parents in the middle of the night. Miriam couldn't think why the two of them needed to go to Ramerupt either, but she forced Joheved back to the task at hand.

When Joheved finally felt that she had the proper penitent words fixed in her memory, she went outside to wait. The full moon lit up the courtyard, reminding her of last month's Purim celebration. How ironic that Miriam, who had shared her fiancé's embraces with impunity, had been too drunk to remember them the next day. Right now, Joheved would have given anything to have her own memory erased in the morning.

Suddenly she heard men's voices. Unable to stand the suspense, she threw herself at her father as soon as he opened the gate. "Oh Papa, I'm so sorry I said all those terrible things to you." Her carefully composed apology had disappeared from her mind. "I'm so ashamed of myself. I didn't mean to show you disrespect." She babbled on, words of contrition and remorse.

"Very well, *ma fille*, I forgive you." Salomon gave her a hug. "I hope you will forgive me for delaying your marriage when I tell you that I have arranged with Meir's parents for a Lag ba-Omer wedding. His mother has sent some fabric for your wedding dress." He thrust a bolt of material at her.

Joheved looked back and forth several times between her father's smile, Meir's beaming face, and the blue silk in her hands. Then she almost knocked Salomon down hugging him in return. She would be wed in a month. In one month!

Meir returned to Ramerupt a few days before Lag ba-Omer, and on the morning of the festival, it seemed as though every member of his extended family came in to offer advice and good wishes while he dressed. It was just as well that the bride and groom fasted on their wedding day; he couldn't possibly have eaten breakfast. Marona had just finished sewing closed the sleeves of his fine new linen chemise when they heard the clattering of horses and clanging of weapons in the courtyard.

Meir ran to the open front door, where the household had assembled to watch Benjamin and several yeshivah students in mock combat with Meshullam and Meir's cousins. It was traditional for the groom to be escorted to his wedding, "just as a king is attended by his guards." However, the encounter was so likely to result in damage that Jewish law held: "If a man or horse is injured when a fellow rides to greet the bridegroom, and he pleads that he did nothing wrong, but rode normally, he is not believed, and must provide evidence."

Meir raced to get a sword and join the fray, but his mother barred his way. "Are you mad?" she said. "After all the work I put into your new silk *cote*, you want to go out there and ruin it?"

He reluctantly replaced the weapon and waited for the ruckus to die down. Then he threw on his mantle and adjusted his ornamented hat. This was it. He mounted his horse, waved good-bye to the servants, and with great fanfare the wedding party set off, accompanied by a wagonful of musicians to provide entertainment on the way to Troyes.

When they crossed the Seine and reached Bishop's Gate, much of the Jewish community was there to meet them. Though it was broad daylight, many of the men held torches. The boisterous crowd escorted Meir to the synagogue, where morning services were in progress. Then, having done their duty for the bridegroom, the torchbearers and musicians left for Salomon's house.

Joheved had spent a restless night. She had been so eager for this morning to arrive, each day looking longingly at her beautiful blue silk *bliaut*. But yesterday, after returning from her first trip to the *mikveh*, reality sunk in. Tomorrow, Meir would be her husband and master. She had seen him angry once, and though he had quickly apologized, maybe he wasn't always so contrite. And would he really approve of her studies?

One worry after another chased through her mind, until she forced herself to concentrate on the prayer she'd recited earlier, before immersing in the *mikveh:* "*Mon Dieu*, may it be Your will that Your presence dwell between my husband and me. May his thoughts be always about me, and about no other, as it is written, 'Therefore shall a man leave his father and his mother and cleave to his wife.' May we be worthy to see children from our children who are committed to Torah and to good deeds. May You hear my prayer with mercy and compassion. Amen." She whispered it again and again, until she fell asleep.

Too soon it was morning and she had overslept. Everyone had already eaten when Mama entered her room, carrying the chemise for her wedding *bliaut*. Mama had spent hours embroidering its neck, sleeves, and hem with blue flowers to match the silken *cote*. Behind their mother trailed Miriam and Rachel, eager to help their sister dress for her finest hour.

While Rivka and Miriam sewed up her sleeves, Rachel brushed Joheved's hair. Her wedding day was the last time her hair would be fully visible in public. Until the ceremony was over, she would be veiled, but afterward everyone would see her long unbraided hair. Just as a new mother's hair was loosened during childbirth, it was best to have nothing constricted upon the nuptial bed. Especially not the bride's hair.

The three sisters took turns admiring themselves in the shiny wall mirror Meir had sent as a wedding present. Joheved stared at the stranger who looked back at her so intently. How grown up she looked, dressed in her wedding finery. Meir was right; she definitely had blue eyes. But her nose was so big, and where did all those freckles come from? She glanced at Miriam and then back at the mirror. She really did look like her younger sister.

Joheved turned slightly, trying to see her profile. Nobody would call her a beauty, but at least she wasn't homely. Look at her—such a serious expression. She stuck out her tongue, struck a few poses, and then laughed aloud at her silliness. She certainly looked more attractive when she smiled.

Miriam was reluctant to spend time staring at herself. Compared to Joheved she was too thin, and all those days in the vineyard with Benjamin had tanned her as brown as a peasant. But she couldn't resist making faces back at Joheved, and when Rachel joined in, the three of them nearly collapsed in giggles. After that, it was impossible to coax Rachel away from the mirror. She stared at her reflection as if transfixed, and only when they heard the musicians approaching was the mirror forgotten.

Her heart beating furiously, Joheved climbed on the white mare and gave one last glance homeward, her gaze focusing on the window of the bedroom she would no longer share with her sisters. When she reached the synagogue entrance, Meir came forward to receive her, and surprisingly, she felt neither eager nor frightened. It was as if she were somehow outside herself, watching.

He took her hand, and as they stood together, the congregation threw wheat and shouted, "Be fruitful and multiply!" Then Mama escorted her up the stairs, while Meir hurried to his seat at the front of the synagogue.

Once in the balcony, the women surged forward to weave flowers into Joheved's hair and help her into her jewelry. Much of it was Leah's, but two items were new, gifts from Meir. Those close enough to see their detail oohed and aahed as Marona fastened Joheved's new girdle and placed the matching headpiece over her veil. Both were fashioned of shining silver, woven into a wide braid, and decorated with delicate silver birds. The eye of each bird was either a pearl or a sapphire, the stone of Issachar, of understanding, and of Torah.

Just before it was time for the ceremony, Aunt Sarah anointed her with perfume.

Escorted by Rivka and Marona, Joheved walked outdoors to the raised platform in the center of the synagogue courtyard. Under the safety of her veil, she stared at Meir with impunity, but his expression was inscrutable. His *cote* was made of the same blue silk as hers, and she could hear people saying that they made a handsome couple.

When she reached his side, he lifted her veil and threw it over his own head as well, forming the wedding canopy. She tried to listen carefully as the *ketubah* and marriage settlements were read to the witnesses, but she knew she wouldn't remember them. The crowd was so large that not everyone fit into the courtyard, so they moved into the street for the *hazzan* to chant the seven wedding benedictions.

"Soon may there be heard in the cities of Judah, in the streets of Jerusalem, the voice of gladness and joy, the voice of bridegroom and bride, the grooms jubilant from their canopies and the youths from their feasts of song. *Baruch ata Adonai*, who makes the bridegroom to rejoice with the bride."

Once the *hazzan* finished this last blessing, Meir took up a cup of wine, drank deeply, and gave it to Joheved. His eyes never left hers as she lifted the cup to her lips. When she was done, Meir turned and threw the goblet at the synagogue's outer wall. The cup shattered and several maidens raced to pick up the shards, possession of which assured them a good marriage.

Immediately the musicians broke into song, and the company, shouting with joy, rushed at the newly wedded couple and carried them to Salomon's house. No sooner did they enter the gate than Benjamin and Meshullam, swinging a loudly squawking hen and rooster over their heads, forced them up the stairs and into Leah's, now their, bedroom.

Suddenly, they were alone. Their mad dash had gotten Meir to the bridal chamber before any demons, confused by the noise, could prevent him from enjoying his newly won nuptial happiness.

Joheved sat on the bed, decked with blooming honeysuckle, and looked around at everything except her husband. This was her grandmother's old room, but it seemed different now, bright and cheerful. Mama had fastened rose-colored hangings on the walls and there was new linen on the bed. On an unfamiliar chest, which Joheved supposed must contain Meir's effects, was a tray holding bread, wine, half a roasted chicken, two cooked eggs, and some fruit preserves. There was also a small dish of salt.

Still feeling unnaturally calm, she tore off some of the bread and dipped it into the salt, then handed a piece to Meir and joined him in the blessing. They ate in silence, listening to the sounds of people celebrating outside. Mixed with the sweet scent of honeysuckle, Joheved could make out the fennel strewn among the fresh rushes and ferns. More protection from demons.

Joheved felt Meir watching her, looked up, and their eyes met.

Those beautiful blue eyes, he thought, the same color as the silk they both were wearing. That was enough waiting for Meir. They were married now, and he should be kissing her, not sitting there staring at her. He pulled her down on the bed, fastened his lips on hers, and reveled in her ardent response.

She pressed her body against his and her perfume, which had first enticed him when they stood together under her veil, smelled stronger now. His hands sought out her curves, but there was no way to caress her bare skin. They were both sewn into their clothes.

Meir broke their embrace. They eyed each other hungrily, and Joheved reached for him again.

"We can't," he told her between kisses. "We have to wait until we can get out of these clothes." He sat up and attempted to replace the flowers his fingers had dislodged.

"We'd better eat our food, then." She offered him one of the eggs.

They finished the small meal and did their best to smooth their rumpled clothes. Joheved wanted to enjoy their privacy a while longer, but Meir pulled her toward the door.

"Come, my bride, the sooner we get down there, the sooner we can leave."

Rachel, who had stationed herself at the bottom of the stairs for this purpose, ran outside to announce the honored couple's imminent appearance. The musicians burst into a fanfare as the newlyweds entered the courtyard, and dancers ran to grab their hands and pull them into the quickly forming circles. Before she knew it, Joheved was going one way and Meir was moving in the opposite direction. She danced with Mama, with Miriam, and finally with her new female in-laws before the musicians finally struck up the tune for a mixed-couple dance and she could be back in Meir's arms.

When the dance ended, the musicians signaled for everyone to sit while they serenaded the bride and groom. Secular songs, particularly love songs, were officially discouraged in Jewish households, yet everyone knew them. The jongleur began with one that was often sung as a lullaby and was rewarded with wet cheeks on many of the older women. Meir's mother was seated next to him, and he could hear her sniffling as she reminded Samuel that she used to sing that song to their son when he was small.

Joheved and Meir remained seated at the head table under the apple tree while relatives and guests chatted with them. The only taint on the happy occasion came when a guest started arguing with Benjamin. In a voice so loud that the musicians' efforts to drown him out were unsuccessful, he accused the students of stealing his chickens. A hen and rooster were missing from his coop, and he demanded their immediate return. Of course this was impossible; the wedding party had eaten them.

Salomon rolled his eyes and stood up, intending to get some coins to pay for the purloined poultry. He knew of the responsa that stated: "Young men with the bridegroom should not steal from anyone, neither chickens nor anything else," and he was fairly certain that his pupils were not ignorant of this rule either. Still it was rude for the aggrieved man to interrupt the wedding banquet. If he had complained in private, Salomon would have promptly reimbursed him.

Then Meshullam stepped in and insisted on dealing with the indignant guest himself. Having made off with his share of birds at other weddings, he knew that Benjamin and the others would be terribly shamed if their *maître* ended up paying for their prank.

The afternoon wore on, with more singing, dancing, and, of course, more eating and drinking. It was almost like Purim, except that Meir and Joheved would be the first, rather than the last, to leave. Samuel must have noticed the couple's increasing impatience, because, just before sunset, he stood up and motioned the musicians for quiet. He raised his cup and toasted the newlyweds: "For a happy life!"

The guests understood the signal and yelled out their good wishes as well. Meir and Joheved rose to thank everyone, and wheat was soon flying at them from all directions. There seemed no escape but to run for the house, with the chants of "Be fruitful and multiply" in their ears. Hannah and Aunt Sarah, having been delegated the task of helping the couple out of their wedding finery, followed discreetly.

Twenty

For Joheved, October and November were delightful months. After months of heat, the weather finally cooled, her nausea and tiredness were gone, and she felt extraordinarily well. The baby was kicking vigorously, and nothing enthralled Meir more than lying in bed with his hand on her swollen belly, waiting to feel his child move within. Salomon was teaching Tractate *Shabbat*, whose second chapter contained a discussion about women dying in childbirth.

Miriam and Joheved made no attempt to hide their interest in the discussion, and for Salomon's pupils, his pregnant daughter's presence brought immediacy to their Talmud studies. Joheved felt an urge to participate in the lesson herself, something she had never done before, and her throat tightened in anxiety. This was ridiculous—Papa and Meir both knew she studied Talmud. Why should she be tongue-tied in front of their students?

The Mishnah began ominously:

> For three transgressions women die in childbirth. Because they
> neglect *niddah*, challah, kindling the (Sabbath) light.

Salomon immediately asked why these three were singled out; why not other transgressions?

Meir was about to answer when Joheved began speaking and the class stared at her in amazement. "Because women are primarily responsible for observing them," she said. "*Niddah* obviously depends on her. And since she makes the family bread, she has the opportunity to remove the small piece of challah that would have gone to the priests when the Temple stood. Finally, she is the one at home, rather than in synagogue, when the Sabbath begins, so lighting the lamp also falls to her."

"These are also mitzvot that men must trust women to perform correctly," Miriam whispered to Joheved. "If a woman neglects *niddah* or taking challah, her husband transgresses as well when he sleeps with her or eats the untithed bread."

"I'm sure whatever you told your sister is something we would all find of value," Salomon admonished her.

Miriam blushingly repeated her comment aloud and added, "And if she doesn't light the Sabbath lamp in time, her family will have to sit in darkness on Friday night."

Salomon held up his hand to get his students' attention. "I want to dispel the notion that death in childbirth is retribution for the woman who has sinned in one of these three ways." He surveyed the room as if daring anyone to contradict him. "Childbirth is so dangerous that a woman may need benevolence from the Merciful One to survive. Even if she has sufficient merit to preserve her in ordinary circumstances, it may not give her the extra protection necessary to save her during the throes of childbirth."

"A woman in childbirth might be in such grave danger that it would take a miracle to save her," Meir said. "Then, depending on the mitzvot she'd neglected or performed, she would either be rebuked or judged worthy of such a miracle."

Salomon nodded while Joheved and Meir exchanged anxious glances. Meir offered a prayer that Joheved would be deserving of such a miracle, while Joheved prayed that her childbirth would be so easy that no miracles were needed.

To prove the point that men also need the Merciful One's benevolence to survive danger, the Gemara now asked:

And men, when are they searched for misdeeds? Reish Lakish said: When they cross over a bridge. Only over a bridge and no more? Rav would not travel on a ferry upon which an idolater rode. Rabbi Zeira would not walk between palm trees when the severe south wind blew. Rav Yitzchak said: If a man becomes ill, the Heavenly Tribunal asks for his merit before they free him.

"So we see that a man, too, is vulnerable in dangerous situations," Salomon explained. "Like a woman, as long as he is in good health, he does not need any special worthiness to remain in this state. But if he takes ill, the burden of proof is shifted to his shoulders."

❧

It was late at night, two months later, and Joheved had never felt so exhausted in her life. Yet she found it impossible to follow Aunt Sarah's advice and relax between contractions. No sooner did one pain recede than the next crescendo began, and it was all Joheved could do to keep her moans from turning into screams. But she would not cry out, just as she refused to curse her husband or her Creator.

Aunt Sarah assured her that all was well. In fact, Miriam whispered to her, unwilling to provoke the Evil Eye, her progress was quite typical. When Joheved had gotten up that morning, she'd felt nothing unusual. But after using the chamber pot, she discovered liquid still dripping down her legs.

Miriam, and then Sarah, confirmed that her water had broken. Joheved insisted that she felt fine, but they sent her back to bed without breakfast. Then the household sprang into action, except for her. Benjamin rode to Ramerupt to get Meir's mother, Salomon hurried to the synagogue to bring home a Torah scroll, and the yeshivah students prepared for a day, or days, of prayers on behalf of mother and child.

Meir carefully hung his tefillin at the head of the bed, and then, to Joheved's chagrin, he went out and returned with her own tefillin, which he silently arranged next to his.

"How long have you known?" she asked, too ashamed to look at him.

"Oh, quite some time," he replied nonchalantly. He didn't want her to worry, not now. "Rachel doesn't always close the door behind her when she comes down in the morning."

"You don't mind?" she asked anxiously, unable to accept what his actions implied.

"Of course not, every mitzvah you perform is to your credit." Couldn't he say something more reassuring than that? *Mon Dieu*, this might be the last conversation he'd ever have with her. *Stop thinking like that! Don't give Satan, the Accuser, an opening.*

Meir fought to overcome his panic, and when he felt calmer, he leaned over and gazed into those incredibly blue eyes. "Joheved, I am proud to be married to such a righteous woman, one who 'runs to fulfill a mitzvah.' " He used the Talmudic phrase that usually applied to an especially pious man.

Once Salomon's tefillin joined the other two, Rivka ushered her son-in-law out. Then she unwrapped Joheved's birth amulet, a small scroll, inscribed with the names Sanvi, Sansanvi, and Semangelaf, the three angels dispatched to capture Lillit. The three were urged to protect, help, deliver, save, and rescue Joheved, daughter of Rivka, from all who seek her harm.

Rivka attached the amulet to the footboard, while Rachel drew a circle in chalk around the bed. Then, with great concentration, Rachel chalked the magical inscription, "Sanvi, Sansanvi, and Semangelaf, Adam and Eve, barring Lillit," on the door and walls, rubbing out and meticulously redrawing any word that didn't meet her standards. By the time she was done, Joheved was feeling occasional mild cramps, but nothing that justified the fuss everyone was making.

Still, she let them dress her in one of Meir's chemises, to share his strength, and his sword, normally stored inside his chest near the bed, now lay on top, ready for battle. She drank Aunt Sarah's medicinal teas and inhaled the sweet herbs burning on the brazier. Surrounded by her female relatives, all babbling excitedly, it was rather like a party.

But that had been hours ago and now it was nearly midnight. Joheved, her hair loose and disheveled, sweat dripping down her body in the heated room, prayed that she would never have to suffer like this again. Everyone agreed that the first child's birth hurt the most. If she could endure this one, the others would be easier. She tensed and clutched Rivka's hand as the next contraction gripped her, but the pain was accompanied by a new feeling, an urge to push so strong that she was forced to obey it.

Aunt Sarah motioned for Miriam's assistance. "It's time, Joheved. Let's get you onto the birthing stool."

The bottomless chair was not particularly comfortable, and with the next urge to push, Joheved was unpleasantly reminded of using the privy. Her labor pains became unremitting; every push was torture, made bearable only by the knowledge that each one brought her suffering closer to its finish. Finally there was a burst of agony, and Joheved pushed with a strength so great that it seemed to come from outside her.

"Keep pushing, keep pushing," Miriam urged her on, her voice high with excitement. "The head is coming now, I see dark hair."

Joheved felt as though her bones were breaking, and the scream she had struggled so long to suppress tore from her throat. Then suddenly, it was over. Another urge to push came, but the pain was nothing compared to her previous effort.

"The head is out now, we're almost there," Aunt Sarah said, standing behind Miriam and letting her apprentice handle this so far uneventful birth. "Here come the shoulders."

Joheved could feel the baby being pulled from her and then the joyous cacophony began. "It's a boy! A boy! You have a son! *Mazel tov!*" The baby let out a cry and the room was again filled with happy chatter; Rivka was sobbing and smiling simultaneously.

The new mother opened her eyes just enough to view her naked, squirming child, loudly protesting against being evicted from his warm abode, then she sank back against the stool. The pain was gone; the bone-wrenching agony was finally over. Joheved could barely speak, but she managed to make the blessing, "*Baruch ata Adonai* . . . Who is good and does good."

She could hear Rachel shouting the news to those below, and she wished she could be there to enjoy her husband's reactions, to hear him make the same blessing a parent traditionally makes at the birth of a son.

Downstairs, Meir and Salomon were being enthusiastically congratulated. Both shed tears and Meir found it difficult to finish the blessing without choking up. When Joheved screamed, he'd jumped up and started toward the stairs, but then he'd stopped, terrified, at the bottom step. For an interminable instant he was convinced the worst had happened, but then there was Rachel, grinning widely, yelling that he had a son. Before he knew it, he'd picked her up and was swinging her around the room. Then Salomon did the same.

Now, after what seemed like an eternity, Rivka was leading him upstairs to see his wife and new son. He took a deep breath outside the door and stepped inside. All the women had gone except his mother, who was arranging fern fronds on the floor. She gave him a fierce hug and then joined Rivka in bidding him good night.

The scene before him filled him with joy. Joheved, her hair neatly braided, was sitting up in their bed, surrounded by cushions. At her breast, propped up by one of those cushions, was their new son, quietly enjoying his first meal.

Meir could feel the tears running down his cheeks. He tried to absorb everything before him, so he could keep this memory like a treasure, to take out and cherish whenever he wanted.

"Oh Meir, isn't he beautiful?" Joheved welcomed him. "Your mother says he looks just like you did when you were born."

Meir approached slowly, reluctant to disturb the baby's contentment. Nearly covered with swaddling, only the infant's small face and a shock of black hair could be seen. "I think you look beautiful," he replied, emphasizing the *you*.

He sat down just as the bells of Matins began to chime. Tonight and every night until the boy's circumcision, Meir was determined to stay up studying Torah in this room. A healthy birth by no means ended the need for protection from the forces of evil; for the seven days preceding the *brit*, mother and child were in great danger. From this moment on, until the boy entered into the covenant of Abraham, neither he nor Joheved would be left alone.

"Are you all right? I mean, are you in pain or do you need anything?" Meir had heard her scream in agony not so long ago, yet she looked perfectly fine now.

"I'm mostly tired, that's all." It was odd, but though Joheved knew she had been in terrible pain earlier, now it was only a vague memory, something she knew had happened to her but could no longer feel. "The baby's stopped sucking. Would you like to hold him?" She lay the sleeping form down next to her.

Meir gingerly picked up his new son. The child was so small; he fit perfectly between his father's palm and elbow. Meir was marveling at the miracle in his arms when there was a soft knock on the door. Meir didn't say anything for fear of waking the baby, but Joheved called out for the visitor to enter.

Salomon walked quickly to where Meir sat, his eyes not leaving the babe for an instant. "I don't want to disturb you, but I can't sleep until I've seen my grandson."

With practiced ease Salomon lifted the child and held him up to the light. "*Baruch ata Adonai . . . Shehecheyanu . . .* Who has kept us alive, sustained us, and brought us to this season." He slowly recited the traditional prayer of thanksgiving, his voice choked with emotion.

Then he handed the bundle back to Joheved and kissed her hand. "Thank you for this precious gift. I'll be back before dawn, Meir, so you can get some sleep."

Joheved watched her father close the door behind him, and her happiness faded. He hadn't asked about her at all; he only had eyes for his new grandson. *What did I expect? How many years has he been waiting for a male offspring?*

But then she felt Meir staring at her, and when their eyes met, she knew that she was uppermost in his thoughts. His loving expression warmed her like a ray of sunshine suddenly breaking through a cloudy sky.

"Shall we name him Salomon?" Meir whispered. A boy was named publicly at his circumcision, and his parents never mention the chosen name until then. If Lillit, Heaven forbid, should come looking for the child, he would be harder to find without a name.

"How about Samuel?" Joheved countered, reluctant to admit that she'd rather not use the name Salomon.

"My sister's little boy is named Samuel." Meir shook his head. "Besides, I think we should use a name from your side of the family. He is your parents' first grandchild."

"Then what do you think of Isaac?" She looked down at the baby and smiled. "That was my grandfather's name." Isaac was also the name of Grandmama Leah's father; it would be a way to remember and honor her too.

"Maybe." Meir nodded his approval, not saying the chosen name aloud. Then he grinned at her. She was alive, the baby was alive—it was a miracle! She returned his smile and closed her eyes.

For a while Meir sat watching her and the baby, asleep together in the large bed. Then he remembered he had work to do. He picked up his text and started to study.

Seven days later Salomon's household was in the kind of joyous tumult they hadn't experienced since Joheved's wedding. The previous night, Joheved had remained indoors with Rivka and an ever-changing group of women visitors while everyone else feasted in the courtyard and drank her family's wine. But today, after her new son's *brit milah* ceremony, Meir and his father would host another banquet, and she would finally be free to go outside and celebrate with the others.

Joheved and Meir wore their nuptial finery, and she was relieved to see that she could still buckle the matching girdle. Even the baby was dressed in sumptuous garments. Rivka had saved a small amount of fabric from Joheved's wedding *bliaut*, hoping to use it for just such an occasion, and her first grandson now wore a fine linen chemise, a blue silk mantle, and a tiny ornamented hat.

The occupants of the synagogue's women's gallery could not restrain their delight at their community's newest member, clothed like a miniature bridegroom. But all their enthusiastic chatter couldn't take Joheved's mind off the fact that soon her precious baby would have his blood shed in front of her eyes.

Suddenly it was time. With great reluctance Joheved made her way downstairs, where Meir was waiting for her. Recently there had been complaints that it was not appropriate for a beautifully dressed young woman to sit among the men, but most people considered it cruel to remove the newborn from his mother's arms at a time when he would most need her comfort. Salomon saw no reason to change things. Baby boys in Troyes had been circumcised on their mother's laps for as long as anyone could remember, and that's the way it would remain.

Meir assisted his wife to the center of the main floor, where two thrones were covered with fine cloth. One was for Elijah the Prophet, whose legend said that after his overzealous denunciation of Israel as breakers of the covenant, the Holy One required Elijah to attend every circumcision to testify that they were indeed keeping it. The other was for Joheved, who would sit there holding her son while the ritual was performed.

The congregation stood as she carried him in. "Blessed be he who enters," they recited, although nobody was sure whether they meant the baby or Elijah.

Meir took his son while Joheved sat down. Once she was comfortable, he pronounced the father's customary invocation, that he was ready to perform the mitzvah of *brit milah*. When he handed the baby back to her, her hands were trembling. As proud as she was to have given Meir a son, at that moment Joheved wished she could be somewhere else. She grasped her son's legs firmly, shut her eyes tight, and took a deep breath. She felt Meir's hand squeeze her shoulder reassuringly. She dare not move a muscle.

Things happened quickly. The *mohel*, the ritual circumciser, made his blessing, "*Baruch ata Adonai* . . . Who commands us concerning circumcision," and immediately, the baby gave out a howl. Joheved let out her breath and every man in the congregation relaxed his clenched thighs—it was done.

As the *mohel* bandaged the wound with a cloth smeared with olive oil and healing herbs, Meir made the father's blessing, *"Baruch ata Adonai . . .* Who commands us to bring our sons into the covenant of Abraham our father." The *mohel* gave Joheved a wine-soaked cloth for the now swaddled baby to suck on, which quieted him enough for the rest of the blessings to be heard.

Now Salomon joined them. Just as it had been his responsibility, representing the mother's family, to host the first banquet, it was his privilege to chant the *brit milah* benedictions. First came the blessing over wine, and Salomon waited until a cup found Joheved's hand before he began. Then there were prayers of healing, one for the baby and one for Joheved. These were followed by the *gomel* blessing for Joheved, for her having survived childbirth, *gomel* being the prayer of thanksgiving said at one's first synagogue visit after escaping from great danger.

Joheved, her terror beginning to dissipate, clutched the precious bundle that was her child to her shoulder and whispered soothing words. The cry of her son, so helpless and unable to pacify himself at her bosom, had produced an unexpected flood of milk from her breasts. Thank Heaven for Johanna, who had handed her some absorbent material to place under her chemise and protect her beautiful silk *bliaut* from stains. Joheved also gave thanks that, unlike her rescuer, mother of twin boys, she only had to endure one *brit milah* at a time.

Surprisingly, her son seemed content with the wine-soaked cloth, so she turned to watch the ceremony's conclusion. Salomon was on the last blessing now, the one announcing his grandson's name. Joheved, indeed the entire congregation, waited with bated breath as Meir leaned forward to whisper the boy's chosen name in his ear. Her father's tears began to flow immediately, and Joheved couldn't help but cry herself as she watched him struggle to control his emotions and finish the benediction.

Salomon gave Meir a long hug and then cleared his throat. "May this child, named in the House of Israel, Isaac ben Meir, become great. As he has entered into the covenant, so may he enter into Torah, into the marriage canopy, and into the practice of good deeds."

The congregation responded heartily: "Amen."

GLOSSARY

Beit Din—Jewish court.

Bimah—pulpit, raised platform in synagogue where Torah is read.

Bliaut—tunic, outer garment worn over a chemise by men and women.

Brit Milah—ritual circumcision, performed when the baby boy is eight days old.

Chacham—Jewish scholar.

Denier—silver penny; a chicken costs four deniers.

Disner—midday meal, usually the largest meal of the day.

Edomite—European non-Jews (Talmudic term for Roman).

Erusin—formal betrothal that cannot be annulled without a divorce but does not allow the couple to live together.

Gehenna—the underworld, where evil spirits dwell.

Challah—special bread eaten on the Sabbath, also that portion of dough that belongs to the priests and is burnt outside of Israel.

Havdalah—Saturday evening ceremony that marks the end of the Sabbath.

Kapparah—ceremony performed the day before Yom Kippur where a fowl is waved over a person's head and his or her sins are passed on to the bird.

Ketubah—Jewish marriage contract given by the groom to the bride specifying his obligations during the marriage and in the event of divorce or his death.

Kuntres—notes and commentary explaining the Talmudic text.

Lillit—demon responsible for killing newborn babies and women in childbirth; Adam's first wife.

Livre—a pound, unit of money equal to 240 deniers.

Matzah—unleavened bread eaten during Passover.

Mikveh—ritual bath used for purification, particularly by women when she is no longer *niddah*.

Mitzvah (plural, mitzvot)—divine commandment.

Mohel—man who performs the ritual circumcision.

Niddah—a menstruating woman.

Notzrim—polite Jewish word for Christians, literally those who worship the one from Nazareth.

Nisuin—ceremony that completes the marriage, followed by cohabitation.

Parnas—leader, or mayor, of Jewish community.

Potach—demon of forgetfulness.

Selichot—prayers for forgiveness.

Shivah—seven days of mourning following the death of a relative.

Sotah—married woman suspected of adultery by her husband.

Souper—supper, evening meal.

Sukkah—booth in which Jews dwell during the harvest festival of Sukkot.

Tahara—preparation of the corpse for burial.

Talmid Chacham—great Jewish scholar.

Tefillin—phylacteries, small leather cases containing passages from Scripture worn by Jewish men while reciting morning prayers.

Trencher—piece of day-old bread used to hold meat (instead of a plate).

Yeshivah—Talmud academy.

Yetzer Ha-ra—evil inclination, usually refers to the sexual urge.

Maggie Anton talks about
Rashi's Daughter, Secret Scholar:

Q. Who was Rashi?

A. Born in 1040 in northern France, Rabbi Shlomo Yizhaki (better known by his Hebrew initials, Rashi) was a great talmudic scholar who studied in Worms and Mayence before starting his own school in his native city of Troyes. Because of his unique take on talmudic study, students flocked to receive the benefits of his vast erudition and distinctive method of interpretation.

Q. Why is Rashi's influence relevant today?

A. Rashi wanted to make being Jewish as easy as possible. His belief in finding the most lenient legal opinion without building "fences around the Torah," and in permitting rather than forbidding, makes him a model rabbi for our times.

Q. How did you get interested in Rashi's daughters?

A. I began studying Talmud with a group of women after my children grew up and left the house. The more I studied Talmud from a feminist perspective, the more curious I become about Rashi's learned daughters and how they managed to study Talmud in the Middle Ages when such study was supposedly forbidden.

Q. Why was Talmud study forbidden for women?

A. This question deserves more than the brief answer I'll give here. In Deuteronomy, Jews are commanded to teach Torah to *"bnaichem,"* a word that even the Orthodox translate as "your children." But the early rabbis used its literal meaning, "your sons," and decided that only men were obligated to study Torah. The talmudic sage Rav Eliezer took this exemption of women one step further and declared that "he who teaches his daughter Torah, teaches her lechery."

Q. So what were the consequences for women who studied Talmud?

A. All societies, Jews included, have disapproved of those who don't follow their norms. Women who wanted to study Talmud were seen as lacking in proper feminine attributes, and because women were thought to be light-headed and incapable of serious study, most Jews at the time believed that those who tried to study Talmud would only learn to be crafty and devious. Since a man typically preferred to believe that he was more intelligent than his wife, the learned woman was left with a limited choice of potential husbands.

Q. What do you see as the legacy Rashi's daughters leaves for modern Jewish women?

A. Rashi's daughters recognized the value of Torah study in the Jewish world and they wanted an education for themselves as well as for their husbands and sons. Like women today, they attended synagogue regularly and performed those rituals usually reserved for men. When modern Jewish women create new rituals and new blessings, we are following in the footsteps of Rashi's daughters and doing what our female ancestors were already doing 900 years ago.